"MY APPROVAL MUST
BE EARNED, SIR!"

Vinny's spirited assertion was only half teasing. "And as for friendship," she went on carelessly, "I doubt you will be here long enough for it to form."

John stood aside, bowing slightly, to allow her to pass. "I am much comforted by the fact that the other members of your family are more welcoming than you," he remarked sardonically.

Vinny felt uncomfortably hot and fluttered her fan energetically. "Mayhap," she retorted lightly, "they have less discernment than I."

Sarah Westleigh has enjoyed a varied life. Working as a local government officer in London, she qualified as a chartered quantity surveyor. She assisted her husband in his chartered accountancy practice, at the same time managing an employment agency. After moving to Devon, she finally found time to write, and published short stories and articles before discovering historical novels.

A MOST EXCEPTIONAL QUEST
SARAH WESTLEIGH

HARLEQUIN®

TORONTO • NEW YORK • LONDON
AMSTERDAM • PARIS • SYDNEY • HAMBURG
STOCKHOLM • ATHENS • TOKYO • MILAN • MADRID
PRAGUE • WARSAW • BUDAPEST • AUCKLAND

ISBN 0-373-51114-0

A MOST EXCEPTIONAL QUEST

Copyright © 1993 by Sarah Westleigh.

This edition published by arrangement with Harlequin Books S.A.

® and TM are trademarks of the publisher. Trademarks indicated with
® are registered in the United States Patent and Trademark Office, the
Canadian Trade Marks Office and in other countries.

Visit us at www.eHarlequin.com

Printed in U.S.A.

Chapter One

Vinny did not wish to be sociable. She had spent most of the day attending to the garrulous outpourings of her mother's morning callers and sought an hour of peaceful idleness, desiring no more taxing occupation before being forced to change for dinner than to contemplate His Majesty's fleet riding at anchor in the sparkling waters of Tor Bay, her brain lulled into drowsiness by the constant buzzing of busy insects.

Watching the two figures picking their way towards her arbour along the scented paths, she let a small sigh of irritation escape her as she set aside the book lying open on her lap. But she could not avoid the meeting, so she shifted her position slightly, straightened the skirt of her sprigged-muslin dress, rearranged the filmy fichu about her shoulders, composed her features into a cool smile of welcome and prepared to be civil to her brother and the tall man limping at his side.

"Vinny!" cried Percy as they approached. "Mama said we should find you here!"

She added a gracious inclination of her head to the smile already in place, while regarding her brother's companion with increasing astonishment. Closer inspection revealed him to be wearing an odd assortment of clothes, none of which fitted. The yellow nankeen trousers stopped far too high above his white-stockinged ankles and sculpted his thighs so tightly that the seams looked likely to burst. And surely that was one of Percy's coats?

Small wonder the waist was high and loose, the shoulders tight and strained, for Percy's more solid figure did not enjoy the athletic grace supplied by the wide shoulders and narrow hips of the other man—and Percy's flamboyant style, the bright shiny blue of the cloth, the high revered collar, the stripes of the waistcoat beneath, did not suit the languid gravity of the person wearing it. The only items of the stranger's clothing which met with her approval were the polished black pumps and the impeccably folded cravat at his throat.

The forced smile of welcome died on her lips as his hooded gaze swept over her. Something about him disturbed her, and it was not the way his eyes lingered on her figure. She was no schoolroom miss to be thrown into confusion by the bold stare of a male creature.

No, the cause was something else. The arrogant lift of his head, perhaps, denying the ridicule invited by those clothes—his manner told her that, although fully aware of the unwonted figure he cut, he held it in disregard. Such odious self-assurance nettled her.

Having completed her own scrutiny, she returned a belated greeting. "Hello, Percy."

"Vinny, allow me to present Mr—hum—John Smith. My dear fellow, this is my widowed sister, Mrs Charles Darling. Davinia Darling," he added, making things clear. "She buried Charles, her late husband, some two years since."

"Mr... Smith?"

Vinny could not keep the incredulity from her voice as she inclined her head again in acknowledgement of the introduction. John Smith as a name seemed as inappropriate to the man as his clothes.

He made an elaborate bow, showing her the top of a head of thick, unruly hair almost as black as her own, though the sun brought out brownish glints in his, not blue.

"Your servant, ma'am."

His light, resonant voice seemed to strike some chord deep inside her. It held a strong hint of laughter. As he straightened from his bow and replaced his curly-brimmed top hat she looked full into his face for the first time. Saw the lines of weariness and pain etched in tough, uncompromising features. And recognised the hollowed cheeks as belonging to someone extremely ill-nourished.

She saw, too, mockery lurking in the depths of his unusual greeny brown eyes. The colour of moss-encrusted bark, she thought fleetingly as she drew herself up and tossed her head to confront the derision, setting the black curls framing her face, and the small spray of silk periwinkles decorating her chip bonnet, dancing.

"You find my name diverting, sir?" she demanded frostily, as antagonism rose to augment the feeling of unease gripping her. How dared this...this ill-dressed creature laugh at her? "I assure you, I did not choose my former husband for the suitability of his surname! Neither, I imagine, did you select your parents for the rarity of theirs!"

"*Touché*, Mrs Davinia—Darling!" he admitted, his firm lips twitching.

His deliberate pause made it sound as though he had called her "darling" and Vinny bristled anew.

"But unfortunately," he went on smoothly, before she could think of a suitable set-down, "I have not the least idea what name my parents bear. My present form of appellation has been bestowed upon me by the military authorities."

For an instant those strange, luminous eyes met hers

again. Amusement had been replaced by loss and confusion. But on the instant lazy lids masked the expression, so that Vinny wondered whether she had imagined it.

"His memory has been taken, Vinny!" put in Percy with a half-laugh. "Don't that take the cake? Just imagine waking up one mornin' not knowing who you are!"

"You have lost your memory, sir?" enquired Vinny faintly. No wonder the man looked confused! She had never met anyone lacking a memory before, and felt quite strange. Her voice softened. "I am sorry. Yet—you can converse?" she puzzled.

He bowed. "Indeed, ma'am. In two languages, though not, alas, in Portuguese, or I might not be in my present straits. Also, I can function adequately and recognise most objects and their uses." A slight frown furrowed his broad brow, and Vinny knew that could she but see his eyes the distress in them would be marked. He spoke slowly, as though in wonder. "Yet my own face is strange to me, I have yet to see a place or person I recognise and I can remember nothing of my life before the moment I awoke in a peasant's hovel in Portugal some three months since."

Vinny's eyes widened. "In the Peninsula? You are a soldier, sir—?"

"He must be, don't you see?" cut in Percy eagerly. "Jackson—you know, the Reverend Mr Jackson, who is chaplain to the Naval Hospital down in Goodrington—he says they think he must have been injured during the storming of Badajoz, in early April. But there were so many dead and wounded, he must have wandered off in the confusion—"

"Back into Portugal, it seems, eventually to find refuge with peasants." The stranger took up his story again, a slightly self-mocking smile touching the corners of his hard, well-sculpted mouth. "They informed the authorities in Lisbon—having bundled me into an ox cart to take me there—that I collapsed on their doorstep delirious some seven days after the battle. I had a congealed mess like a broken duck's egg on my head, burns down one shoulder and arm, and somehow I had badly sprained my knee, which still, alas, gives me pain. My uniform, I have been informed, had been virtually scorched or torn from my back, and what remained was so faded and ragged, not to mention filthy with mud and blood, that they burnt it."

Vinny's quick gasp of horror brought a small smile to those fascinating lips.

"They could not afterwards describe any detail of colour or insignia. I owe them my life," he went on sombrely, then added, his voice betraying a note of self-disgust, "I must have presented a deplorable sight. I wonder they thought me worth saving."

"So you see the Army has no idea to which regiment he belonged, or of his rank, though since he is quite clearly a gentleman they have assumed he held a commission."

Percy spoke eagerly. His dearest wish was to join the Army, or at least the militia, but his father, Lord Marldon, flatly forbade his only heir to do any such thing. Even duties in the local militia could lead to unnecessary danger, in his opinion. What if Napoleon should finally manage to invade? But such strictures did not prevent Percy from consorting as often as he was able with those who were in, or attached to, the Army—or even the Navy.

Despite her instinctive antagonism, Vinny could not prevent quick sympathy stealing over her for the stranger, one so obviously proud, struck such a lowering blow in the service of his country. Her eyes became near-black pools of concern as they rested on his face.

He saw nothing but pity in them, an emotion he could not accept. Clenching his jaw, biting back the bitter words he knew he would afterwards regret, he scorched her with an angry, resentful glare.

And then that infernal sense of stupefaction assailed his mind again, as though he was foxed. He lowered his lids swiftly, knowing his eyes would give him away. At that precise moment it seemed vitally important that she should not become aware of his confounded weakness.

Confusion had been total at first, his brain scarcely capable of stringing two thoughts together. He had fought this disability as fiercely as he had fought other, physical battles, and with the passing of time his thought processes had improved, had become rational except during those moments of dark impenetrability, which still persisted.

Accustomed now to operating without his full memory, in many ways the past seemed immaterial. Once his body was completely fit again the lingering fuddle-headedness would go; of that he was convinced. Then, doubtless, he would be able to carry on from the present to create an agreeable future. He would have no choice.

But this girl-woman, with her wide-apart, ebony-dark eyes sparkling like jewels in their nests of black lashes, her clear, vivid features, soft mouth, willowy figure and undoubted spirit, had disturbed some half-forgotten memory of sexual challenge, of pleasurable dalliance. She had taken him in dislike—his misplaced sense of the ridiculous had not helped his cause—and insulted him with her pity. He felt an urge to conquer her hostility, to make her retract her commiseration, to hold her helpless in his arms...

The prospect appealed, but he had no further opportunity to indulge his fancy. She was speaking in a frigid voice which told him she had seen and resented his fierce rejection of her pity. He forced his distracted mind to focus upon her words.

"I trust you will soon be fully recovered, sir. Are you to join us for dinner?"

She made the polite enquiry hoping Percy had not been stupid enough to ask this disturbing creature to eat his mutton with them, for he plainly belonged in the barracks. She fluttered her fan vigorously, feeling the need for cooling air on her hot cheeks. For all his elaborate bowing and scraping, his proud air, he lacked the manners and address of a true gentleman.

"He is to stay, Vinny! Mama and Papa are quite willing to offer Mr—hum—Smith bed and board while he recovers from his ordeal. He is not physically indisposed, d'you see, and a hospital is no place for a well man. Besides, the Navy needs the bed for its own sick and wounded. They intended moving him to the small hospital attached to the barracks at Berry Head, but this is a far better plan. Mr... Smith will stay with us while he regains his strength, and we shall try to help him to recover his memory."

"I see." Vinny snapped the folds of her fan together and stood up. She was not surprised to find that she had to raise her eyes a considerable distance to reach the man's firm, clean-cut chin, which she addressed with tart courtesy. "In that case, we shall no doubt meet again shortly, sir. But since you are plainly quite capable of arranging your own affairs you need expect no assistance from me in your quest for a memory."

She dipped a curtsy which was almost—but not quite—an insult and swept off, clasping her novel and fan in one hand and twirling her parasol angrily in the other.

"Damme," muttered Percy ruefully, eyeing his sister's departing figure through his quizzing glass, "can't think what's eatin' her, my dear fellow; she ain't usually so waspish. But never mind, she'll come round—you see if she don't."

Upon which optimistic note he took his companion's arm and the two men followed Vinny back to the house.

Changed and dressed for dinner, Vinny descended from her bedroom determined to be no more than civil to their guest. Since she was a little early she expected to find the drawing-room empty, but discovered the intrusive stranger already in occupation. He stood by one of the windows gazing thoughtfully at the panorama of Tor Bay spread before his eyes, studying the myriad ships riding at anchor in the sheltered waters, the billowing sails of other vessels taking advantage of tide and breeze to enter its havens or to depart thence for more distant shores.

Annoyance brought her to an abrupt halt. Instinct inclined her to make an instant and hasty retreat. But, hearing the sound of light footsteps approaching, he turned and made a bow. She could not avoid the encounter without appearing quite lacking in conduct. She trod reluctantly into the room, startlingly aware that he looked different. For some reason her limbs began to tremble in a most strange manner.

"Mrs Darling! I had thought myself unforgivably beforehand, but I collect I was not mistaken in the hour at which you dine."

Vinny glanced at the ornate clock ticking on the Adam mantel. "It lacks a quarter of the hour, sir. The covers will be laid at four."

Controlling her voice presented considerable difficulty. She could not imagine what had come over her. Never before had she been so embarrassingly aware of a man's physique. She could scarcely remove her eyes from his shapely lower limbs, encased now in white satin knee-breeches and silk stockings. She forced her gaze upwards, only to be confounded anew by the way he stood before her, the picture of arrogant, languid elegance, dressed in what she recognised as evening clothes belonging to her father. The outfit was too grand for the occasion, but justice demanded she acquit him of blame for that.

The high collar of the snowy cambric shirt was swathed by an exquisitely tied cravat and someone—Percy's valet,

Thomas?—had taken his hair in hand. Its arrangement now represented a creditable imitation of the latest "windswept" style. The dark blue superfine of the coat would have pleased even Beau Brummell, though scarcely the fit. Although the Viscount was more nearly the stranger's size than his son, her father nevertheless lacked this man's breadth of shoulder. The silver-grey brocaded waistcoat which completed the outfit served to accent the whiteness of both frilled shirt and breeches.

She was back to them again. She quickly averted her eyes, conscious that his easy grace cloaked powerful, lithe strength, and that he exhibited none of the bored affectation assumed by so many of the men who moved in first circles. Because he had never moved in them himself and had not, therefore, acquired the habit, she told herself witheringly.

She held that thought firmly in mind as she took a steadying breath, berating herself for reacting like a silly, simpering miss, for becoming flustered by his suave masculinity. He was, after all, merely another male creature, one whose consequence was in doubt, and one she did not particularly like.

"I was admiring the view," he remarked conversationally.

Vinny forced her eyes beyond him to the scene framed by the window. She could not keep a certain defensive bite from her voice when she spoke.

"We Sinclairs regard it as the best in England, and peculiarly our own."

"And therefore not to be shared with guests?" he suggested mildly.

She flushed, realising he had been aware of her barbed incivility. Ignoring his question, she posed one of her own.

"Why did the Navy bring you here?"

He shrugged, undismayed by her abrupt enquiry. "Some official in Lisbon singled me out as a special case and put me aboard the first vessel sailing for these shores. It happened to be a frigate bound for Tor Bay."

"You would have been better served to travel on a hospital ship," she suggested tartly. "From that, you would have been taken to a more suitable, military establishment."

"I was not in need of any particular medical attention," he retorted, his manner changing to one of cool reserve in the face of her pointed displeasure. "And I believe there to have been less likelihood of my contracting an infection, though there was some risk of fever, as there is on every ship."

At that moment there came a welcome interruption of the tête-à-tête in the form of Clarissa Sinclair, Lady Marldon. Shorter than Vinny, and growing plump in middle age, she had nevertheless kept her vigour and the most part of her looks.

"Mr Smith!" she exclaimed, her voice, though slightly breathless from hurrying, warm with welcome.

Thus addressed, their guest made his duties.

"Dear Mr Smith," went on Lady Marldon effusively, "since we shall regard you as one of the family during your stay at Preston Grange, I have ventured to order dinner set in the style we usually adopt when we dine alone. I trust you will not think us lacking in courtesy."

"Ma'am," he replied with another bow, "your generosity in offering me the hospitality of your home is more courtesy than I deserve, and to be entertained as a member of your family I consider the greatest honour possible."

A very pretty speech indeed, Vinny thought scornfully.

"We are all so delighted to have you with us, my dear sir. Your presence will enliven our quiet life in a most pleasant manner. Do you not agree, Vinny, dear?"

"Of course, Mama," murmured Vinny dutifully, resenting the trap unwittingly set by her parent and angrily aware of the ironic gleam her response had brought to Mr Smith's disturbing eyes.

"And I see you have been well fitted-out!" Clarissa went on to exclaim in approval. "Lord Marldon has absolutely refused to wear those evening clothes since our return from Sackville Street, where we stayed for our daughter's come-out. How long ago was that, Vinny, my love?"

"Six years," replied Vinny reluctantly.

"You know your dear papa," went on Clarissa gaily; "I gave him up many years ago! Never happier than when he has mud under his boots, or is riding about the estate on horseback seeing to things. So you see, Mr Smith, he can well afford to part with some portion of his evening wear! I had the gravest difficulty in convincing him of the necessity for his presence in London for our daughter's come-out, and now I cannot persuade him there even to visit her in her own establishment!"

"And you do not come yourself," chided Vinny, glad of the excuse to change the course of the conversation. "I am aware of how much you enjoyed yourself that Season. You must know how much I would welcome a visit from you."

"Oh, I am getting too old for such junketing! Besides, how could I leave your papa? He would be quite lost here on his own without me."

Despite the presence in the house of a large staff, Vinny knew that her mother spoke the simple truth. Lord Marldon depended upon his wife to provide all the small comforts, the personal attentions, and a degree of companionship which no servant could provide.

However, "I'm sure he could manage for a few weeks," she protested.

"But I am content here, my love. We do not lack for

society in this area, you know. I declare, we are as gay here with dinners and balls as anywhere!''

"I collect that your son does not share his father's contentment with the simple pleasures, ma'am,'' put in Mr Smith.

"He is still young!" exclaimed Clarissa. "All young men are the same! They think of little but excitement and change, and think nothing of careering about the countryside at any speed in their carriages! The times I have had to listen to an account of the virtues of a new curricle! So well-sprung, so wondrously appointed! And as for his horses...'' She finished on an eloquent shrug.

At that moment the man they were speaking of came in, closely followed by the distinguished figure of Lord Marldon. From his wife's description, thought Vinny, anyone might be forgiven for imagining him a typical country squire, with few pretensions to gentility. But her father was far from an ignorant farmer. His aristocratic breeding was evidenced by his bearing, his culture by his manner and address.

With the arrival of the two men the party passed through into the elegant Adam-style morning-room and sat at the damask-covered table, while servants placed the covers in their appointed places. Vinny found herself seated opposite her brother and the stranger.

Despite her mother's claim to be making no fuss, additional silver gleamed in the soft candlelight and extra footmen were needed to lay and remove the quite excessive number of covers provided for each course.

Her parents appeared not in the least concerned to be entertaining a person about whom they knew nothing, whose ancestry might be anything. Or nothing. But then, neither of them had ever been top-lofty, she thought fondly, as she helped herself to a plump trout from the nearest cover and began to eat. She did not consider herself to be so, either. However, five years in London society had taught her to be careful in her choice of friends and acquaintances. Here it did not matter so much, but people of little or no consequence were inclined to presume, given half a chance.

She looked up from her lavishly decorated and crested bone-china plate to find Mr Smith's gaze resting thoughtfully upon her.

Their eyes held for a moment. And then he smiled.

Her breath stopped in her throat. Colour began to creep up her neck and invade her face.

His features were transformed, softened, lit. She had never imagined him able to look so young, so...engaging. His eyes were gleaming with the humour he did not seem able to suppress for long, and for a dreadful moment she imagined he was laughing at her. But it was self-mockery he was offering to share.

"This is quite the best meal I have eaten within memory," he declared, the wry dig at his own condition not lost on her. "I must request Lady Marldon to convey my congratulations to her cook. I doubt I have ever tasted a finer saddle of mutton."

The tide of heat retreated as fast as it had risen, leaving Vinny feeling acutely uncomfortable. "You must congratulate my father, too, sir," she managed to reply. "The meat comes from our own flocks."

"Like the mutton, do you, m'boy?" asked Lord Marldon from the bottom of the table. He had sharp hearing, especially when the subject under discussion concerned him, though in truth the table was not so large as to put him beyond normal earshot. "You must take out a saddle horse tomorrow, see the estate and the home farm. Plenty of good cattle in the stables. Sinclair will show you, if I'm not about. Get him to take you over to his place at Westerland one day; you'll approve, I'll be bound."

"Thank you, my lord. I should enjoy that—if I find I am able to ride horseback."

"Of course you are. Strange officer who ain't able to get on a horse," grunted his lordship.

"I shall soon discover. It is one of the more acceptable elements of my affliction that skills I acquired in the past remain with me."

"You must show him the summer-house," put in Lady Marldon eagerly. "I do declare it is the prettiest place on earth!"

"It is built in the style of a Grecian temple," explained Vinny with a smile she could not restrain. The summer-house had been an extravagance of her mother's, built before the turn of the century at the same time as the interior of the house had been refurbished. Designed in the classical style then all the rage, it looked, in her daughter's opinion, quite out of place in the Devon landscape, though Vinny would never dream of saying so, and could not deny its intrinsic beauty.

Percy became full of plans for the morrow, and Vinny relapsed into silence. Mr John Smith, whoever he was, was showing himself to be quite at home in genteel society, more than able to hold his own in first circles. Her earlier assessment of him as being without conduct or address had been quite out. That opinion, she acknowledged honestly, had been born of nothing but pique.

Now, with the cloth removed and the dessert covers in place on the lustrous mahogany of the dining-table, she contemplated him from behind her thick, dark lashes. How deftly his long, sensitive fingers dealt with the consumption of a peach grown in the glasshouse! Her own hands were dripping with juice, while his appeared quite dry and clean. She used her finger-bowl and napkin hurriedly.

As she and her mother left the gentlemen to continue their conversation over port and brandy, she was acutely aware of his eyes on her retreating form and suitably annoyed with herself for her strong reaction. She lifted her head higher. The little lace cap perched attractively on the knot of hair atop her head should tell this encroaching stranger that she was a mature woman who would stand no nonsense. And if she had, for some reason, chosen to wear one of her more becoming gowns that evening—a cream silk with a small russet design printed on it—the fact had nothing whatsoever to do with his presence.

"Mama," she said as the ladies settled to their needlework, "I wonder at your inviting a stranger to stay with us. Why, we have no idea who he might be!"

"But, my love," replied Clarissa artlessly, her eyes blinking owlishly from behind the spectacles she now needed for close work, "how could we refuse? He came by his affliction in the service of his country! And he behaves in *such* a gentleman-like manner! The Army believes him to be an officer! Of the highest rank, I dare say!"

"They would know who he was, if that were the case," retorted Vinny shortly. "I cannot understand why his identity is not already discovered."

"They lost so many officers at Badajoz, my love. Why, Percy tells me that the Ninety-fifth regiment alone lost twenty-two! And so few of the bodies could be recovered from that terrible ditch. So dreadful!"

Her mother's rather plump face in its frame of white lace had dropped, and for a moment she looked quite overset. Vinny was immediately at pains to console her.

"Do not upset yourself, Mama. Percy says it was worth the sacrifice, for Lord Wellington entered Salamanca in June."

"You are quite right, my love," cried Clarissa, rallying. "And you must see why we could not refuse our hospitality to poor Mr Smith?"

Vinny sprang up and impulsively kissed her mother's

soft cheek. "Of course I do! I am being old-maidish in the extreme!" "Missish" would be a more accurate description of her behaviour, she thought impatiently. "But I do hope he regains his memory before long," she added, "for at the moment I hold entertaining tedious beyond measure!"

"He need not disturb you, my love. Your dearest brother will provide all that is needed in the way of amusement; of that you may be sure."

Vinny resumed her seat, picked up a length of blue ruched ribbon from her satinwood work-table, cut off a length of matching silk and threaded her needle. She was stitching bands of the decoration around the plain hem of an older dress to bring it into fashion. She could neither draw nor speak more than a few words of French or Italian, but one essential female accomplishment she did have was skill with her needle. That evening, however, she found it difficult to concentrate. The work was lying under her idle hands when the tea tray arrived and the gentlemen joined them.

"Play for us, Vinny," requested her father once the tray had been removed.

Vinny, even more accomplished at the pianoforte than with her needle, rose obediently and moved to the instrument, uncomfortably aware of the stranger's presence. It should not concern her, for she was quite used to performing in company. The fact that it did brought more of her resentment down on the head of *poor* Mr Smith.

"What shall I play?" she asked, riffling through the leaves of her music book.

"A little Handel?" suggested her father.

"Make it something lively, Vinny!" protested the Honourable Percival Sinclair urgently. "Give us a song or two."

New light was thrown on the music as their guest walked

over and used the flame he carried to ignite the two candles already standing in sticks at either end of the keyboard.

"Thank you," acknowledged Vinny stiffly.

She opened her music book at random and sat down on the stool, composing her features with difficulty. Her hands were trembling and it needed all her skill and determination to play the opening bars of a lively French ditty, which she had copied out in London only weeks before, without striking wrong keys. Her voice was not as sure as usual, but she got through the first verse somehow, wishing with all her might that the creature standing at her shoulder throwing the light of his candle on the page would go away. But he showed no inclination to leave her side, and gradually her agitation died and she began to perform with more normal assurance.

John Smith stood slightly behind her stiff back, very much aware of the little lace cap bobbing in time with the music as she sang. Provoking creature! Why did she resent his presence so? Did he appear of so little consequence in her eyes that she disdained him? His lips tightened on the thought.

It was damnably inconvenient not knowing whether he had an income or any assets other than what little the Army was prepared to offer him in back pay, or whether he possessed a family—a wife, even, and children. But attempting to remember his father and mother brought only a feeling of acute discomfort, of disorientation; and as for his having a wife—he had not previously given that possibility serious consideration, instinctively dismissing the idea that he could possibly be wed, for he did not feel leg-shackled—although at his age... Whatever that was. The doctor reckoned him to be a little above thirty, and he had no reason to quarrel with that opinion.

He felt instinctively that he belonged in company such

as this. Yet without proof, how could he blame society for suspecting his origins?

He gazed down at the tender curve of her nape and knew an urge to kiss it. What would she do? How would she react?

Used to having someone turn the pages for her, Vinny nodded her head when the time came and he roused himself from his reverie sufficiently to execute her implied request with an assurance which suggested he had performed the same service on many previous occasions. Another piece of knowledge to add to his growing store.

She followed the French song with a couple of English folk tunes, her confidence rising. She had almost forgotten his presence behind her until she chose a popular ballad and he began to hum the harmony in a husky, light baritone which blended pleasingly with her soprano and sent a shiver of appreciation down her spine.

Vinny lost the last vestiges of nervousness as she became engrossed in the music. The rare luxury of making it with someone else, and to such advantage, held her spellbound through song after song, until at last they were interrupted by the arrival of supper.

Her mother clapped delightedly and Percy voiced loud approval. But it was her father's quiet, "Thank you both, that was excellent, and gave us quite extraordinary pleasure," that afforded her the greatest satisfaction.

She looked up into the hard face of the man who had contributed so much to that excellence and pleasure, seeing him with new eyes. "You can sing," she murmured, and then added sincerely, "You have a fine voice."

"So it would seem. I am sure you do not need me to tell you how much pleasure your own exceptional talent provides. Thank you, ma'am."

The others were occupied with the serving of supper. Her face was raised to his, her eyes in their dark nests glowing softly. He seemed to hesitate only fractionally before his lips came slowly down to touch hers in a light yet lingering caress.

Vinny clutched the edge of the keyboard as her senses swam. Her whole body seemed not to belong to her. Her heart was hammering uncontrollably in her breast.

He straightened, removing his overwhelming presence to a safer distance. His eyes held a strange, questioning expression as they scrutinised her flushed face, saw the dazzlement and confusion written there. He waited, as though unsure of his next move.

That moment's hesitation gave Vinny the time she needed to pull herself together and to speak first. She trembled yet, her heart still beat fast, but otherwise she was recovered from that unaccountable spasm.

"Really, sir," she whispered fiercely, "you forget yourself!"

"Perhaps," he admitted huskily, "I do."

"Either that or you are nought but a rake!"

His hand shook slightly as he set his candle down. "How should I know?" he demanded, a hint of humour returning to his tone. "'Twas a strong compulsion, whatever drove me to such reprehensible conduct. Perhaps I am a rake—but I think the explanation may simply lie in the fact that many months have passed since I last enjoyed the pleasure of female society. I believe your charming company has quite gone to my head."

It was far from an apology, and his last remark had been made on a breath of laughter. Yet the charm he exuded almost overwhelmed her.

"No doubt the last female society you enjoyed was that of some Spanish *señorita!*" exclaimed Vinny tartly, determined not to be seduced from her dislike.

"Not too closely, for they smell of garlic," he responded immediately.

They stared at each other. Then he masked his eyes.

"It seems you remember *them!*" snapped Vinny, crushing down a strange feeling of excitement. She had triggered that snatch of memory! But his recovery was of no conceivable interest to her! "Well, sir, whatever your excuse," she went on swiftly, "I would have you know that I am no light woman who will fall easily into the arms of the merest passing male!"

"Let us not come to cuffs," he suggested easily. His momentary disorientation appeared to have passed, for he met her eyes quite steadily, and gravely. "I did not and do not think you such. Be assured of my deepest respect, ma'am. In return, I would value your good opinion, and hope I may count you a friend."

"My approval must be earned, sir!" Her spirited reply was only half-teasing. He had set her emotions into a scramble and she had no intention of making things easy for him. "And as for friendship," she went on carelessly, "I doubt you will be here long enough for it to form."

"Come along, you two, supper!" called Percy.

Vinny rose from the stool. The man known as John Smith stood aside, bowing slightly, to allow her to pass.

"I am much comforted by the fact that the other members of your family are more welcoming than you," he remarked sardonically.

Vinny felt uncomfortably hot and fluttered her fan energetically. She knew she was in the wrong, but refused to admit it.

"Mayhap," she retorted lightly, "they have less discernment than I."

Chapter Two

Vinny awoke next morning full of spirits. Despite all the aggravation of the previous evening she had slept well. She drank her chocolate quickly and sprang out of bed, calling for Flora, the new lady's-maid who had entered her service earlier in the year, to bring her clothes immediately.

"It is such a splendid morning, I shall go for a walk before breakfast," she announced. "I had better wear my half-boots, for I may encounter rough ground beyond the park."

"You intend to venture so far afield?" asked Flora doubtfully.

"I shall be quite safe, I assure you! This is not London, and I shall be on Marldon land the entire time!"

"I would rather walk in London, ma'am! I should feel a great deal safer!" declared Flora. "I cannot feel secure in the country. What if some gypsy should attack you, madam? Or a cow!" she added anxiously.

"There are no gypsies on this land and cows are quite harmless, Flora. You will have to accustom yourself to woods and fields and animals if you are to be happy in my service, for I spend several months of each year here."

"Yes, ma'am. I have no wish to leave your service," Flora assured her mistress, removing the last curl paper from the short hair framing Vinny's face. "It is just that I have never been from London before. My previous mistress spent the entire year at her Berkeley Street residence."

"I know that, Flora, but she was elderly and fixed in her ways. When you applied for this position I warned you that my habits were different. Surely you must prefer it here! You must appreciate the fresh sea air and the wonderful views!"

"I'm not saying I don't, ma'am, but 'tis empty and lonely to my way of thinking."

Vinny laughed, and watched with approval as Flora, an experienced woman in her late twenties, pinned up her back hair in a loose knot and arranged the curls becomingly about her face. "You will become accustomed," she assured her. "That is excellent, Flora. I'll wear my oldest bonnet, the one with the small brim and blue lace trimming."

"It becomes you very well, madam, and will match your spot muslin, to be sure."

Vinny knew this. Although she did not wish to dress up for her expedition she wanted her clothes, however old, to add to her sense of well-being, not to diminish it.

She set out briskly, determined on a good hour of exercise. A gentle breeze blew in from the sea to freshen the air, making the morning perfect for walking. She crossed the extensive pleasure-grounds surrounding the house without pause for admiration of either bloom or view, entered the shrubbery and passed through it to stride briskly along the shadowed pathways of a wood. On the other side of that she took an invigorating breath, lengthened her stride and embarked upon a passage across open parkland. She found it difficult to remember when she had last felt so alive, so full of energy. Only yesterday she had been quite out of spirits.

On she strode until both cornfields and pasture, the latter dotted with grazing animals, beckoned enticingly a short distance ahead—and she came to the ditch which divided the park from the farm and kept the animals from straying to forbidden ground.

She had forgotten the ha-ha. To encounter Flora's dreaded cows she would have to make a detour to find a path from park to farm fitted with a gate or cattle-grid. Her enthusiasm for walking across farm land waned. But it was too soon to return and she still had an excess of energy to expend. She turned to follow the course of the ha-ha. Time enough to decide whether to cross it or not when the possibility arose.

Meadows, dotted with beech and chestnut trees, old oaks, hornbeams and towering elms, gave way to shrubby coverts here and there, but it was not until she skirted a plantation of Scots pines that she found what she sought. She glanced at the watch pinned at her breast to find that, if she were not to miss breakfast, time would no longer allow exploration of the fields beyond the cattle-grid. And the exercise had made her hungry. She turned her back on the farm and entered the cathedral-like shade of the towering trees.

A bed of pine needles covered the track, deadening the sound of her footsteps. A hush pervaded the wood. Few animals or birds chose to make their homes among the conifers. Yet such was her absorption in her own swift progress that she failed to notice the approach, from a crossing path, of someone with a faster, heavier, uneven stride, until collision brought her to an abrupt and staggering halt.

Steely arms encompassed her as John Smith, off balance himself, clutched her to him in an effort to prevent her being sent sprawling headlong to the ground. Most of Vinny's breath had been knocked from her lungs, and the remainder expelled in a gasp of shock as the odour of herbs mingled with fresh, manly sweat threatened to overwhelm her—and she realised who held her in such a firm embrace.

"Mr Smith!" she panted, pushing at his chest. "Let me go this instant!"

His arms dropped immediately. He stepped back and bowed. "My apologies, ma'am." His chest rose and fell as he filled his lungs with much needed air. That he had been taking energetic exercise was plain from the perspiration which beaded his brow and lip. His short hair dripped with sweat.

He wore nothing but those yellow trousers and a shirt, which, being unfastened for most of its length, displayed an embarrassing expanse of chest sparsely covered with black, curling hair. Moisture ran in rivers from the hollow at the base of his neck and down the channel formed by his breastbone. Having retained much of the deep tan acquired in Spain, his face and hands appeared dark in contrast to the pale skin of his body.

Vinny felt the trembling in her limbs again, but this time she could account for it by shock.

"I did not hear you coming," she excused herself, though her tone implied censure.

"Nor I you." He smiled. She looked delightful, her small, vivid face, pink with outraged modesty, framed by the brim of her saucy little bonnet. "But I cannot pretend to regret our—encounter," he told her with a widening grin. "You were taking exercise?"

"I was enjoying a solitary walk, sir," she informed him repressively. "If you will excuse me, I must return to the house with all speed if I am to change in time for breakfast."

"Ah! Then so must I. I thank you for the reminder."

He bowed again. "I will not inflict my company upon you now, ma'am, but no doubt we shall meet at the breakfast table."

He veered from his previous path to take her more direct route back to the house, easing into a long, loping stride while she stood fuming at his effrontery. She found her legs still quivering as she followed at a more sedate pace.

Vinny had decided to ignore their guest, since his presence was unwelcome to her, but, with the other members of her family determined to take him to their bosoms, she found herself unable to keep to her resolve.

Lord Marldon and Percy were both to escort the visitor on a tour of the estate.

"You should accompany us, my dear," said her father. "You will enjoy the outing."

"I think not, Papa." Vinny sought rapidly for an excuse. "I have already taken exercise this morning, and must be here to help Mama receive her morning calls."

"Do not remain behind on my account!" protested Lady Marldon immediately. "I am expecting no one in particular, and will convey your apologies to such as may call."

"Do come, Vinny," cajoled Percy. "We shall make a splendid party, and can take a nuncheon at the farm. It must be an age since you last enjoyed Mrs Goodwin's baking!"

John Smith merely regarded her from hooded eyes, the slightest of smiles touching the corners of his firm lips. He knew quite well why she was reluctant to join the party, and her discomfort amused him.

It was that smile rather than any other persuasion that made her drop her resistance. She would show him that his presence did not disturb her one iota!

"Very well," she agreed, "if you are certain, Mama?"

"Quite certain, my love. It would be a sin to remain

indoors on such a lovely day when you could take your horse for a ride.''

''And if Mr Smith's physical condition will allow, after his earlier strenuous exercise?'' Vinny went on to enquire sweetly. ''I had thought his knee might cause him pain.''

''Nothing that I cannot endure,'' he replied promptly. ''I must regain my strength as speedily as possible if I am to resume a normal life.''

''Well said, sir! Don't do for a young man to get soft,'' approved Lord Marldon. ''Sinclair could do with a little more exercise.''

''I often take my horse out *and* I follow the hounds!'' protested Percy in an injured tone.

''When you are here,'' growled his sire, his censure reinforced by the lowering of his heavy brows. ''I doubt you did much horseback riding when you were in London with your sister.''

Vinny had no intention of entering into a family disagreement. Her father was right, but she would not take sides. ''I shall have to change,'' she informed the company, rising from her chair. ''Excuse me, please.''

''I'll have your horse saddled and brought round for you, my dear,'' promised her father, diverted from his grouse against his son. ''We shall all be ready to start in half an hour.''

At the appointed time, Vinny emerged from the house to the sound of horses' hoofs crunching on gravel. The men were already gathered at the door. She noted Mr Smith eyeing her topaz riding habit and the small matching hat with its plume of feathers. A smile of approval touched his mouth. Vinny ignored him.

As the grooms delivered their charges the riders descended the steps. Percy claimed his black stallion while Lord Marldon indicated to Mr Smith that the large grey had been saddled for him. Vinny moved towards the mare carrying a side-saddle. She had ridden Beauty since the animal had been a lively young filly, regularly before her marriage, less often now.

John Smith, clad in a pair of her father's riding breeches—and boots borrowed from a groom—approached the grey confidently. He stroked its nose and spoke softly into its ear before gathering the reins and mounting neatly from a nearby block. He settled in the saddle and patted the horse's neck. Then he wheeled it about and smiled gravely at his interested audience.

"I believe I am a horseman," he announced.

"We knew you must be! But cavalry?" asked Percy eagerly as he mounted his own horse. "Could you make a charge?"

John Smith shook his head. "It seems unlikely. I do not feel I could do battle on horseback."

"That cuts down the number of regiments to which you could belong," grinned Percy. "Must have been foot. Must try you with a musket some time."

John Smith shrugged. "I find I am familiar with fire-arms. I imagine every soldier is trained to use a musket, just as every officer should be able to ride a horse. Such experiments prove nothing."

"Quite right, my boy. Do not let my son engage you in such useless exercises!" urged Lord Marldon. "Are we ready? Then follow me!"

For most of the way Vinny rode beside her father, conscious of the two other men following closely behind, or riding abreast where space allowed. The paths, the rides, the fields were all familiar to her, yet she saw them now through new eyes, wondering how Mr Smith regarded them, whether he was impressed by or critical of the Marldon estate. His face gave little away. He rode easily, conserved his horse's energy, gentled him, urged him on where necessary in the manner of a man born to the saddle.

Galloping across a field, the others strung out behind him, Percy suddenly hallooed and shouted, "Jump the hedge! It's safe enough! I've done it many a time!"

He raced at the line of low bushes cresting a ridge of earth to form a typical Devon hedge, taking the obstacle with great panache, rising in his saddle and whooping with exultation as his stallion sailed over—but the animal stumbled on landing and he lost his seat, sliding to the rough pasture-land unhurt and unrepentant. The reins had not escaped his grasp and he leapt back into his saddle on the instant, grinning widely as he urged the stallion on.

John Smith, close behind but not too close, steadied the grey before putting it to the jump, which the horse took neatly and cleanly, earning a hefty pat as reward. Lord Marldon, less adventurous than the younger men, chose a low spot in the hedge to make his jump, and Vinny followed her father over. Exhilaration brought an added sparkle to her eyes and success a laugh to her lips as she slapped her mare's neck.

"Well done, my Beauty!" she congratulated her horse warmly, and was answered by a toss of its head and a little whinny of pleasure.

"You enjoy riding," observed Mr Smith, drawing alongside.

Vinny made her voice cool. "I do, sir. Though I do not keep a riding horse in London, so the enjoyment is all the more keen when I visit my old home." She paused. Honesty forced her to continue. "You, sir, are an excellent horseback rider."

He acknowledged her compliment with a small bow of his head. "Your brother put his horse to that jump at too fast a pace," he remarked. "No wonder the animal pecked on landing."

"You are entitled to be critical, sir."

He glanced at her quickly, aware that once again he had

aroused her quick antagonism. Moments before she had been full of happy enjoyment. Now her expression was closed. Shutting him out. He sighed impatiently.

"I did not intend my observation to express censure," he told her coolly, "but my unexpected knowledge. I am continually astounded by such new discoveries—my ability to read music and to sing last evening," he pointed out drily, "today my ability to ride."

"I wonder," said Vinny, attempting to mask a quite unwelcome curiosity behind forced raillery, "what your next great discovery will be?"

"Ah!" exclaimed John Smith, recovering his good humour and treating her to an irrepressible grin. "Possibly that I am well versed in the art of making love to beautiful women?"

The treacherous colour rose in Vinny's cheeks. The feathers in her saucy hat quivered indignantly. "That, sir," she informed him icily, "I have never for one moment doubted. My doubt has been over your delicacy in mentioning it and your choice of females on which to practise your so-called art!"

"Spanish *señoritas*," he murmured innocently.

Vinny did not deign to answer, but spurred her horse forward along the farm track. John Smith considered her stiff back thoughtfully. At the least he had succeeded in cracking her cool façade.

Reaching the farmhouse, they dismounted. The horses were watered from a deep trough, and set free to graze in a nearby enclosure. The farmer, who managed the Home Farm on his lordship's behalf, was occupied in some distant field but his wife emerged from her kitchen to greet the party effusively.

"My lord! And Miss Vinny! Why, it be many months since I last had the pleasure of welcoming you, miss!"

"Madam," grinned Percy, putting an arm round the

motherly shoulders to give them a squeeze. "You must remember, dear Mrs Goodwin, my sister is now Mrs Darling, and a widow, too!"

"Oh, ma'am!" The woman, flustered, dipped a curtsy and rushed on. "You must forgive me, ma'am, and I was that sorry to hear of your loss, but you will always be Miss Vinny to me! And you, Mr Percy! How can I think of you as a grown man when I remember you as a little lad, coming into the kitchen to beg a piece of my cake?"

Vinny smiled, her affection for an old friend, even though one sadly neglected of late, overcoming her annoyance at being shown up in a childish light before the stranger.

"There is nothing to forgive, Mrs Goodwin. How are all your children?"

"Well enough, I thank you, ma'am."

She had no chance to expand on her favourite topic, for Percy exclaimed, "Cake! Mrs Goodwin, have you some for us now? I vow we are all quite famished!"

"And thirsty, I'll be bound! Aye, Mr Percy, I've plenty of good fruit cake, and cordial for Miss—Mrs Darling, and small ale for his lordship and yourself—but what of the other gentleman? Will he take ale or cider?"

"Our visitor? Of course, you have not met Mr... Smith." Percy could still not use the other man's assumed name without hesitation.

John Smith was recalled from a reverie to be introduced, and to confirm his liking for both cake and ale.

"If you'll just sit yourselves down on those benches, I'll fetch it out in no time at all."

Mrs Goodwin disappeared indoors and Lord Marldon eased himself down on the nearest bench. A rustic table stood between it and the seat Vinny chose, and there, only moments later, the farmer's good lady placed the tray of victuals.

Percy and Mr Smith strolled over to partake of the refreshments. To Vinny's consternation, the latter put one foot up on the bench, scarce a yard from where she sat, and bent forward, leaning one arm on his leather-clad thigh while he took a deep draught of his ale.

Vinny bit elegantly into the wedge of moist fruit cake, chewed carefully, and told herself his nearness made not the slightest difference to her enjoyment. But the cake went down in an uncomfortable lump, and the cordial did little to cool her heated face. The intruder seemed quite unaware of the discomfiture his close presence caused her. And, although she was doing her best to hide her discomposure, the fact that he made no attempt to remove himself seemed to Vinny to illustrate his total lack of sensibility. She greeted a general move to resume their ride with relief.

The remainder of the excursion passed without incident, so far as she was concerned. Mr Smith kept his distance, probably because Percy demanded his attention; but, whatever the cause, his absence from her side was most welcome.

On returning to the Grange, Vinny repaired immediately to her room to rest and change for dinner. Mindful of the previous day's pre-meal encounter with the intrusive Mr Smith, she took care to arrive in the drawing-room almost on the stroke of four. Dinner passed uneventfully. Not until the gentlemen joined them afterwards did any new challenge to her composure arise.

Percy pulled out the card table. She was used to playing with him of an evening, and he fully expected her to take her place at the baize-covered board. She hesitated, tempted to plead the urgency of her needlework, but the lure of a game of chance overcame her reluctance to sit at a small table with Mr Smith, who was naturally to be one of those taking a hand.

"I suppose you can play *vingt et un?*" drawled Vinny provocatively.

"The rules returned to me during my voyage aboard His Majesty's frigate," he answered in his most unruffled manner.

"And casino? Whist?"

He shook his head slightly. "I am certain the rules of those games will return with similar ease," he assured her confidently.

"We'll begin with *vingt-et-un,*' announced Percy. "With a changing bank, I suggest. Cut the pack, Vinny. I'll deal for banker."

Vinny watched the cards fall and was unsurprised to see a black jack turned up before Mr Smith.

"Your bank, my dear fellow," confirmed Percy.

John Smith gathered the cards together and began to shuffle for the first deal. "The upper limit of the stakes will be half a crown," he announced. "In truth, I am short of funds, as you may imagine."

"We'll accept your pledges," grinned Percy.

The other man shook his head. "I never hazard more than I can afford."

"Really, sir! I did not expect you to exhibit such a poor spirit!" exclaimed Percy in some disgust. "There is little sport if no risk is taken!"

"I shall be venturing all the money at my command," declared John Smith quietly. "I will not risk more."

"My dear fellow—" Percy had begun, when Vinny intervened.

"I find that a sensible decision, brother. We seldom play for more than half a crown when we game together. There can be no reason to raise the stakes now. I accept Mr Smith's terms."

John Smith appeared rather surprised, and Vinny was no

less astonished herself to be championing their guest. But on this point she found herself in full agreement with him.

Percy shrugged. "Well, I shall raise the limit to a guinea when I hold the bank."

"Then I shall reluctantly abandon the game."

"I agree," put in Vinny quickly. "You stand in need of greater prudence in your gaming, Percy. You know Papa will be displeased if you run into debt again."

"I am scarcely likely to do that, with such paltry stakes as you propose!"

Lord Marldon had refused to join in the play, but was reading near by. He lifted his head to regard his son over the rims of his spectacles.

"Sinclair knows I'll fund no more of his excesses. You are quite expensive enough as it is, my boy!"

"I do not greatly exceed my income as a rule!"

"But you know I will not tolerate any further extravagance on your part."

Vinny wished she had not been so outspoken, for Percy was visibly embarrassed at being so chastised before the other man. But he was inclined to recklessness in all his ways, and had been unable to meet his debts at the end of the Season just past. Although he had a small independence of his own, their father controlled the chief part of his income.

"I shall not play beyond my means," he informed the company stiffly.

"Nor ours, if you please! Do let us begin!" cried Vinny in an attempt to turn the subject.

Mr Smith resumed the shuffle. Vinny watched his long fingers manipulating the pack. He executed the feat with admirable dexterity. At some time in the past he had spent many long hours practising. He offered her the cut. She kept her hand steady with an effort and was careful not to make accidental contact with his.

Percy was far too rash to be a good player, and Vinny could usually run out the winner. That evening, holding the bank or not, Mr Smith played with a combination of skill, acumen and luck which defeated both his opponents.

By this time Percy had regained his good humour and congratulated the other man as he gathered up his winnings.

"Don't you wish you'd risked setting a higher stake?" he demanded with a laugh.

"No. I am more than satisfied with the amount I have won, and neither you nor Mrs Darling will feel your losses, I believe."

Absorbed in the game, Vinny had managed to forget her aversion to being in close contact with him. As she had when singing on the previous evening. Rising from the table, she retreated with all speed in order to render quite impossible a repetition of the outrageous behaviour he had exhibited on that occasion.

But she need not have worried. Mr Smith did not so much as look in her direction.

The doctor had proclaimed the gentleman fit, the Army had discharged him with a subaltern's back-pay. There could be no excuse for his lingering on at Preston Grange—apart from the earnest entreaties of the other members of her family for him to remain. Vinny seemed to be the only one who considered he had outstayed his welcome.

"My dear Vinny, we cannot allow the young man to launch himself into the world at large without his memory," her father had remonstrated when she voiced her opinion.

The sun streamed into the library, illuminating the rank upon rank of leather-bound volumes surrounding them. Countless happy hours had been spent there, browsing among her father's collection. Yet now, while Lord Marldon wrote at his desk, she sat irresolutely scanning some illustrations in a book recounting great voyages of discovery, but not truly seeing anything.

On such a beautiful day both would have preferred to be riding out on horseback with Percy and the man John Smith, but for different reasons had chosen to remain behind. Business kept her father desk-bound. Vinny found herself tied indoors simply because of her aversion to their guest's company, which seemed to grow, rather than diminish, with time. He annoyed her and made her uncomfortable and so she shunned him as far as possible. In return, he largely ignored her presence, vexingly continuing with his pleasures as though she did not exist.

Such a situation could no longer be tolerated. Vinny slammed the book shut, earning a reproving glance from Lord Marldon.

"That man has been with us for more than a month now, and will never recover his memory while he remains here," she stated flatly. "He needs to visit London, ask at the Horse Guards for information, move about in Society and discover whether he is recognised—"

"A capital idea, my dear!" exclaimed her father. "Why did we not think of it before? You shall take him to your Town house and see what you can do! And, although I deplore the fact, Percy will leap at the chance to accompany you!"

"Papa, I had not intended—"

"Nonsense, child! You have been in remarkably low spirits of late, and such an enterprise must restore them. We will suggest it the moment they return."

"Dear Papa," sighed Vinny, "I know your intentions are of the best, but I really have no wish to be in London at the moment, or to aid Mr Smith in his search for his memory. I am quite persuaded that he can manage without my assistance!''

''I believe you to be in error, my dear. He needs every support you and I or anyone else can give him. And, you know, your manifest avoidance must distress him, though he manages to hide it. I can see no reason for your taking against him, and confess a failure to understand your attitude—which I consider unfortunate to the point of rudeness. Your minds met over the question of gaming, yet you find excuses to avoid taking a hand, and your voices blended so well together on the only occasion you consented to sing.''

Vinny drew a deep breath. That her father should find it necessary to make such a long speech of criticism concerning her behaviour came as a shock. Yet her avoidance had been instinctive. Most things about Mr Smith sent uncomfortable shivers down her spine, seemed to set her teeth on edge—his voice, his hands, his mere proximity. No wonder she resented his presence!

''I cannot help it,'' she muttered uneasily. ''I feel he is encroaching.''

''I am sure he does not intend to,'' the Viscount assured her gruffly. ''Think about it, Vinny. Whatever his origins, he is a splendid young man. Now his dress has improved—''

''Bought with funds won at our card table!''

Her father eyed her coolly. ''Is that your reason for refusing to play recently? That you cannot bear to lose a modest sum of money?''

''No! Of course not!'' She could not possibly admit to the truth. She hesitated. ''But—''

She was saved from thinking up an excuse by her father's cutting in. ''He has also received his subaltern's back-pay from the Army,'' he reminded her curtly. ''Do not condemn the gentleman for accepting and spending what is rightfully his!''

''I don't.''

''Forgive me, but it sounded as though you did.'' Lord Marldon eyed Vinny critically before carrying on. ''Since he has been with us Mr Smith has recovered much of his fitness; he is no longer the emaciated creature he was when he arrived—''

''Which I find hardly surprising, considering the vast quantities of your food he consumes!''

''Which I do not for one moment begrudge, daughter!''

When her father called her ''daughter'' in that tone, Vinny knew she had earned his severe displeasure.

''I am sorry, Papa, but—''

''No excuses, Vinny,'' ordered her father curtly. ''Your attitude grieves me. Society owes him a debt, which you can help to repay.''

Vinny wanted to protest, to ask why she should be called upon to pay, but could not bring herself to argue further with her father.

Besides, he was right. Her behaviour had been foolish. She had allowed her irrational feelings to overset her normal composure and good manners. All she need do was pull herself together, take the fellow to London, set him on his way and then forget him. Whoever he turned out to be.

''Very well, Papa,'' she agreed briskly. ''I will do as you suggest, although most of fashionable society will be out of Town at present. Perhaps we should travel to Brighton, instead.''

''No, no, I am certain London is the place. Clubs and things, you know. The staff might remember...''

''So they might. I will leave it to you to broach the subject, Papa. The suggestion will look better coming from you.''

And if I distance myself from it, it will be easier to leave him in London with Percy and return here, she added silently. Then I shall be rid of the disturbing creature once and for all.

A thought which failed to give her the satisfaction she had anticipated.

Chapter Three

And so it was arranged. Vinny, endeavouring to present a cordial front, was surprised by the dispatch with which her suggestion was put into operation. Percy leapt at the idea with unconcealed alacrity, eager to return to the pleasures of Town life. The other gentleman greeted it with cautious optimism.

Several days elapsed in feverish preparation. A messenger was sent ahead to warn her staff in Portman Square of her imminent arrival, with guests. Although the exchange of visits in a provincial backwater was not as prolific as in the fashionable centres, receiving and returning calls could still consume vast quantities of time and energy. A tiresome morning spent in making her farewells once more sent Vinny in search of peace, this time in the coolness of Lady Marldon's celebrated summer-house.

The sound of approaching footsteps disturbed the quiet buzz of the summer's day. One of her father's spaniels panted into the welcome shade of the stone edifice, his tail waving in greeting. A man hesitated on the threshold, a lean dark silhouette against the glare of the sun, straight as the Doric column beside which he stood.

"May I join you, ma'am, or will my intrusion prove a disturbance?"

Mr Smith. She could not conceive of a greater disturbance, but the merest pretence of good manners dictated that she should not refuse his request.

"Not at all, sir." She gestured with her free hand. "Please come in."

"Thank you, Mrs Darling." He strode forward and bowed. "I confess to having sought you out, for I wished to express my thanks. 'Tis vastly civil of you to offer me the hospitality of your house in Town, ma'am."

"Not at all," murmured Vinny.

Having paid his addresses, her visitor squatted down and concentrated on stroking the abjectly devoted spaniel, who was rolling on the floor at his feet begging for attention.

"Your assistance is most unexpected—but nevertheless welcome," he said.

For a moment Vinny imagined those sensitive fingers on her skin, and the familiar tingle ran down her spine. She instantly averted her eyes, straightened her shoulders and set the notion aside, and so was able to answer him with a fine show of affability.

"I always do my best to please Lord Marldon," she informed him. "Besides, I thought his suggestion an excellent one. You cannot spend the remainder of your life waiting for something to happen. Your memory needs jogging, and London seems the appropriate place to seek those who might be acquainted with you."

"The Peninsula would doubtless be better," he remarked with a fleeting, regretful smile, "since those of my fellow officers who survived are still over there."

"Were none merely wounded?"

He shrugged, his brown eyes with the green flecks resting on the dog, but not seeing it. "If so, they have not been brought to Goodrington. It is, after all, a Naval hospital, and my delivery there was by chance. Others have probably recovered in hospitals in Spain, or perhaps they are at Army establishments, or even at their homes, convalescing. Wherever they are, they are not accessible to me. I do not suppose I knew many from outside my own regiment, and since I cannot say which that was..."

"One officer from among four divisions," she mused as he trailed off, her interest caught up in his problem despite herself. "The Fourth, the Light, the Fifth and the Third, wasn't it? Do you know how many regiments were involved?"

He shook his dark head. "I did not even remember the number of divisions."

"We can discover. And then trace any officers who are known to be back in England—"

"Mrs Darling," he said soberly, meeting and holding her eyes as he looked up, his hand stilled on the spaniel's head, "I have long admired your brain. I see I shall have it to thank for my recovery, when it comes."

Vinny flushed at the praise, wondering fleetingly whether her father had, after all, attributed the entire scheme to her. "I doubt it is brains you need, sir," she protested, picking nervously at the yellow muslin of her skirt, "but plain common sense."

"And you have plenty of that, too," he immediately retorted, accompanying his remark with the merest hint of a smile.

The dog shifted and whimpered, its long tongue seeking his hand, begging for more fondling. The sensitive fingers responded, pulling gently at the silky ears, but still the man held her eyes with his.

"Come, sir," she cried, ignoring the heat which suffused her face, "I believe you are attempting to flannel me!"

"Do you not find it preferable to our remaining at

odds?'' he demanded, the incipient smile breaking out in earnest.

She looked into teasing, luminous eyes and knew that she agreed. A man without a memory, coming to them in such unusual circumstances, he had necessarily become an object of curiosity, even compassion, however much she might resent the former and he the latter. How long she had wanted to become better acquainted with him she could not have said. But the desire had been there, waiting to surface at the merest hint of an excuse.

''And you do not find such attributes a disadvantage in a female?'' she asked uncertainly, aware that he was eyeing the most unladylike copy of Adam Smith's *Wealth of Nations* which she held in her hand. He was not to know that she had not been reading it, but allowing her thoughts to wander.

''On the contrary, I find them quite fascinating,'' he returned quietly.

Vinny took a deep breath and stood up, smoothing down her skirt. ''Then you are in the minority among your sex,'' she informed him tartly. ''Most gentlemen desire their females to be decorative and accomplished in needlework, music and the arts, but do not require them to use their brains.''

''It must be unutterably wearying to be forced into a union with one incapable of carrying on a lively and informed conversation, or of discussing a problem intelligently.'' He too stood up, no longer teasing. No more than a yard separated them. Vinny dropped her eyes from his.

''It is,'' she told him briefly as she fled past him into the sunshine, clasping her book against her breast like a defensive shield but leaving her parasol in her haste.

Outside, she paused to take several more deep breaths.

''I believe you forgot this.''

He was beside her again, the dog at his heels. She tucked

Adam Smith under her arm, took the yellow silken shade from John Smith and quickly opened it, raising it to shield her face against the sun. It also served to hide it from him, a duty her deep-brimmed bonnet had failed to perform.

He obviously intended to escort her back to the house. As they paced along together, the dog scurrying and snuffling among the undergrowth, he made no attempt to revert to the subject which had caused her disquiet, but sought her knowledge of trees and shrubs, and admired the climbing roses and the lavender bushes and all the other blooms which gave their perfume to the summer air.

Vinny found his company diverting. Perhaps the projected journey to London would seal a friendship she could no longer deny would afford her pleasure—if only she knew who he was, if he did not so often irritate her and if he did not have such an unfortunate effect upon her composure!

She had travelled down in her chaise, posting with four hired horses for speed. Her own team had been brought down at leisure, for use during what she had anticipated would be a protracted visit to Preston Grange.

Her horses had been put to. A footman handed her up to join Flora, already seated inside.

The equipage appeared to meet with Mr Smith's approval. Looking modestly dashing in the best outfit obtainable from the local tailor, he ran his hands over the four beautifully matched chestnuts and exchanged some knowledgeable remarks with her coachman-cum-postilion, Ellis.

At Percy's insistence they were to make the journey at leisure, using their own horses all the way, and were therefore limited in the distance they could travel each day. The only sensible way to cover a great distance was by chaise, using post horses; but Percy had been reluctant to forgo the pleasure of driving his new curricle and costly pair of "splendid goers."

"The weather is set fair; we shall not find it a tedious journey, I'll vow!" he had declared. "Let us regard it as an excursion! You enjoy an excursion, Vinny!"

"But not in a chaise!" objected his sister. "If I had my barouche-landau here 'twould be a vastly different matter!"

However, she did not press her point, and Percy had his way. The weather continued fine, and Vinny felt more than vindicated in her earlier objection to the plan as she entered her carriage. The soft top of the barouche-landau would have folded back, while the interior of the closed chaise was already stifling. She would rather have suffered the discomfort of dust than endure the stuffy atmosphere prevalent inside the chaise, even with the window dropped. The men would enjoy all the fresh air possible in the open curricle.

Percy could be so selfish at times! She had not wished to travel to London in the first place, she reminded herself petulantly. She would abandon Ellis and her own animals at the next stage and hire four fresh post horses with postilions and press on ahead.

The human reason for her present discontent moved to wish her a comfortable journey. He bent an elegant leg, encased in tolerably well-cut buff pantaloons, to place a shining hessian boot on the step of the carriage, while extending a green-clad arm to rest his hand on the window-ledge.

"Sinclair tells me we are to lie tonight at the White Hart in Exeter, where we can be assured of reasonable accommodation and sufficient good stabling."

"That is what we agreed."

"Then farewell for the present, ma'am. His horses are

not yet put to, but doubtless we shall overtake you on the road.''

"Do not allow Percy to drive foolishly," she begged anxiously, her ill-temper overridden by concern. "You would surely have been better advised to travel with me, or on horseback—"

He laughed, and for some reason her spirits lifted at the sound. "Can you picture Sinclair riding sedately in a chaise, or accompanying it on horseback for that matter, when he can drive his new curricle and hold the reins of such a prime pair? And think of the crush were we to join you inside! And your maid, forced to travel with the luggage!"

Flora stirred beside her, and Mr Smith gave the woman a sympathetic smile before returning his attention to her mistress.

"No, Mrs Darling, it would not do, and you must not expect a young blade like your brother to consider safety first!"

"Nor you, I think, sir," she returned with a rueful smile. "But do have a care; the roads are not good, despite the tolls exacted from travellers!"

"I promise you, ma'am, we shall take the greatest possible care, and shall be anxiously awaiting your own safe arrival in Exeter."

He stepped back to sweep her a courteous bow as she gave Ellis, splendidly attired in postilion's uniform and already mounted on the nearside leader, the office to proceed.

Percy's being absent meant that she was not able to caution him personally on his driving, which she supposed must be a good thing, since he would not have taken the slightest notice of anything she said. Strangely, she was comforted by the knowledge that Mr Smith would be with him. Something about the man gave her a great sense of reassurance. He took risks, but not recklessly. He would find a way to prevent Percy from doing anything foolish. Why she was so certain of this she did not know, but the conviction had been borne in upon her, however reluctantly, over the weeks he had spent at Preston Grange.

A third vehicle, an old carriage of Lord Marldon's, drawn by hired horses, had lumbered off some hours previously, carrying most of their combined luggage and Percy's personal manservant, Thomas. His groom had been entrusted with the reins. It should arrive in Exeter slightly ahead of them, and Thomas had been detailed to procure the best rooms available while the groom arranged stabling for their horses and a change of animals for himself.

Her chaise had not long been on the turnpike road before Ellis was waiting his opportunity to pass an overladen cart. With that obstacle behind him he made excellent time, despite stopping often to rest the horses at the summit of a hill. Vinny began to wonder where Percy's curricle could be.

To her relief it caught up while her own team was resting, midway to their destination.

"Trouble with the harness," Percy amiably explained his tardy arrival.

"I wondered where you were," confessed Vinny, walking across to greet the new arrivals, having alighted to enjoy the air and to stretch her legs. "I do believe it would be a deal more pleasant if we travelled together. I should greatly appreciate company upon the road."

"A capital notion," applauded Mr Smith as he stepped down from the carriage, setting the light vehicle bouncing upon its huge springs. "I am to take the ribbons for the next stage, and shall follow your chaise with pleasure."

"Well, I don't know—" began Percy dubiously.

"My dearest brother," urged Vinny, "I know you relish speed above everything, but would you leave me alone on the road with no protection but Ellis and the young stable-boy riding the wheeler?''

"You've never mentioned being nervous before," grumbled the Honourable Percy gloomily, "but I suppose—if you don't mind, my dear fellow…?"

"Mrs Darling's wish is my command," said Mr Smith with exaggerated gallantry.

"Fool," grinned Vinny, feeling more light-hearted than she had since her come-out. "But I shall value your company, Percy."

"Oh, very well, then." He shrugged somewhat irritably. "I dare say the cattle won't mind."

He went to inspect his horses. The servants were either busy or had wandered off in various directions.

"But not mine?" enquired John Smith softly, harking back to her last remark to Percy, while steering her towards the rear of the curricle and leading her to stroll a short distance along the road.

"Yours too, of course," responded Vinny a little curtly as she stepped at his side. She did not want him thinking she actually enjoyed being with him, however true it might now be. "But mostly I shall value being certain that Percy is driving sensibly."

"How old is your brother, Mrs Darling?"

"Six and twenty, sir. Why do you ask?"

"And you, ma'am? To how many years do you own?"

"Three and twenty." Vinny flushed. "Not that I believe it to be any concern of yours, sir!"

"On that I entirely agree," he assented evenly. "But do you not think Sinclair, three years your senior, capable of living his own life? He is not as lacking in common sense, or prudence, as you make him out."

"You are impertinent, sir!" gasped Vinny. "You have no call to lecture me—"

"None at all!" He smiled his charming, disarming

smile. "I have no doubt you wish me at the Deuce, but I thought only to ease your mind, for I am aware that you worry for him."

That smile had its effect. Vinny's ruffled feathers began to settle down. "Then I forgive you, sir, and in return ask you to understand my concern. You may not be aware of it, but my husband died as the result of a driving accident."

He paused in his walk, bringing her to a standstill too.

"No, I was not. I had thought that…"

"You had thought what, sir?" she prompted.

"That Charles Darling had been an elderly bridegroom, and died of some affliction peculiar to the aged," he admitted, beginning to walk forward again and looking more uncomfortable than Vinny remembered previously seeing him.

"He was Percy's age," she told him quietly as she kept pace at his side, "and had rather less sense than that with which you credit my brother. I did not marry an old man for his money."

She saw the flush tinge his cheekbones. "My apologies, ma'am. Though I believe 'tis quite the done thing, and brings no discredit to a young lady to marry a fortune, wherever it may be found."

"No," agreed Vinny tightly. "In my opinion it brings greater reproach to the elderly man who seeks to buy youth and beauty he can no longer command by his character and address."

"Not an accepted view, ma'am, but one with which I fully concur."

They walked in silence for several moments.

"Did you love your husband?" asked John Smith abruptly.

"Love?" Vinny was startled and rather discomposed that he should ask. "Young ladies of my station seldom marry for love, sir," she retorted sharply, "even when they do not marry for a fortune. But I held him in esteem and affection, he was vastly good-natured, we dealt well enough together.''

''I see.''

''Do you, sir?'' asked Vinny, without expecting or seeking an answer. She went on quickly, ''But, in deference to your opinion of Percy, I release you both from your promise to keep me company on the journey.''

''That is a promise from which I for one desire no release,'' he told her lightly. ''I can see no reason for us to scurry off, only to suffer a tedious wait for you to join us at journey's end. To travel in company will be most agreeable. And, for my part, I shall willingly exchange places with you on occasion, so that you may enjoy the fresh air.''

She rewarded this piece of gallantry with a brilliant smile. ''Thank you, sir.''

Before she could say more, Percy, turning from his inspection, called after them. ''My bays are recovered, and Ellis says your cattle are, too. Shall we get on?'' he demanded.

''I am quite ready,'' responded Vinny quickly, hiding the disturbance Mr Smith's words had provoked. For his tone and manner had invested them with a subtle meaning she could not miss.

As the journey proceeded, Vinny began to look forward to the intimate dinners shared with her brother and Mr Smith, served in private inn parlours while the servants ate in the public rooms. With the experience of many journeys over the same road behind them, Percy and Vinny knew which inns to patronise and which to avoid. She no longer held any idea of posting ahead.

Afterwards, the three of them enjoyed a stroll or a game of cards. Vinny still found Mr Smith's company disturbing, but no longer necessarily irksome. She had learned to control her responses, to a degree. She joined in the play with enthusiasm and found the contest stimulating.

One evening she outwitted both her brother—which was normal—and their companion—which was not—and took the greatest of satisfaction in so doing.

John Smith smiled slightly as he opened his purse to honour his losses. "You have a talent for the cards, ma'am. Since you would seldom take a hand at Preston Grange I had not realised you played so skilfully."

"Should've warned you," grinned Percy. "My sister can be a demon at the card table when the mood is on her—though, like you, she refuses to play high or deep."

"I gamble with what I trust is skill and restraint," said Vinny primly.

"I would appreciate the opportunity to recover some of my blunt!" grumbled Percy, who stood in debt to both. "Let us play one more hand! And for God's sake raise the miserable limit you always impose on the stakes!"

"You are certain to fall ever-deeper into the suds, my dear fellow, with your sister on such good form tonight. I should wait for a more favourable occasion."

"I've been doin' that for weeks," protested Percy in a pained voice, "and what good has it done me? Your pockets are plump, while mine are almost to let! I must hit a winning streak soon!"

"We have had this discussion before. *You* can afford your present losses," put in Vinny decidedly. "Mr Smith's funds are still limited."

"But that is not the reason for my caution," put in John Smith quickly. "I am not, I trust, nervous on my own behalf. My inclination lies in quite the reverse direction— but recent experience now confirms my instinctive reluctance to gamble without restraint or thought for the cost. It shows me that I invariably—" Here he broke off and bowed his head in amused deference to Vinny. "Almost invariably,'' he corrected himself with a smile, ''have the luck and skill to win, and some inner demand I cannot explain dictates that I moderate the effect my good fortune may have on others. I cannot tell you why. I only know that it is so.''

Vinny experienced a warm glow of appreciation. She had seen more than one person ruined at the tables by a ruthless opponent, and deplored the prevailing morality which encouraged it.

Percy shrugged. ''You don't need to be tender-hearted on my account! But if you won't oblige, I'll go and look in the public rooms. There may be a game in progress there.'' He held up a hand as Vinny opened her mouth. ''No, my dear sister, I will not gamble all I possess. Neither will I rook some guileless servant. But if you are done for the night, I am not. I will see you at breakfast tomorrow.''

Left alone with Mr Smith, Vinny did not attempt to hide her anxiety.

''I do wish Papa would allow him to take up a commission in the militia,'' she lamented. ''He could expend his reckless energy in drilling, and practising manoeuvres.''

''He might as easily ride hard and gamble to excess among his fellow officers,'' pointed out her companion mildly.

''You speak from experience, sir?'' interposed Vinny sharply.

For a moment he looked confused. ''I do not know,'' he confessed.

Vinny sighed, partly in regret over her brother, partly in disappointment that Mr Smith's memory had not been jerked into action. Then she addressed him with a wry smile.

"You must think me quite idiotish, worrying over Percy as I do."

"It is a little stupid, yes, and I believe you have been led astray by Lord Marldon's excessive concern. He holds his son on too tight a rein. Yet I think Sinclair a lucky man to be the recipient of so much affection."

A bleak look flitted across his face, gone almost before Vinny saw it. Yet it told her more of this man than she had formerly understood. Much as he might attempt to cover his disability, it affected him deeply, not least in the loss of human affection. Vinny tried to imagine herself in such a circumstance. Without family or friends one would be lonely indeed. Quite lost.

Impulsively, she placed her small hand upon his arm. "You will regain your memory," she assured him earnestly, "and when you do you will find yourself the object of similar affection."

This time he recognised her compassion for what it was. Not pity, but genuine concern. He took the hand and lifted it to his lips. They were dry and cool on her tender skin. She felt their touch as a pain in her breast.

"I wish I could be certain of that," he said.

She recovered her hand with a degree of reluctance, but prudence demanded a hasty retreat.

"I must bid you goodnight, sir."

"Goodnight, Mrs Darling."

He watched her leave the room, wishing he had the right—an excuse—to detain her. He could not remember whether he had ever felt for any other woman as he felt for her. But what exactly did he feel?

He attempted to sort out his emotions, without conspicuous success. He did not know what to make of himself, or of her. Clever, talented, opinionated, provoking, temperamental, yet at her best deeply caring and compassionate, Davinia Darling represented a mixture of qualities which bewitched—and confused—him more than his loss of memory had ever done.

One moment he wanted to shake her, to bring her down from her top-lofty perch, the next to take her in his arms and make love to her until they were both senseless. He desired her company, yet was wary of allowing an attachment to grow.

What use for a man without family, memory or fortune to nourish a *tendre* for a Viscount's daughter, a wealthy widow who, by all accounts, had no desire to engage the attentions of even the most eligible of noble gentlemen? A woman with no intention of marrying again, and no apparent wish to engage in an *affaire de coeur?*

She would prove difficult for any man to manage, he acknowledged, and wondered whether Charles Darling had been up to handling such a high-spirited filly. Vinny—he thought of her as Vinny, though it would be imprudent as well as inexcusable to address her as such—had not apparently derived much pleasure from that union.

But he could handle her. Could waken her tempestuous nature into passionate response. He had felt it to be so from the first moment he had set eyes on her exquisite figure and enchanting face—and experienced futile anger at the comic figure he cut in his borrowed garments, countering it with stupid humour over her name. But the bad start was behind them now. Perhaps…

He shook himself out of his unsettling thoughts. Domesticity had never been one of his virtues or desires in the past—it could not have been, or he would surely not have chosen a military career. It did not particularly appeal now. And to even consider offering the Honourable Mrs Charles Darling anything less than marriage to someone bearing a respected name struck him as ludicrous.

Yet he found her company tantalising; she touched some chord in him that desired to protect, to serve…

The best service he could render her, he supposed rather sourly, was to ensure that Sinclair did not overstretch himself tonight. He let himself out of the quiet parlour to seek the boisterous, rancid atmosphere of the inn's pot-room.

Percy was nowhere in evidence. An enquiry of mine host, a stout man with sweat beading his florid face, begot a sly glance in the direction of the back stairs.

"He went off with one of my serving wenches," the man informed John Smith, slanting a knowing leer his way. "I could find a pretty one for you, quick as a nod, sir."

This obliging offer met with a brisk shake of the head. John Smith silently cursed the Honourable Percival Sinclair, abandoned his friend to his dubious pleasures, and sought his own less than comfortable bed.

Chapter Four

The bustle of arrival subsided. Her guests had been settled in their apartments and dinner eaten in the small dining-parlour. Vinny presided at the tea table, set up in the morning-room, which she used as an informal drawing-room when not entertaining, in buoyant mood. It was, after all, pleasant to be mistress in her own household again.

"Tomorrow," she reminded her brother, "you have promised to escort Mr Smith to the Horse Guards." She looked from one man to the other. "We are, I believe, agreed on the information you may hope to acquire."

"A list of all those officers missing after Badajoz," agreed Percy, "but how are we to decide which one is Mr... Smith?"

"Someone there may recognise him," said Vinny sturdily, "and if you discover the whereabouts of any wounded returned to this country we may arrange to visit them." She turned to her guest. "Have you still no glimmer of remembrance, sir?"

"None," admitted Mr Smith regretfully.

She handed him a cup of tea, which he carried to his chair. They drank in silence for a while, each retired into privy thoughts, until Percy stirred.

"Let us visit White's tonight!" he suggested brightly. "Ain't much sense in waitin', is there? Might as well go now. Then we can try somewhere else tomorrow evenin'— Watier's, Brook's and Boodle's will all require a visit!"

He was already on his feet, eager to make use of such an excellent excuse for enjoying himself in the way he preferred. Vinny fought down a quite unreasonable sense of disappointment before risking a glance at Mr Smith. If he was willing, she would not attempt to prevent their departure.

"Is that your desire, sir?" she enquired. "I believe my brother is anxious to re-acquaint himself with old haunts, and perhaps to engage in a more interesting game than we should offer him here."

John Smith had seen the initial drop in her countenance. He could scarcely count her disappointment as due to the prospect of losing his company. For, since she quite doted upon her brother, Sinclair's imminent departure and possible ruination at the tables would be more than enough to account for her displeasure.

He answered in carefully penitent tones. "I fear that, before launching myself into Society, I require an evening in which to recover from the journey. I must confess to finding the thought of meeting someone who knows me, and being forced to confront my past, a daunting one. One I would rather face after a night's rest."

"I consider that very poor-spirited of you, my dear fellow!" exclaimed Percy. John Smith merely smiled. Percy shrugged good-humouredly. "But as you like. I shall nevertheless go myself, and hope to discover who is still in Town."

"A most useful exercise, Percy," applauded Vinny. "I shall be making visits in form tomorrow morning, and leaving cards if I am not received. We must contact as many of our circle as we are able."

"The sooner the better," agreed Percy, all eagerness to be off. "Must do what we can to get your memory back, my dear fellow."

"I am obliged," murmured John Smith. "I can only offer my regrets at appearing indolent in my own cause, but I truly cannot relish the thought of facing a large company this evening, and must beg of you to be discreet, not to make much mention me or my…indisposition. I have no doubt that I shall become an object of extreme curiosity and would rather defer the favour of having so much attention bestowed upon me until I can no longer avoid it."

Percy acknowledged the apology with an airy wave of his hand. "We agreed not to make a great work of it, didn't we? Trust me! I shan't say a word tonight!" With a final grin, he departed with boisterous speed.

Mr Smith's eyes had clouded. The furrow between his brows deepened. Vinny saw his confusion grow, and regretted the return of a condition from which he had of late seemed free. She had thought him merely using exhaustion as an excuse not to go out—in fact she had suspected him of noticing her own discontent at the proposed expedition, and seeking to banish it by persuading Percy to remain in. Which was why she had so quickly agreed to Percy's departure. She would *not* be considered an overly protective, fussy female!

But she must have misjudged the man's motives. He had been expressing the simple truth. Even if not physically, he was mentally exhausted. And why she should suffer renewed disappointment, because she had thought him showing consideration for her feelings when he was not, she could not imagine!

Neither could she imagine why anxiety should gnaw at her as she watched him struggle for a return of normality— or what passed for normality in his present state of mind. But his disorientation passed as swiftly as it had come, and long before she had settled her feelings in her own mind. He smiled at last, if somewhat thinly. "I am sure you will forgive me."

Vinny smiled back. "Of course. The bustle of London bemuses you, sir?"

"I find it does, although Portman Square is quiet enough. I do not imagine I have had much occasion to visit Town in the past. I cannot feel dealing with its problems to be foremost in my experience."

"So our efforts to find someone here who recognises you may be worthless!"

"I fear so, though I cannot be certain. And I collect that not everybody spends their entire life in the capital?"

Vinny laughed. "By no means! The majority retire to their estates for at least half the year! We must hope you have made acquaintances in the country who are presently in Town!"

A new smile curled his lips, and that teasing look entered his eyes. "Perhaps Dame Fortune will smile on me in this enterprise, as she does at the card table!"

"She certainly smiles on you there, sir!" agreed Vinny with feeling.

"You did not object to your brother's visiting White's," he remarked quietly.

She shook her head. "His previous indiscretion was relatively small, and Lord Marldon made a great piece of work of it. Papa is, I fear, overly severe in his attitude— he expects too much of his heir... It puts me to the blush to admit it, but I am obliged to you for setting me right on the matter."

"And I am flattered that you should value my opinion."

On this happy note they relapsed into cordial silence. Mr Smith laid his head back against his chair and closed his eyes. The dying rays of the evening sun slanted through the window. Although not falling directly upon his face, the light revealed his features to be quite drawn again.

They were alone. Sharing an intimacy which would appear quite improper in certain circles. But Vinny consoled herself with the thought that widows enjoyed a licence denied to other single ladies.

She settled back in her own chair, content to watch his now familiar features in repose. Lines of experience and weariness only made the general assemblage more interesting. His nose was nothing special, straight but a little thick at the end. His mouth—that was a different matter. Her nerves tightened as she studied it. Well-formed, the bottom lip full but firm, its general hardness softened in relaxation; it promised... She caught her own lower lip between her teeth and drew in a breath before moving her eyes to examine the lean, squarish chin which denied any suggestion of softness. Tough, she had thought his face, and uncompromising. Belonging to a man brought up in a hard school. That initial assessment had proved to be correct—yet he could show such gentleness, such consideration on occasion. And, hard school or no, it had not erased his humour, his appreciation of finer things, or compromised his manners and address...

She caught her thoughts up sharply. What was she doing, sitting in apparent domestic peace sighing over a man about whose background she knew nothing for certain?

She sprang to her feet, and as she did so his heavy lids lifted. Dappled green eyes regarded her enquiringly. Vinny stepped briskly into shadow and pulled the bell-rope. "I will take supper in my room," she told her guest imperiously. "Yours will be served here, unless you prefer—"

"Indeed, ma'am, I do not require supper. I too shall retire in but a moment." He stood up, his eyes holding hers. Then he took her hand and raised it to his lips.

Vinny's reaction to this gesture was obscured by the

arrival of a servant. She quickly withdrew her fingers, gave her orders, bade him goodnight and made her escape.

The gentlemen set off in Percy's curricle immediately after breakfast. Vinny followed a few minutes later in her barouche-landau, Ellis up on the box and a liveried footman in attendance. She did not step down from her carriage at any of the residences at which it paused until she was assured of being received. She made several brief but satisfactory calls. Where the occupants were from home her footman carried her card to the door and delivered it to a servant.

She returned to Portman Square full of optimism and eager for news. But by the time the two men finally put in an appearance she had almost given them up, and was about to change for dinner. Percy's gloomy countenance told her that success had not yet been achieved.

"Well?" she demanded.

"We obtained a copy of the list of names." Percy flung down a sheet of paper. "Er—Smith don't recognise one of 'em."

"To my regret, they mean nothing," confirmed John Smith. His momentary frown turned into a expression of elation as he addressed her eagerly. "But Sinclair has failed to inform you of the most important thing! News from the Peninsula—we had it direct from the Horse Guards! Wellington was forced to abandon Salamanca in July—"

"Oh, no!" exclaimed Vinny.

"Yes, but wait! His army was in retreat when Wellington saw his opportunity to engage Marmont's French one, and won a famous victory! Salamanca is ours again, and Wellington advanced to take Valladolid! But the greatest news has just this day arrived—he is marching on Madrid!"

He was a soldier to his core, thought Vinny, watching the animated face, free now of gloom, alight with joy in the success of unknown and temporarily forgotten comrades-in-arms.

"Great news indeed!" she exclaimed. "Mayhap this endless war is almost over at last!"

"Do not set too much store by that, dear ma'am. He has to face attack from two French armies to the north, and two, even three, from the south! But Napoleon himself is engaged elsewhere. Our Commander-in-Chief will not be taken by surprise; on that you may count."

"You speak with great authority, sir," she observed. "As though you remember Spain and know the man."

"I studied the action on maps as it was explained. It made complete sense to me, though I could not visualise the terrain. As for the man—I feel I do know him," he admitted slowly, "yet not personally. I can picture him no more than anyone else, yet—impertinently, perhaps—I imagine I know his mind."

"Yet you do not know your own!"

"Indeed I do, ma'am!" he protested, a note of aggression entering his voice. "'Tis my memory only which is impaired!"

"To which I referred!" she retorted sharply. "And which was, if you remember, the original subject of our discussion! Did you obtain news of the wounded from Badajoz?"

Percy intervened to answer her, waving yet another piece of paper in the air. "Very few have been returned home, so far as they know, though I wouldn't set too much store on the accuracy of their records—a couple of men to Scotland, and three to Ireland! Not one they can name is nearer than Aberdeen!"

"Are there no English officers in the Army?" exclaimed Vinny in exasperation.

"Unless the records are as incomplete as Sinclair believes, all those involved are either dead or missing, or still in Spain," supplied Mr Smith calmly.

"You must travel to Aberdeen," she announced decisively.

He lifted his chin and stared at her down his nose. "I fear it most likely to prove a wasted journey."

Vinny realised that, however much he might appreciate a tutored and enquiring mind, he resented being organised. She temporised. "There can be no need to undertake it immediately."

"Just so." He bowed, acknowledging her tacit apology. "For the moment I am content to pursue other lines of enquiry. I will make the journey only as a final resort—"

"So we've agreed on doin' a round of the clubs after dinner," cut in Percy. "Just look in, don't you know, no gaming."

"Although," said John Smith with a shrug, "I suspect I may not have been in command of the means to join the leading clubs—and Mrs Darling has already inferred that London may be unfamiliar to me."

"Still, we can leave no stone unturned! And as to expense, there are plenty of coffee houses and lesser clubs we can quiz later."

"I shall expect to receive morning calls from tomorrow," announced Vinny. "If Mr Smith would consent to be present—"

"Oh, I say, Vinny! That's the outside of enough! You can't expect us to sit around over a pot of scandal broth listening to a roomful of old gabble-grinders—"

"I shall be glad to engage to be present, ma'am. But Sinclair has no need to suffer on my account."

The quietly spoken words brought a flush to Percy's cheeks. "Well, I dare say it will depend on who comes," he admitted. "If Lady Hartwood brings her daughters...

The Hartwoods are in Town, you know. Saw Sir Jonas last evenin'."

"And you cherish a *tendre* for Miss Hartwood," smiled Vinny, remembering her brother's light-hearted pursuit of former months. "Depend upon it, if she knows you are in Town, she will call. But have a care, brother. You must not make your attentions too plain, else she will think your interest fixed and expect an offer."

"That's the trouble with females," grumbled the Honourable Percival. "Can't accept a fellow's admiration without expecting him to get himself leg-shackled! But, since I have no intention of makin' her or anyone else an offer, I shall behave with conspicuous discretion."

"You," accused Vinny severely, "are a shocking flirt!"

Her brother grinned, but did not attempt to deny the charge.

The immediate days ahead organised, Vinny began to plan an evening supper party, to be held within the month. In the interval between rising and breakfast the following morning she wrote out a list of those she would invite— were they yet in Town. Cards of invitation would have to be ordered, printed and delivered, amusements organised.

Folding doors between the morning-and drawing-rooms could be opened to make space for some dozen couples to stand up in elegant surroundings. Card tables could be set up in the small dining-parlour beyond the morning-room and downstairs in the reception-room off the hall where she received and entertained those morning callers not invited upstairs to the morning-room. Supper would naturally be served in the dining-room. She had entertained in such a way on numerous occasions, but seldom with so much enthusiasm. After all, the sooner Mr Smith discovered who he was, the sooner her life would return to normal.

With such a pleasing prospect before her she ate a hearty breakfast. Callers could scarcely be expected to arrive so early, and immediately they had finished eating Percy proposed a visit to his tailor's to fit their guest out in clothes suited to town life.

"No," objected Vinny quickly. "Do not take Mr Smith to your tailor, Percy. Your style is not, I collect, to his taste. Am I not correct, sir?"

"Er—"

Vinny watched delicacy of feeling and honest opinion vie for possession of John Smith's features and took pity on him.

"Weston will fit Mr Smith out famously," she told her brother. "He will count it a favour to serve any acquaintance of Lord Marldon."

Percy took the implied criticism of his own sartorial elegance in good part, merely grinning and remarking, "My father's dress certainly fitted you better than mine, my dear fellow! So I bow to my sister's view. Weston it shall be. We should return before your morning visitors have departed, my dear Vinny."

"I have most severe doubts on that point!" grimaced Vinny. "I am fully aware of the time a visit to the tailor can consume! However, I see the necessity for Mr Smith to renew his wardrobe. Tomorrow will be time enough to begin attendance here."

"If I may be allowed to voice an opinion, I have one outstanding objection to this scheme," stated John Smith in a rather tight voice. "It may have escaped your notice, but my funds are limited. I cannot afford an expensive tailor."

"Oh, but my dear fellow, if you are to mix in first circles, you must dress accordingly!" exclaimed Percy, and added, "Don't concern yourself about the blunt. He will not expect to be paid!"

"Really? I should not have thought his establishment a

charitable institution,'' remarked Mr Smith with biting sarcasm.

"What Percy means,'' said Vinny, exercising extreme patience, "is that payment may be deferred until you are in better funds. You should have little difficulty in supporting such expenditure if you engage in regular gaming.''

"I have not the slightest desire to embark upon a career as a professional gambler!''

"Naturally not! But until you discover your true circumstances you cannot afford to be too nice in your conscience!'' she retorted, just as sharply as he had spoken. "Come, sir! Indulge us! You would,'' she added in a more placating tone, "appear to the greatest possible advantage dressed by Weston.''

Mr Smith had risen to his feet. He paced across to the fireplace and turned his back on the empty grate. His manner suggested that he was attempting to overcome considerable agitation of spirit.

"I will not allow expediency to overturn principle,'' he told her at last. "Much as I should wish to oblige those who have shown me nothing but kindness, and who have rendered me every assistance within their power—'' he bowed to both sister and brother in turn "—I will not compromise. I need to be in command of the means to meet a bill before I commit myself to the expense. I fear,'' he finished decisively, "that I must decline to visit Weston for the moment.''

Percy regarded him as though he were mad. "But my dear fellow,'' he remonstrated, "everyone runs up debts; it is the done thing, you know—who could cut a dash, otherwise?''

"I have no wish to pretend to be other than what I am. Anyone who has known me will recognise me in any outfit I care to wear, I dare say.'' He brushed a speck of fluff from the sleeve of his green coat and ran his eyes down an impeccably clad leg. The buff pantaloons fitted almost to perfection. "I do not believe my present apparel will bring you into disgrace. And Lord Marldon has most kindly extended the loan of his evening dress."

Twice now he had set his mind against a course of action planned for him. Vinny recognised an obduracy of spirit which, considering his situation, astonished as much as it annoyed her.

"I collect, sir," she said tartly, "that you will not be forced into anything, and will not bow to pressure, however well-intentioned. That has become transparently clear."

"I believe I am entitled to hold strong opinions and to keep to them."

Part of her honest soul rose in admiration of such strength of purpose, even if it did border on arrogance.

"Perfectly, sir. Perhaps you would care to take over the direction of your course of enquiry. I am very willing to leave you here and return to Devon. My servants will be at your disposal, and no doubt my brother will elect to remain with you."

He reacted instantly and swiftly, striding across to where she sat to sink to one knee in penitent homage.

"I beg of you, do not allow my stiff-necked utterances to persuade you to leave!"

He lifted her hand and carried it to his lips. On this occasion there was no interruption to disguise the effect. The strange, piercing quiver which ran up her arm reached her breast.

"I need your help, ma'am," he admitted huskily, "and in most matters am entirely at your disposal. But on certain points I must solicit your understanding."

"You will not accept orders, you will not gamble to excess and you will not stretch your pocket beyond its means," offered Vinny with a wry little smile. She retrieved her hand and clasped it in her lap. She had not wanted to leave. Part of her still wished that he had a less unsettling effect upon her nerves, but a growing part was beginning to enjoy the stimulation his presence brought. The thrill when he kissed her hand had not been at all unpleasant. He still knelt at her feet and his lips, curving now in an answering smile, were near enough for her to touch. She had only to lift a hand...or to lean forward...

As his gaze caught hers his strange eyes darkened. He sprang to his feet and bowed.

"You have it exactly, ma'am. I do not know why I am as I am, but I fear I cannot help my nature. I believe I may be obstinate."

"And arrogant, sir!"

"I say, Vinny, do stop bein' so waspish! Poor fellow is doin' his best to apologise," protested Percy, breaking in on what had become an intimate exchange.

"I was funning," explained Vinny. "I believe you understood that, sir?"

Mr Smith gave a delighted chuckle. "I did, Mrs Darling! And it gives me the greatest of pleasure to confirm your diagnosis! I believe I am an arrogant fool to impose my opinions upon you as I do! But I cannot help it!"

"I might wish you could—but I should admire you less if you did not hold to your principles, sir!"

"Well, then, there you are!" exclaimed Percy fatuously. "I propose takin' a walk. Acquaint you with the streets round about, What do you say?"

"I am perfectly agreeable, if Mrs Darling has no objection?"

"None. Just do not allow Percy to keep you above an hour!"

They were being deliberately considerate and polite to each other. Why could she not enjoy the same relationship with him as she did with other gentlemen of her acquaintance? wondered Vinny irritably as she watched the two depart.

With a sigh of frustration, she settled down at a writing-table. Her parents would be anxious to know of their safe arrival. She finished the letter, sealed it and had just given it to a footman to post when her first caller was announced. Others followed, coming and going in quick succession.

As she had predicted, Miss Hartwood had persuaded her mama to bring her to Portman Square. They were accompanied by her younger sister, Miss Arabella Hartwood, and another young lady introduced as Miss Rosedale, a cousin of the sisters whom Lady Hartwood had been persuaded to chaperon for a few months, and who had already taken up residence with her.

This was, on the surface, a generous gesture, since, despite their acknowledged beauty, liveliness of spirits and abundance of suitors, neither of the Miss Hartwoods had contracted an engagement during the previous Season. Rumour had it that they were waiting to fix the interest of gentlemen of more consequence than had so far offered. Percy, as heir to a viscountcy, would do if he could be brought to the point, since Miss Hartwood found him attractive—though a duke would have been preferable.

But Vinny immediately recognised the reason for Lady Hartwood's sanguine acceptance of the young cousin into her household. Miss Rosedale would offer little competition to her daughters.

Vinny scarcely gave the quiet girl more than a cursory glance as she acknowledged the young lady's respectful curtsy. She registered brown hair, nice eyes and a gentle smile before her menfolk arrived to cause a thrill of anticipation and confusion among the Miss Hartwoods.

John Smith's introduction, as Vinny had foreseen, created quite a stir.

"My dear sir," gushed Lady Hartwood, eyeing the handsome figure he cut with approval, "such a misfortune to befall a brave officer! Do you tell us that you can vouchsafe no knowledge of your history? That you have no ability to claim kinship with anyone?"

"I do, ma'am," he returned with a slight smile. "To my knowledge I have no history and no distinguished connections."

"But you must have, sir! Come now, do not be shy! Confess! You are bamming us! Do you not agree, Mary?" she demanded of her eldest—but, without waiting for an answer, sped on with her speculation. "Confess!" she repeated. "There is a scandal in the family! You therefore wish to deny all knowledge of it and reject the relationship!"

"You are quite out, ma'am. But you must think what you will. I have nothing further to add," responded Mr Smith with icy courtesy.

Quite undeterred by his manner, Lady Hartwood swept on. "You are determined to retain an air of mystery!" she declared. "Nothing so distinguishes a gentleman—particularly a gallant officer—in the eyes of young ladies as to have some puzzle buried in his past! Is that not so, Mary? But beware, sir! *Parents* are not so easily gulled by fine manners and an enigmatic air!"

"Were I looking for a wife, I might well heed such a warning, my lady. However, since I am not, I shall feel free to hold to the truth."

If Lady Hartwood recognised his frigid reply as a setdown she chose to ignore it, while making it the signal to turn her attention to Vinny.

"And what do you make of your guest's condition, Mrs Darling? Or are you privy to his secrets? If so, we must depend upon *you* to discover them!"

"I can assure you, ma'am, such a course would bring

you little enlightenment. Mr Smith has been equally unable to confide in us.''

"And yet—you are prepared to introduce him into Society?" cried Lady Hartwood, quite outraged.

Vinny smiled, surprised at the degree of sympathy she felt for Mr Smith, while admitting admiration at the way he had dealt with Lady Hartwood's impertinence.

"Mr Smith is self-evidently a gentleman, ma'am, and the acquaintance is approved by Viscount Marldon. I need no other recommendation.''

Percy's attention had been quite taken up in an attempt to capture Miss Hartwood's interest. Hers had wandered to the conversation, and her gaze, resting upon Mr Smith, held a mixture of curiosity and admiration. Should *he* wish to fix her interest he would have little need to exert himself, thought Vinny rather sourly. Although Mary Hartwood had indicated her readiness to receive Percy's more formal addresses—which he was reluctant to make—she had never looked upon him with her blue eyes so full of limpid invitation as they were now. Her sister, too, was eyeing Mr Smith eagerly, assessing his attractions, his consequence and his possible income.

Looking rather piqued at being deprived of the young ladies' interest, Percy spoke more aggressively than usual. "Probably ain't much more to know, if you ask me.''

"Which we did not,'' said Vinny sharply.

"Only funnin',''️ he informed the room at large, and happened to look across at the new female Lady Hartwood had brought with her.

Like Vinny herself, her brother had barely spared the newcomer a glance when introduced, but now Vinny saw his expression change. His eyes seemed to widen and then glaze over as he met the girl's clear, honest grey gaze.

Startled to see his reaction, Vinny looked at her again. Miss Rosedale, too, had been following the exchanges with

Mr Smith, but her thin-featured, unremarkable face showed none of the avid speculation, none of the visible admiration expressed on those of her cousins, though intelligent interest and sympathy were evident. Combined with the light shining from her clear eyes, the effect was quite startling. A slightly faded mouse had been Vinny's first impression. She was forced to revise it somewhat. But Percy looked as though he'd been hit over the head with a cudgel!

She addressed the girl at the first opportunity, asking how she liked London.

"I find it noisy and confusing, ma'am," Miss Rosedale returned with a quiet smile, "but interesting and enjoyable, too. The museums and libraries are of particular interest to me, and of course I am most grateful to my aunt Hartwood for introducing me into Society."

Such a reply, which combined honesty and common sense, showing appreciation without once going into raptures, and expressed her gratitude to her aunt, could not but increase Vinny's favourable impression.

Lady Hartwood quickly brought the conversation back to herself and her daughters and Jane Rosedale said virtually nothing more during the remainder of the visit, apart from words of assent and farewell. Yet Vinny saw that Percy's interest had grown rather than diminished.

She glanced at Mr Smith, afraid that his eyes, too, would hold a dazzled expression. But to her shamed relief they did not. They met hers brimming over with suppressed laughter, which exploded into a deep chuckle as the door closed behind her guests.

"I fancy we are in for some ripe entertainment, once the mamas gather," he remarked. "Are they all as extraordinarily indelicate as Lady Hartwood, pray?"

"Many are," Vinny admitted. "But you will be safe from serious attention if you confide the state of your resources. Fortune counts for everything."

"Then perhaps," said Mr Smith with another chuckle, "I should bless my straitened circumstances. I should not enjoy evading the attentions of fortune-hunting mamas for long!"

A night's sleep had clearly enabled him to rise above his reluctance to be the object of so much curiosity. He could view it now as a rich joke.

"You would soon learn the art," grinned Percy, his pique quite overcome by some other emotion which caused him to appear subtly subdued. "I will willingly be your tutor!"

"How you have survived so many Seasons without being caught—" began Vinny.

"I never met a woman like Miss Rosedale before," said Percy simply.

Dumbfounded, Vinny stared at her brother. "Then I did not imagine your interest?" she asked faintly.

"No, my dear Vinny. I believe I am caught at last," said Percy.

He appeared quite serious. Vinny drew a breath. "I will make a point of seeking her out, encouraging her company," she promised at last. "We know nothing of her."

"Just by lookin' at her I know all I need," declared Percy with absolute assurance.

"Sensible fellow," applauded Mr Smith. "Meet the right female, attempt to attach her, and damn what anyone else thinks."

"Is that your philosophy, sir?" asked Vinny, concealing a quite disturbing anxiety to know his answer.

He looked at her with that in his eyes which brought a rush of colour to her cheeks. "It certainly is now," he told her. Then he laughed. "Whether it has always been so is more difficult to tell."

"One thing that is *not* difficult to tell," responded Vinny, with an asperity designed to cover her con fusion, "is that neither Lady Hartwood nor Miss Hartwood will be pleased at your change of heart, my dear brother!"

Chapter Five

Had it not been for the presence of the mysterious and charismatic John Smith, Percy's defection might well have caused greater consternation among the Hartwood ladies. As it was, Lady Hartwood's determination to cozen information from the latest arrival on the social scene, and the Miss Hartwoods' preoccupation with vying for his attention, conspired to ensure that none of them noticed Mary's former suitor's paying his addresses to their mouse of a cousin.

If Percy was not pleading with Vinny to visit the Hartwood establishment in Harley Street, her daughters were pleading with Lady Hartwood to visit Portman Square. Vinny began to suspect Mr Smith of enjoying the attention lavished upon him. Mary and Arabella were by no means the only young ladies of their acquaintance to show a disquieting interest in the inscrutable, gallant lieutenant—the rank at which he admitted to having been discharged.

"The Hartwoods are monopolising you," Vinny complained one evening, after their return from a social engagement. "Wherever we go, they descend upon you and claim your attention. You are not meeting as many of the other members of Society as I would wish."

"Enough have seen me, I believe, ma'am, to enable me to feel reasonably certain that I did not move in these circles before joining Lord Wellington's campaign."

"He's right, y'know, Vinny," said Percy. "We've scoured the clubs and no one recognises him, not even one single servant, and some of 'em've been about for years. Seems to me we're on the wrong track."

"He seems comfortable enough in it," retorted Vinny acerbically. "The young ladies do not allow either his lack of background or his straitened circumstances to dampen their interest! Lady Hartwood spoke truly when she predicted that his air of mystery would attract notice! Though it would be as well to regard her caution," she went on, turning to the man in question. "Any young lady with a substantial dowry to bestow will be well guarded from an imprudent marriage."

He gave her an ironic bow. His lips retained their pleasant curve, but his eyes were cold. "My answer to that, ma'am, remains the same. I am not seeking a wife."

"Just as well," shot back Vinny, "for I doubt you would win one! But since you visited Weston's this morning, I collect that your financial position has improved. You have made enough at the tables to meet his bill?"

"Your inference is correct, ma'am." The coldness had invaded his voice.

"Ordered two new suits, one for mornin', the other for evenin', purchased shirts and cravats and visited the bootmaker, too. You won't recognise him in a few days' time!" laughed Percy. He yawned hugely. "I'm off to bed. Goodnight."

"Pleasant dreams," Vinny wished him as he left the room.

"He'll enjoy those," remarked Mr Smith as the door closed behind Sinclair. "No doubt Miss Jane Rosedale will figure in them largely."

"You have noticed?"

"Why should I not? He is a changed man, and speaks of little else!"

"I know. Amazing what love can do, isn't it?" remarked Vinny, a little wistfully. "But Lady Hartwood and her daughters seem not to have done so. They have been too occupied in claiming *your* attention, *Lieutenant!*"

"Do I detect a measure of reproach in your voice, Mrs Darling?"

"Of course not!" denied Vinny vigorously. Her dark eyes sparked a challenge. "Why should your success concern me?"

"Indeed, ma'am. Any more than your own popularity should trouble me," he countered smoothly.

So he *had* remarked her court of admirers and the succession of eager partners with whom she danced, despite *his* never asking her to stand up with him! Since their arrival in London he had shown her nothing but the minimum of attention demanded by good manners, and this had piqued her. She had suspected him of being too absorbed in his own enjoyment during their evening engagements to observe her activities. That he had not sent a small thrill of triumph shivering along her nerves.

"In fact," she shrugged, feigning indifference, "you have done Percy a service. He has been able to court Miss Rosedale without interference from the Hartwoods."

"So—you have no reason to object to my enjoying the interest my unfortunate condition has brought upon me."

"None at all, sir!" Realising her rebuttal had been far too sharp, she moderated her tone. "Although I believe Lady Hartwood to be still convinced you are faking your loss of memory, and nobody else knows what to believe!"

Shadows obscured his face. Vinny could not quite make out his expression. "Amnesia is a condition only more recently diagnosed,'' he said slowly. "They probably believe that, if I am speaking the truth, I belong in Bedlam.''

"You are not mad!''

"Not so long ago I would have been considered so, according to the doctor who examined me. But people must make up their own minds. Their opinion is not important to me." His voice sounded indifferent, but as he shifted in his chair the light from a nearby branch of candles fell across his features, revealing a brooding expression. He looked up to give her a wry smile. "I am only surprised— and grateful—that you and your family did not question the truth of my assertion.''

That smile betrayed his vulnerability. Vinny hastened to reassure him. "You came directly from the hospital, recommended by the Reverend Mr Jackson! And the confusion in your mind was more evident then.''

"I am comforted to know that the improvement is noticeable. But—'' he paused to eye her from beneath heavy lids "—the time has come for me to travel to Aberdeen. We have exhausted London's possibilities, I fancy.''

Vinny's expression veered between outrage, exasperation and something that looked very much like disappointment.

"Would you leave London before my evening party, sir? Which, I may point out, I have organised entirely for your benefit!" she added hotly.

"I thought I would be falling in with your previously expressed wish,'' he rejoined blandly, his eyes still carefully scrutinising her face.

"*That* was before I had organised a soirée!'' exclaimed Vinny, not sure whether he was roasting her or not. Aggravating creature! Why had he ever entered her life? "If, after that, you still need to travel there, or anywhere else for that matter, Percy and I shall be glad to accompany you on the journey.''

"I doubt whether Sinclair will wish to leave London at present," pointed out Mr Smith gravely. "And I cannot allow you to risk your reputation by accompanying me without a chaperon. I shall travel alone."

He sounded so insufferably, arrogantly complacent! Vinny almost exploded. Her eyes glared indignation, but she kept her voice level.

"You will do no such thing, sir! And I must say that as a young unmarried girl I accepted the restrictions set upon my freedom with grace. As a widow, I confess to finding them vastly irksome! I am, however, aware that my reputation would be in shreds were we to travel alone together, even accompanied by servants. Since I have no desire to flout the conventions and give the scandal-mongers food for gossip, I shall rely on Percy's accompanying us. Not," she added hastily, "that I wish to journey to Aberdeen any more than I did to London, and certainly not before my supper party. I shall be forced to cancel the invitations, which have already been sent out! Really, sir, your decision is most inconvenient! But you need someone with you who knows your condition."

"I believe I am now recovered enough to fend for myself, Mrs Darling."

"Pshaw!" Vinny's temper boiled over at last. Ungrateful beast! She leapt to her feet and lifted her fan as though threatening to beat him over his arrogant head with it. "You really are the most...most difficult, aggravating creature I have ever known!"

"And you, ma'am, are the most managing female I have ever had the misfortune to meet!" He rose from his chair in a single lithe movement. They stood, barely a yard apart, glaring at each other.

Vinny caught her breath. The expression in his eyes sent the blood coursing through her veins. It held so much more than the anger evident in his entire stance. She had caught glimpses of some half-hidden emotion before. Now, at last, she recognised it for what it was.

She clenched clammy hands on her fan. His gaze smouldered on her mouth. Quite clearly he was tempted to kiss her. She licked her dry lips, knowing she wanted him to. Her response burst over her like a shower of sparks from a firework display. All the tension, the trembling, the feelings of frustration, the swift anger, were due to one cause and one cause alone. She wanted him to kiss her as much as he apparently wanted to do so. Such alarming physical attraction had never struck her before, and she had refused to recognise it.

Because she had not dared to, for where could it lead?

Why now? cried her heart. Why for a man without memory, name or fortune?

She gathered all the will-power at her command and took a bolstering breath, standing her ground, facing him and his devilish attraction down.

"The cancellations will be sent tomorrow," she told him abruptly. That was surely retreat enough.

At the sound of her curt tone his tension visibly snapped. The fire in his eyes died, leaving them coolly assessing. She should have been glad to see the danger recede, but instead Vinny felt a contrary sense of disappointment. His emotion had been too easily dissipated. Hers still boiled within her.

"I have no wish to cause you inconvenience, ma'am."

Aware that his voice had thickened and that it trembled slightly, John Smith cleared his throat. His admiration for her fierce spirit and enchanting person had almost overwhelmed him, made him do something he would bitterly regret. Mastering his desire had taken a supreme effort, rendered more difficult by the glimpse of a similar emotion mirrored in her lovely, startled face and the unconsciously provocative moistening of her full lips. But how quickly she had recovered!

The wisdom of his almost unconscious decision to avoid closer intimacy was now proved beyond doubt. The fire which he had suspected—and now knew—could so easily be ignited between them could do nothing but consume: his pride, her position in society.

But he had not intended to cause her distress and attempted to remedy his mistake. "Shall we leave this discussion until after your party?" he suggested quietly.

His words merely served to inflame her further. "You do not wish it cancelled? Why do you not make up your mind?" she demanded furiously.

He managed a lop-sided grin. "I plead the privilege of my condition. Besides, apart from the lure of your charming company, which it seems I shall be unable to avoid, I feel no great enthusiasm for undertaking a journey on what must, almost certainly, be a wild-goose chase."

"Then why did you suggest it?" she snapped.

Why had he? To nettle her? "Because I felt I should," he retorted brusquely. "I am, after all, imposing on your hospitality most blatantly."

Vinny let out a pent-up breath. She had ceased to regard him as encroaching and now he was accusing himself of the same fault! But his awareness did prove that he possessed finer feelings. Not that she had ever truly doubted it—at least not recently.

She sighed. "You are not imposing," she told him wearily, and shrugged. "I confess to having become completely involved in your most exceptional quest. I shall not rest until you have regained your memory."

His heart kicked in his chest. He drew in a sharp breath. She cared what became of him! The discovery brought pleasure and unexpected pain.

"That may never happen," he reminded her grimly, "but—your concern is not unwelcome."

He accompanied this statement with such a smile as to make Vinny's heart miss a beat. And to force her to seek an answer to a most pressing question. Why *was* she so determined to pursue the quest, so reluctant to allow him to do so on his own? Because she feared she would lose him unless she kept him close? How could one lose what one had never had? Common sense told her there was danger in following her present course; she should let him go—but she did not have the resolution to withdraw.

"I must bid you goodnight, Mr Smith," she managed. "Tomorrow Ellis shall drive us in Hyde Park again. We may meet someone new in Town."

"I shall be at your command, ma'am." He bowed with all his normal elegance, his resonant voice light and completely under control again. "Goodnight."

No more was said about travelling to Aberdeen. Vinny absorbed herself in the plans for her social evening and the days between sped past until there was none left.

She dressed before dinner, which was laid later in London than at Preston Grange. She had ordered a simple meal, for her staff had been busy all day preparing exotic supper dishes. Descending the stairs, she admired anew the restrained elegance of her home, the dainty plaster leaves and scrolls embellishing delicately coloured walls and ceilings, the sparkling mirrors, the gleaming chandeliers. The servants had been busy for days cleaning and polishing until no smear, no speck of dust, was visible anywhere.

On the landing she caught a glimpse of herself in a mirror and paused to fiddle with the neckline of her dress. As she passed on she wondered whether either of the gentlemen dining with her would notice her new gown. The rose-pink silk of the petticoat and paler gauze of the overskirt had caught her eye in Grafton House and her mantua-maker had made them up to a design cut low in the bodice, revealing the soft swell at the top of her breasts, while the skirts fell in folds from a waist gathered high beneath them. A concoction of deeper pink ribbons and white lace added interest to both hem and neckline, while a matching decoration had been entwined among the shining curls gathered high at the back of her head. A single strand of pearls glowed warmly about her neck.

To John Smith she appeared enchanting. Desire leapt in him, as it always did at sight of her vibrant features, her slender figure shown to advantage by quick, impulsive movements. But tonight the low cut of her gown, more than merely hinting at the fullness of her breasts, her vivacity, which had contained some new, special element since that night when he had almost succumbed to temptation, sent the blood coursing through his veins.

He ached for her. Yet in all honour he could make no move to win her. He thrust his hands beneath the tails of his new, exquisitely cut black evening coat lest their trembling betray him, veiled the expression in his eyes and schooled himself to greet her with an exemplary bow and cool courtesy.

It was left to Percy to voice the admiration both men felt.

"I say, Vinny, you look fetching tonight," cried her brother, and immediately switched to the subject uppermost in his mind. "I wonder what Miss Rosedale will be wearing? Some drab gown made in the country, no doubt, probably sewn by herself. But d'y'know it makes not the slightest difference to how I feel about her?" he added, as though amazed at himself.

"Neither should it," Vinny told him severely. "Dressing in the first style of fashion is not everything! If marrying a woman for money is not your object, then the ability of your beloved to make her own gowns should cause you nothing but pleasure! And I am certain she will gladly add more agreeable colours to her wardrobe, given the opportunity.''

"You do like her, Vinny, don't you?'' asked Percy with unaccustomed hesitation. Until now, his pursuit had been carried on without reference to any but his own feelings. Suddenly, he appeared to need reassurance.

"Of course I do! I am quite in raptures over her! Have I not sought her out whenever occasion allows? I find her a most pleasant, sensible girl. But it would not be correct to invite her here without her cousins. I only wish I could!'' Vinny waved an expressive hand to indicate her regret. "She exhibits an enviable degree of sensibility and is certainly no antidote!'' she went on, since Percy clearly expected more approbation from her. "She has a charm of face and manner which have, after all, fixed your interest, my dear brother. You have been an assiduous morning caller in Harley Street of late, and have even taken to drinking what you are pleased to term scandal-broth!''

Percy pulled a rueful face. "I vow I have drunk enough tea to sink a ship!''

"But have you succeeded in attaching her?''

"I believe so! Have you not noticed how she smiles when I approach? How readily she consents to stand up with me to dance? You've seen it, ain't you—er—Smith? You admire her, don't you?''

John Smith, jerked from the contemplation of one woman's perfection in order to praise another's, rose to the occasion with enviable poise.

"She welcomes your attentions with a smile no man could doubt, my dear Sinclair. As for her virtues, I leave the contemplation of those to your own good sense. Which, I may add, has improved vastly since you have made her acquaintance.''

"She don't approve of gaming," admitted the Honourable Percival, but without the gloom Vinny might have expected. Percy had discovered alternative excitements to add the necessary spice to his life.

"But you still gamble," observed Vinny.

"Can't expect a fellow to give it up altogether," Percy protested, his colour high. "But I keep to—er—Smith's rules now. No high stakes, no sittin' at the tables all night..."

"Between you," murmured Vinny softly as she accepted Mr Smith's immaculate black arm to pass through to dinner, "you have wrought a miraculous change in my brother."

He smiled, careful to keep his expression neutral. Both were aware of the vibrations emanating from the light touch of her fingers on his arm.

Both were equally determined not to acknowledge them.

The evening would be similar to many others they had attended during the past weeks, except that the party was hers, with Percy acting as host and John Smith the guest of honour.

A light rain had begun to fall, and darkness descended early that evening but, despite this, a small knot of poor people had gathered to see the splendid carriages and brilliantly attired personages arrive. Blazing flambeaux spluttered in the shelter of the porch, lighting the flight of steps up which, under the protection of large umbrellas, footmen ushered the guests from carriage to door.

The congestion of coaches outside soon converted into a congestion of people inside the house. Vinny stood in the receiving line with Percy and Mr Smith, proudly conscious of the way her rooms appeared to advantage in the light cast by myriad candles set in chandeliers and sconces. Pleasant strains of music coming from the drawing-room—

a pianist, harpist and violinist had been engaged to accompany the informal dancing later—reassured her that the musicians had arrived. She had already checked that in the rooms set aside for cards the tables had been laid out with their separate candles and unbroken packs.

"How thankful I am that so few people thought it unwise to risk the damp night air," she remarked as the first rush of guests thinned.

"Jane ain't here yet," said Percy gloomily.

Soon afterwards Sir Jonas and Lady Hartwood were announced, his corpulent person splendidly clad in maroon velvet, her taller, angular figure as elegant as a purple silk gown, an extraordinarily long ostrich feather head-dress and three strings of pearls could make it.

She dipped her duty curtsy and Vinny evaded the feathers by swaying backwards.

"My lady." Percy, his gloom dispelled, was not so lucky. His greeting ended in a sneeze as a feather caught his nose. He recovered quickly. "You know our guest of honour, Mr... John Smith, I believe, ma'am?"

"Silly boy!" chided Lady Hartwood with a gay little laugh. "You know quite well he has us all consumed with curiosity!"

Mr Smith evaded the feathers with consummate ease and only the twitch of his lips betrayed to Vinny the inner laughter struggling to escape as he made his grave bow. Unfortunately she caught his eye, and only good breeding prevented them both from dissolving into fits.

How distinguished he looks, she thought. How well black suits him! And the immaculate white at his throat, emphasising the darkness of his sunburned skin!

Her attention was reclaimed by Lady Hartwood.

"But here are our dear daughters!" she exclaimed, having performed her own duties. "Mary, Arabella, make your curtsies!"

The two young ladies moved eagerly forward. Miss Hartwood, a vision in lemon muslin, possibly having noticed that Percy's attentions were flagging and not wishing to lose the prospect of an excellent match, gave him a languishing glance before turning the full brilliance of her greeting on Mr Smith. Arabella, only slightly less lovely in pale blue, barely troubled to acknowledge her host before passing on to the guest of honour and distinguishing him with her most beguiling smile.

"Oh!" exclaimed Lady Hartwood as an afterthought, "And here is dear Jane Rosedale! So kind of you to invite her!"

"The party would not have been complete without Miss Rosedale, ma'am," responded Vinny, smiling at Jane with a warmth she would have found it difficult to extend to Mary or Arabella. This girl had a quality of character she could only admire. Her quiet composure hid a sense of fun which Percy had speedily uncovered. Mary would have ruined him within a year—had he not managed to evade her lures—but Jane promised to be his salvation. "Miss Rosedale, you are most welcome! We must have a comfortable coze later, when everyone else is engaged at the card tables!"

Jane's delightful smile, half-shy, half-assured, made all those who regarded it forget the elderly white muslin in which she was attired. "I should be greatly honoured, ma'am. I do so admire your lovely home. I am afraid my background is far less elegant. A country parsonage can scarcely compete."

She passed on to be greeted eagerly by Percy, warmly by Mr Smith. As was to be expected, she had grown in assurance since that first morning visit, thought Vinny. Percy's interest must have helped. He had speedily discovered that her father was a clergyman who held a living of no more than eight hundred pounds a year, her mother, Sir

Jonas's sister, having scorned several wealthy suitors to marry for love. Jane could scarcely be regarded as the catch of the coming Season, though she did possess a small dowry, left her by her maternal grandmother.

"Come, Jane! Do not linger!" remonstrated Lady Hartwood. "Come and sit here, with me!"

Vinny saw the girl trail dutifully behind her benefactress and take her seat among the chaperons. Mary and Arabella easily escaped their mother's attention and hovered near by. Watching with veiled interest, Vinny wondered whether Lady Hartwood had at last noticed that her niece had managed to fix the interest of her daughter's former admirer, and issued a warning. When the receiving line broke up and Mr Smith, as guest of honour, escorted his hostess out to lead the dance, she became convinced of it. Mary immediately engaged Percy's attention, making it impossible for him to ask any other female to stand up with him.

Vinny felt a thrill of excitement as she took her place opposite Mr Smith at the head of the set. They had seldom stood up together before. Of course, the country dance kept them at arm's length but from time to time they were forced to clasp hands, and then Vinny felt the warmth of his strong fingers creep up her arm to invade her heart. He smiled. She smiled back. The distance between them seemed to dissolve. He moved with both dignity and grace. She decided she had seldom enjoyed a dance more.

"So far, a successful squeeze," he remarked when the steps brought them together.

"Of course. My parties are always successful," she told him, accompanying the words with an impish smile. "Did you not know that I am an accomplished hostess?"

"I had heard a rumour." He chuckled, a rich sound which sent a quiver along her nerves. "An invitation to one of the Honourable Mrs Charles Darling's soirées is always much sought after.''

''Then your gratitude at my throwing one especially for you should be profound.''

Too late, she realised that her teasing had brought a reminder of that night when he had declared his intention of leaving. This was their first moment of intimacy since then. That it should occur in the middle of a line of other dancers did not seem to matter. Mossy brown eyes met ebony in a moment of intense communication which left Vinny breathless.

''I can assure you, ma'am, it is.''

No more was said. The movements of the dance led them apart again, and when it ended he escorted her back to her place, leaving her with a bow. But for quite a while afterwards Vinny moved among her guests in a daze.

She had little time or inclination to follow the fortunes of the young couple who had previously been uppermost in her mind, though she did notice that Percy had managed to engage Jane's hand for at least one of the dances.

An excellent cold collation was served for supper. Her chef and kitchen staff had done well, producing an attractive array of cold meats, pies, patties, tarts and an assortment of syllabubs and jellies to tempt the appetites of her guests.

Afterwards, remembering her promise, she managed to detach Jane for a few moments, taking her up to her boudoir on the pretence of a need to re-pin her hair. Vinny wasted little time on pleasantries, but came straight to the point.

''You must be aware of the fact that my brother has become sincerely attached to you, Miss Rosedale. Forgive me for asking—but do you return the sentiment?''

A becoming tinge of pink stained Jane's pale cheeks.

"Indeed I do, ma'am! But—he has not spoken—I scarcely dared hope…"

Reassured as to the girl's feelings, Vinny felt it permissible to expand on her brother's. "I believe him to be serious, Jane—if we are to be sisters, I shall call you Jane! But your aunt and cousin will be disappointed, I believe. If you should find it impossible to remain with them, after Percy has made his intentions plain, then be assured of a welcome here."

Jane expressed unbounded gratitude, but did not think the offer would be necessary. "My aunt Hartwood is perhaps a trifle top-lofty and over-ambitious for her daughters, but I do not believe her to be vicious, ma'am. She will not treat me unkindly."

"I am glad to hear you express such an opinion," said Vinny, stifling her own doubts, and the two women descended the stairs in perfect understanding and harmony.

A few of the younger guests were still dancing, but, since most of the gentlemen had deserted the ballroom in favour of the card tables, Vinny decided to go through to the small dining-parlour to watch the play. She sent Jane down to the reception-room on the ground floor, where she knew Percy would be presiding over the tables, and entered alone.

John Smith, backed by a bevy of young ladies which included Arabella but not Mary—the latter presumably in renewed pursuit of Percy and therefore downstairs—held the bank at *vingt-et-un*, his table being patronised by Sir Jonas. Several people stood, or lounged on chairs, watching the play and placing bets on the hands. Lady Hartwood sat ensconced at a nearby whist table.

The younger ladies grouped behind John Smith gave way before their hostess's determined advance. He seemed to exude some magic charm which drew her to him despite herself, she mused wryly. His touch during that first dance had ignited her blood, and her nerves were alive, tingling with expectation.

Expectation of what? she wondered, as he continued with his game, apparently quite unaware of her presence. She longed to reach out, to touch the vibrant black head bent in solemn scrutiny of his cards. A stack of guineas stood before him on the table. He had won a considerable sum despite playing for stakes below the modest house limit she had set—for no one would leave her house bankrupt if she could prevent it!

A short while after her arrival one of the players, a newcomer to London at that time—though Vinny knew the Earl from former visits—pushed across the coins he had just lost, shaking his head.

"Reminds me of a young fellow I knew at Oxford," he remarked. "Never met his match at cards! Had extraordinary skill and the Devil's own luck!"

Vinny shifted closer. "You knew this other gentleman at Oxford, my lord?" she enquired somewhat breathlessly. "May I enquire when?"

His lordship raised his brows in surprise at her intervention, but soon lowered them in a frown when he noticed the strain in her eyes. His rather puffy face screwed up into thought. "Years ago, ma'am. Let me see…went up in ninety-five. Must've been a year or so later this young sprig arrived to empty all our pockets!"

John Smith sat through the exchange as though turned to ice. His easy, graceful attitude had not changed, but he seemed frozen into it. Vinny could not see his eyes, but imagined they would hold the old, bemused expression.

"What was his name? What became of him?" she enquired quickly.

"Eh?" His lordship appeared puzzled by her persistence. He shrugged his heavy shoulders. "Devil knows! I don't!"

The room was small. Play had ceased at all the tables. Lady Hartwood leant forward, agog with curiosity. "Is it him?" she enquired in a loud, penetrating voice.

"Is what him?" asked his lordship, more muddled than ever.

"Smith!" she exclaimed. "Was it Smith you knew?"

Chapter Six

Vinny placed her hand on John Smith's shoulder. His muscles contracted under her fingers, but otherwise he did not move.

The Earl looked from Lady Hartwood to Vinny and down to the silent man sitting opposite him.

"Smith?" he muttered. "No, his name wasn't Smith."

Lady Hartwood opened her mouth to speak again, but Vinny beat her to it. Anything to keep that woman silent!

"You possibly have not been in Town long enough to hear," she explained quickly. Her heart was thumping and she found it difficult to speak at all, but it seemed easier to dash words out than to consider them carefully. "Mr Smith is not really Mr Smith; he does not recollect his true name, or who he is. We were wondering, my lord, if you might recognise him as your young acquaintance?"

Her voice husked to a questioning halt. His lordship's bloodshot eyes drifted from hers back to John Smith's face. He pursed his moist lips and sucked in a breath.

"Young puppy," he muttered. "Was an arrogant young puppy. No interests beyond horses, carriages, gambling and drink. No heart. Take a fellow's last guinea without a scrap of compunction. Fond of the ladies, too. Good-lookin' youngster. Women thought so, anyway. Bits of muslin all over the town.''

"But was it Smith?" Lady Hartwood had left the whist table and come across to shoo her daughter to a safe distance from a creature who might own such an undesirable reputation. Her feathers shook in agitation as she brayed out her question again.

"Couldn't say, my lady." The Earl considered the immobile John Smith anew. "Don't look much like him. Taller. Thinner. Older, too, of course. Like me!" He neighed with embarrassed laughter.

No one else joined in. Sensing the tension gripping his audience, he sobered and shrugged.

"Fellow disappeared. Scandal, hushed up. Some chap threw himself into the Isis if I remember rightly. Pockets to let. Woman involved, too. Never did hear the chief of it. Didn't concern me—not interested."

Vinny found her voice rather difficult to produce. "And you do not remember his name?" she managed.

"Who? Chap who drowned himself?"

"No! The one who caused the scandal," she cried, regaining her usual facility of speech as exasperation momentarily overcame the mixture of emotions causing her stomach to churn and her throat to contract.

"No, ma'am." The Earl's brows drew together, registering affront at her tone, but he answered civilly enough. "Younger son of some noble house, I believe." He snorted a half-laugh. "Weren't most of 'em, up at Oxford?"

Desperation lent an abrasive edge to her voice. "But surely you must remember—" she began.

"No must about it, ma'am!" he interrupted irritably. "Memory never much good at names. Can't call it to mind. Wasn't Smith, though."

"Hartwood! I think we should leave at once!" cried the baronet's lady. "This is no place for Arabella—"

"That seems rather unnecessary, my dear," remonstrated Sir Jonas mildly. "We were just enjoying a splendid game—"

"And how much have you lost?" demanded his wife in a scorching tone calculated to wither any resistance.

Sir Jonas answered with surprising spirit. "Very little, my dear. We are not playing for high stakes—"

"As you well know, I do not allow high stakes in my house, ma'am!" Vinny took the initiative again, controlling her voice by a supreme effort of will. Her outward coolness astounded her, when she considered the turmoil raging within. The hand on John Smith's shoulder had become a prop to sustain her as she teetered on shaking legs. "I can assure you," she went on, "that, even were Mr Smith proved to be this young man his lordship once knew, it would signify nothing."

In an attempt both to give reassurance and to bolster her own frailty, her fingers tightened on John Smith's shoulder. "The gentleman *we* know bears not the slightest resemblance in character or looks to the youth of whom his lordship speaks," she informed Lady Hartwood icily. "Since we have known him, Mr Smith has done nothing to earn our censure, and he remains my honoured guest."

Done nothing to earn censure except to kiss and tease me, whispered a treacherous voice in her head. But, rather than produce a feeling of renewed indignation, her memories made her the more determined to support him.

"You appear excessively anxious to defend this creature," observed Lady Hartwood venomously. "I have often suspected there to be more to the relationship between you than you would have polite Society believe!"

While Vinny stared in outrage at the spiteful woman, the Earl spoke into the silence.

"I say," he muttered uneasily. "Didn't intend to set the cat among the pigeons..."

Vinny felt all the tension drain from the muscles beneath her hand. John Smith moved at last, rising to his feet and smiling with an easy, assured grace that tore at her heart, for she knew how much its achievement must cost him.

"But you have not, my lord," he denied. "Lady Hartwood has long indulged a fancy that I have some discreditable secret hidden in my past, though until now it has not prevented her from throwing her daughters at my head." A small gasp of outrage greeted this statement, which he ignored. "True or false, this revelation will suit her as well as any other," he went on smoothly, "and if, now, she takes me in aversion, refuses to allow the young ladies into my company and casts doubts on the character of my hostess—well, since she is a...*lady*... I can do no more than express regret—not for my own sake, but for the sake of Mrs Darling and all those whose continued friendship I rely upon to see me through my difficulties, and who will be distressed by the aspersions she has seen fit to cast."

This last he addressed to Vinny, accompanying his words with a small but elegant bow.

Vinny felt the colour burn her cheekbones. She had sought to convey her continued support, and he had acknowledged his need—and his readiness to defend her, by implication, in a duel. She shuddered inwardly at the thought of his courting such danger on her behalf. She would not want that. But the tenuous thread already binding them together suddenly strengthened, making her aware that breaking such a bond would be painful.

And yet...his very words and actions proved how entirely capable he was of fighting his own—and her—battles, how little he in truth now needed her assistance...

Lady Hartwood had drawn herself up in silent, regal affront. John Smith sketched her a slight, mocking bow and turned to the gentlemen still sitting at the card table. "Shall we resume, sirs?"

A mutter of assent greeted these words. John Smith took his seat and began a new shuffle and deal, his hands seemingly steady as rocks. Vinny's trembled quite visibly, and she tried to disguise the fact by gripping the back of a chair and fluttering her fan.

"You wish to leave, ma'am?" she enquired politely of Lady Hartwood, who lifted her sagging chin in haughty disdain.

"Since my spouse appears determined to continue with his game," she responded tartly, "I shall take the carriage, which may return for him. Please be kind enough to have it called."

"Will you not reconsider, ma'am? There can be no possible reason to suppose Mr Smith and that student in Oxford to be the same person."

But her ladyship, from being the coy inquisitor, had become the implacable judge and jury.

"There is no certainty, of course, but until it is proved otherwise I shall remove my daughters, and my niece, from any possibility of contamination."

"That is your prerogative, ma'am." Vinny turned to Arabella standing mutinously silent behind her parent. "Miss Arabella, it distresses me to see you depart in such a manner."

"I have no wish to leave, ma'am—"

"Arabella," boomed her mother imperiously, "you will come with me!"

"Yes, Mama," muttered the girl dutifully.

"I will instruct the footman to have your carriage brought round immediately, and to inform Miss Hartwood and Miss Rosedale of your decision," said Vinny coldly.

Several other chaperons decided it was time to leave and rounded up their charges. Guests were arriving and leaving all the time, since many attended several functions in one evening and others considered the night too damp to risk being out too late, but this exodus smacked of desertion. Vinny watched her party dwindle with mixed feelings. She desired solitude in which to quell the unruly responses of her body and to examine her own reactions to the events of the evening, but disliked the way some of the *haut ton* had responded to what was, after all, a most tenuous and probably erroneous clue to Mr Smith's past.

Word, of course, spread among the guests, and the scandal-mongers had a famous time. But, in general, John Smith having made an excellent impression over the last weeks, people reserved judgement. Especially the men, who were less disposed to be shocked by the information the Earl had imparted.

In the early hours, when the final chariot had left, the last coach rattled from the door, Vinny heaved a sigh and addressed her brother.

"I fear you will have to visit the Hartwoods alone in future, Percy. Her ladyship will not admit Mr Smith, and I collect my welcome in Harley Street would be cool. But I have offered Jane Rosedale my hospitality should things become too difficult for her there."

"It is I who should be apologising," said John Smith wearily. "My presence has caused you nothing but inconvenience and pain. I believe I should leave."

"Oh, no!"

"Don't even think of it!"

Vinny and Percy spoke as one. Mr Smith smiled slightly.

"You are both generous and kind. But I have caused you enough trouble—"

"Do you believe," said Vinny savagely, "that I care that—" she snapped her fingers "—for what a few stupid old women think? Or that I will be intimidated by what they may say or imply? I shall conduct myself and my affairs according to the dictates of good breeding, morals and manners and, provided I do not offend against those, I shall do as I wish!"

"Couldn't agree more; spiteful old cats can go to the Devil for all I care!" vowed Percy. "Sooner Jane can get away from that female she calls her aunt, the better I shall be served."

"She will remain while she can," Vinny told him, regaining her composure with an effort. "She is not unhappy there, and I imagine you may call as often as you like, provided you do not make your preference too obvious. Be circumspect, brother. Do not ignore Mary and Arabella.

"All very well for you to advise," grumbled Percy morosely, "but Mary has begun to demand my attention again. And with—er—Smith's absence, both the young ladies will be lookin' to me...but as long as Jane understands..."

"She does, and returns your regard. Be patient, Percy. As for you, sir—" she turned to the other man, who stood nearby apparently deep in his own thoughts "—I imagine you will wish to travel to Oxford. At least it is not so far distant as Aberdeen!"

"No."

The denial was irrefutable. Vinny looked at him in surprise. Weariness was etched in the lines upon his face. His dappled brown eyes, sometimes clouded, sometimes cool, sometimes vibrant with life and laughter, sometimes filled with an emotion she could not comfortably face, were now distant, opaque, hiding his soul.

Her heart missed a beat. Some memory had stirred; she felt sure of it. A memory he had no desire to face.

"You do not wish to pursue this lead?" she asked bluntly.

"No."

Again the monosyllabic response.

"You should," she persisted softly.

He shifted his gaze to her direction, but did not focus his eyes. "I shall not go," he stated with finality. "I will bid you goodnight."

His brain was in turmoil. Vague, painful memories, shut away in some part of his mind he could not reach, struggled for release. But if that young man were indeed he, he wished to remain in ignorance. At least until he had more salubrious memories to cushion the horror.

"The Deuce!" muttered Percy as the door shut behind him.

"It *was* him," said Vinny faintly. "It must have been, or he would not be so disturbed. And his reluctance to gamble bears it out...he's afraid of repeating a tragedy, although he doesn't know it...or didn't... Oh, Percy, I hope he is all right! Go and make certain!"

"If you like. I'll look in on my way to bed. You comin', Vinny?"

She sighed. "Yes."

The once glittering chandeliers glinted vaguely, reflecting the dim light given off by the few candles still alight. A footman stood ready to douse those the moment they retired.

"You're fond of him, ain't you?" Percy remarked as they picked up a candle each to light their way up the stairs. "Better not go fallin' in love."

Vinny gave a hollow laugh. "Do not be so foolish, Percy! As if I would!"

"Don't suppose you'd be able to help it." He grimaced. "Hits a person like a blow on the head."

"You should know!" quipped Vinny, with another forced laugh.

"As you so inelegantly express it, I do speak from personal experience," Percy assured her solemnly. "It ain't altogether pleasant, either, when there are obstacles in the way. Makes for anxious, sleepless nights—"

"You?" exclaimed Vinny in disbelief. "You suffer from sleepless nights?"

Percy grinned, the light from his candle illuminating his handsome, cheerful face as they halted outside her bedroom door. "Not many, not me! But I have known others quite pine away from languishing after some impossible love. And—er—Smith is quite impossible, you know."

"Why?" whispered Vinny.

She knew, of course. Hadn't she been telling herself so for weeks past? But she needed Percy to confirm her opinion.

"If he *is* that fellow from Oxford, he's a reprobate. If he's not, we don't know who he is. Nice enough chap, but no background. In either case, not for you, Vinny, my girl."

"But...if he remembers, and he's not..."

"Don't do to dream, Vinny."

She sighed, and nodded. "You'll...make sure he's all right?"

"Said I would. Leave him to me." He clapped her on the shoulder with brotherly affection. "Go to bed, go to sleep, and forget the fellow."

Easier said than done, thought Vinny as Flora undressed her, brushed her hair and tidied the room before leaving her mistress lying staring at the tester above her head. She had never felt less like sleep. Every nerve in her body was at full stretch. The churning in her stomach had resolved itself into a dull ache interspersed with lurching spasms of anxiety. Her mind buzzed, going over the events of the evening time and again, wandering back to the moment they had met, reviewing all their encounters, the bad and the good. Imagining the feel of his arms, his lips on hers...

Percy had kept his promise. She had heard the sound of voices, the reassuring cheerfulness, the closing of doors.

But still she could not quell her anxiety. Her longing to see for herself.

On a sudden impulse, she threw back the coverlet, sprang from the bed and snatched up her dressing-robe. Her bare feet made no sound on either rug or wood as she left her own room to stand outside the door of her guest's. Strain her ears as she might, she could hear nothing.

What had she expected to hear? The sound of pacing? The echo of manly sobs? The creak of the bed under a restless sleeper? A wry smile touched her lips. She was behaving in a quite ridiculous fashion! Should she be seen, her reputation would be in shreds! She removed her ear from the panel and turned to go.

Her feet refused to obey her command. They remained firmly planted where they were. And her hand went out to the ornate knob. Turned it.

It was the work of a moment to push the door open. The impulse to see him sleeping had been too strong for her rational brain to resist. The candles were extinguished but moonlight filled the room. She pushed the door wider and as the window came into her view she saw him standing there, his hands spread wide, resting against the jambs, his muscular body illuminated, sculpted in silver. Her little gasp came at the same moment as a hinge protested. He spun round, muttering an oath.

"What the Devil are you doing here?"

The harsh, abrasive voice sent a contracting shiver through her. She felt ready to sink with mortification at being discovered, but refused to run away. She did the opposite and stepped further into the room.

"I merely wished...to make certain that you...had recovered...from...earlier..."

She was ashamed of her faltering voice, but at least she had stood her ground. He stalked away from the window, but the room was so full of light it scarcely mattered. She could see him every bit as clearly as before.

He was naked to the waist. The mat of fine hair she had glimpsed once before was revealed to her absorbed gaze, as were the muscles of his shoulders, the taut outline of his ribs, the beginnings of a flat stomach where the hair disappeared beneath his evening breeches. And she could see where the satin-smoothness of his skin gave way to tender-looking patches of stretched and rutted scarring spreading over his left shoulder and upper arm. He had said he had received burns. Now she was faced with the evidence. She bit on her bottom lip to stop the sudden rush of tears. It became suddenly difficult to breathe.

"You must think me singularly weak, if you regard it as necessary to invade my room on such an errand! Percy," he sneered, "has already evinced his concern. Or was it yours, ma'am?" he demanded, with sudden perception.

"Mine, yes!" she admitted with renewed spirit, though her voice shook treacherously. "Is it so despicable, to show concern for a guest under my roof?"

"Thank you for the reminder, ma'am!"

"That was not my intention, sir!"

The thin summer dressing-robe concealed little of her slender body. At sight of her his disturbing, chaotic thoughts had been overwhelmed by a flood of physical desire which he found it difficult to subdue. He took refuge in arrogant, angry pride.

"Was it not? I have to inform you, ma'am, that I must refuse to remain under this roof if you continue to insist on treating me as an invalid!" He threw back his head on the strong column of his neck and emitted a snort of disgust. "I have no need to be either nursed or mothered! As I shall take great pleasure in demonstrating, should you choose to remain in my room longer."

He lowered his head and took a purposeful step towards

her. His jaw set hard, his lips twisted into a cynical smile, his eyes swept up and down her trembling figure, making his intention perfectly clear. Vinny gasped, clutching her robe more firmly about her body.

"There is no call to be crude, sir!" Tears threatened anew, but from a different cause. She sniffed hard to stem the flow. "I had no intention other than to satisfy myself of your well-being! For that I risked my reputation! You, sir, are not worthy of my concern, let alone my good name!"

She gave him no chance to reply, but stormed out of the room, shutting the door behind her with a rather loud bang which she afterwards hoped the servants had not heard.

Having dropped into an exhausted doze around dawn, Vinny awoke heavy-eyed, on edge and depressed. Flora swept back the curtains, revealing a fine morning.

"Drink your chocolate, ma'am, before it gets cold," she admonished, for her mistress lay inert.

Vinny sat up reluctantly, attempting to banish all thought, since the only ones to enter her head were so embarrassing, so unwelcome. The chocolate did comfort her fluttering stomach a little, and eventually she dredged up a smile as she slid from the bed and allowed Flora to minister to her.

"You must be tired after yesterday, ma'am," Flora chattered on as she dressed her mistress and arranged her hair. "So many people came! The evening was a great success!"

Vinny made no response. She was in no doubt that every servant in the place knew of the confrontation in the dining-parlour and that speculation was rife. But Flora was too well-trained to remark and Vinny was certainly not going to satisfy curiosity or invite comment.

She filled in the time before breakfast with thinking.

Some drastic action was required to resolve the question of John Smith's true identity. He could not go on living in limbo. His life would be ruined. And scenes like that of the previous evening could be repeated. He would be driven insane, and so would she.

She had to know. Had to discover whether there were any hope... For Percy's warning had come too late. She had not realised it before, but his words had struck a nerve, forcing her to acknowledge that her attraction to John Smith—whoever he turned out to be—went far deeper than the mere physical.

She loved him. She longed to be able to share her life with him, to fill the nursery with beautiful babies he had fathered.

She had never felt that way about Charles Darling. In fact she had been glad when... She pulled her thoughts up. It did no good to dwell upon the past. The future beckoned. Except that it was clouded by uncertainty. Not least the uncertainty of *his* feelings. He admired her, but did he love her? But until they discovered his past—all of it, even the parts he did not wish to acknowledge—she could do nothing to try to win his regard.

He had been that student at Oxford; of that she had little doubt. Which, according to the Earl, meant that he was of noble birth. And that he had wasted his time at Oxford gambling, pursuing women and drinking to excess. He had been a rake.

A little, fond smile curved her lips. How easily she could visualise that silly young man! Thinking it genteel and manly to copy others of perhaps higher rank and apparently exemplary character! And though she must condemn his behaviour then, she could only admire the man he had become. He must have run away, hidden himself in the Army and spent the intervening years, a reformed character, campaigning against Napoleon.

Not being hungry, she skipped breakfast and went down late, hoping to avoid both men. She succeeded. The morning-room was empty, too.

"Has Mr Sinclair gone out?" she asked the footman.

"Yes, ma'am. He left in his curricle half an hour ago."

"And the other gentleman?" She forced herself to calmness while she awaited his reply.

"He ordered a horse saddled and went out around nine o'clock, ma'am."

"Thank you."

Dismissing the man, she sat down at her writing-table. Mr Smith had been out for almost two hours. She wondered where he had gone. But an idea simmered in her head, putting other thoughts to flight. She took out a piece of paper, trimmed her quill and dipped it in the ink, then began to write.

Information Sought. Gentleman, ex-Army Officer, suffering from loss of memory due to wounds received in the Peninsula, seeks to discover his identity. Six feet tall, dark, about thirty years of age. No particular distinguishing marks. Eyes brown, flecked with green. Information to Box No:....

She sat back, brushing the underside of her small chin with the feather while she read over what she had written. It seemed all right. The details were flimsy and could fit a hundred men, but someone might recognise a missing relative and contact the box number. Most newspapers accepted advertisements. She would put it into as many as possible. She ticked them off on her fingers: *The Times,* the *Mirror,* the *Whitehall Evening Post,* the *Gazette,* the *Recorder,* the *Courier*...she would try them all.

So absorbed was she in her occupation that she failed to notice his return. The first she knew of it was the sound of the door opening. She whirled round, flushing guiltily, pushing the piece of paper beneath the blotting pad.

"G-good morning."

He bowed faultlessly. "Good morning, ma'am."

A tinge of colour burnt his cheekbones, though whether it had been put there by exercise or embarrassment she had no way of telling. The awkwardness stretched between them until she felt she would snap.

"D-did you enjoy a good ride?"

"I thank you, ma'am yes. We enjoyed an excellent gallop in the park."

"We?" she asked sharply.

"The horse and I," he responded drily. He had not changed from his riding clothes. As he strode across the room he brought the odours of fresh air, horse, wool and spices with him. She loved the tang given off by the soap he used, and breathed in the scent of him like a seeking hound.

He did not smile. A furrow drew deep lines between his brows as he stared at the edge of paper peeping out from beneath the blotter. "What were you writing?" he demanded.

"Nothing."

"Then why hide it from me?"

"Because it was private!" she snapped defensively.

"'Nothing' is private?" he enquired sceptically. "Mrs Darling, I suspect you are up to something. If it concerns me, I want to know what it is."

Vinny shifted uncomfortably. "W-why should you think it concerns you, sir?"

He gave her a smile, but not a friendly one. "Because you took such care to conceal it from me. Your entire attitude screams guilt. Let me see it." He held out an imperious hand.

Vinny drew a deep breath. He would have to know what

she had done sooner or later, but she would rather it were later, when he could not prevent the advertisement appearing.

"You forget yourself, sir," she said, equally imperiously. "You have no right to demand any such thing!"

"No?" he drawled.

His voice was the only slow thing about him. His hand shot out to snatch up the paper as Vinny's moved to cover it. The shock of the contact sent a wave of reaction through her body and she drew back with a gasp of dismay. Touching her did not deter Mr Smith, however. His hand closed over hers and briskly removed it, so that he could extract the piece of paper with his other. He did not let her go, but maintained a steely grip on her fingers while he perused what she had written.

Having finished, he crumpled the paper in his hand and jerked her to her feet, pulling her close so that his angry face almost touched hers.

"How dare you?" he snarled. "How dare you advertise me as though I were a prime piece of horseflesh being put up to auction?"

Chapter Seven

Vinny stared into his furious face, speechless with guilt and an angry frustration she could not express. Eventually she found her voice.

"We have to do something!" she exclaimed. "You refuse to follow up the best lead we have! I hoped to find another!"

"It is you who forget yourself, Mrs Darling," he gritted. "My life and my mind are my own! I will not have decisions taken out of my hands in such an arbitrary manner!"

"Then what do you suggest we do?" she demanded hotly.

"I suggest you keep to your decision of last night, ma'am, and remember that I am not worthy of your concern!" he snarled. That final gibe of hers had hurt. "Unless—" His eyes narrowed on her mouth. He wrenched her against him. "Unless you would in truth prefer this!"

Vinny struggled to evade the arms tightening about her, but he only clamped her to him the more fiercely. Despite all her squirming his mouth claimed hers in a hard, punishing kiss.

He was hurting her, suffocating her—but it did not seem

to matter. She barely had time to wonder how long she had wanted him to do just this before her mind ceased to function under the onslaught of unbelievable sensations. The taut strength of his frame pressed against her, unaccountably melting her bones. Her lax muscles moulded themselves to his hard length, her limbs no longer belonged to her. Had he not been holding her so brutally close she would have crumpled to the floor.

She hung limply in his arms, unresisting as fire streaked through her veins. Somehow, she found the strength to extricate her arms from their imprisonment between their bodies and link them behind his neck, pressing herself closely against him. Little sounds of pleasure rose from her throat as her tongue curled with his. And gradually, feeling her spontaneous response, the fierceness of his attack gentled. His arms loosened their iron grip, allowing his hands freedom to roam over her body, to trace her spine, to cup the swell of her breast...

How long they stood engrossed in the pleasure of the embrace neither afterwards knew. The man had begun to kiss her as a vent for his anger, a punishment for her wilful, reckless actions, a release from all the frustrations of his condition; but her response changed everything.

He had been fighting the desire to kiss her for weeks—nay, months. Now she was in his arms and returning his kisses with all the innocent ardour implicit in her transparent eyes and the full, sensuous curve of her lips. He would vow she had never been awakened like this before...

His mouth left hers reluctantly, but they both needed air. He sought instead to trace the contours of her cheeks and jaw. With a murmur of pleasure she allowed her head to fall back. Her lids were closed, concealing the expression in her eyes, but her arousal was displayed in the colour staining her cheeks, the shallowness of her breathing. The slender column of her neck invited the caress of his lips and the low-cut gown revealed impossibly seductive curves...

He drew a harsh breath and consciously allowed his passion full rein as he lowered his head to kiss his way down her throat to the tantalising swell above the neckline of her dress. The exquisite sensations his touch inspired brought a gasp to Vinny's lips. She wanted them to go on and on, while the moist warmth of his mouth held her entire being in thrall—until she became conscious of where their passion could lead...and she was not ready...could not allow...

"No! Please, John, stop..."

Her breathless plea faded to a halt, but it was enough to arrest John Smith, whose pulse leapt with renewed vigour on hearing her call him by that name. It sounded strange, unfamiliar, yet sweet. If only he knew his true appellation! To hear that on her lips...

"Vinny!" he breathed. "Oh, my dear!"

She backed away as his arms dropped, her face a bright red as she hurriedly adjusted the neck of her gown and realised how much liberty she had allowed him. Her breath was coming in quick, shallow gasps and her entire body seemed to be on fire. She ran her tongue along her swollen lips and blushed anew. Everyone would be able to see how thoroughly she had been kissed—if the servants had not already witnessed the scene through the partly open door! If so, her reputation would be tattered beyond repair! And what must *he* be thinking of her? No lady would have allowed...would have responded with such complete lack of modesty...he must hold her in utter disgust for displaying such unrestrained ardour...

"Your behaviour is despicable, sir!" she cried, her inclination to sink with mortification hidden beneath a show of outrage.

But his breathing was every bit as bad as hers. She watched his hands shake as he ran them through his rumpled hair.

He shut his eyes to cut out the sight of her, so desirable, so vulnerable in her confusion, and drew a deep, calming breath. Silently, he berated himself for allowing his self-control to escape him. He could not allow her to know how much he needed her, needed her concern, her affection—her love. For he could offer nothing in return. Except, perhaps, to awaken her to the joy she could find if she allowed her passionate nature its freedom. But she had already made it plain that she would not welcome any such revelation, for no gentlewoman could admit to feeling desire...at least not before marriage...and even then... But he was convinced that Vinny would not be like that... which made his present position the more frustrating.

He executed a rather stiff bow. "I offer my sincere apologies, ma'am. My behaviour was, as you point out, inexcusable."

Dear God, he—his voice—had become so formal! When he had called her Vinny, and his dear, she had thought her heart would burst with happiness. But he had kissed her in anger, not love. Because she had annoyed him again. And she had accused him...

"I—no," she admitted unevenly. "You did it to punish me, because I had made you cross." She found it impossible to take refuge in continued anger, and tried to strike a playful note instead. "You could scarcely throw me across your knees and spank me!"

To her relief he laughed, albeit a trifle harshly. "Don't tempt me!" he growled.

"Oh!" She hadn't thought of her words as provocative, and suffered renewed mortification. "I did not mean—"

He interrupted her quickly. "I know you did not. Forgive me again. I scarcely know what I am saying and had better keep silent, or I fear I shall put you to the blush once more."

Her foolish action had caused his anger. She had to admit that. And although she still found his reluctance to pursue his quest most aggravating and his presence disturbing—sometimes she found him exceedingly vexing, like now, when he had quite taken the wind from her sails with his apology—she was becoming daily less inclined to be at cuffs with him. Or to drive him from her house. For, after all, she loved him.

She hesitated a moment. Then, looking down at her clasped hands, she said stiffly, "I apologise for attempting to…to…" she swallowed rather noisily "…to make decisions for you," she went on awkwardly and patted nervously at her chignon, which had suffered from his rough handling, studiously avoiding his searching eyes the while. She drew a steadying breath before daring to meet them squarely. She needed it, for there was that in them which took it away again.

However, she managed to struggle on. "I must go to my room to tidy my hair and change into a walking dress. I intend to visit Lackington's bookshop, in Finsbury Square. You have not been there yet, I believe. May I beg for your escort?" she asked formally.

He had himself perfectly in hand now. He made his usual, easy bow. "I shall be honoured. I am entirely at your disposal, ma'am."

"I will order the carriage to be ready in half an hour."

"I too must change, ma'am. I fear I exude a quite regrettable odour of horse."

"I like the smell of horse," said Vinny enigmatically as she left the room.

Infuriating, tantalising, delightful, surprising creature! thought John Smith as he prepared to follow her up the stairs. Although she had tried to pretend it had, his unforgivable behaviour had not offended her! She had changed since that first time he had succumbed to the impulse to kiss her. Then, she had been outraged. Or had appeared to be. Today, although she would never admit it, he would swear she had enjoyed their encounter as much as he!

Messrs Lackington, Allen & Co were open for business in the Temple of Muses, Finsbury Square. Entering its portals always gave Vinny a thrill. Every available inch of wall in several rooms, and in the huge domed gallery above the enormous circular mahogany counter, was covered in shelves full of books of every description. Women by the thousand patronised the booksellers to purchase the novels they could not find in the circulating libraries. Vinny went there to browse mainly, though if a volume caught her eye she was often tempted to buy. Her father's library was one of the things she missed most in London, and she was slowly building a small one of her own, although she fully realised that it could never compete in any way with one collected over generations.

The outing was not proving a success, she had to admit. Memories of their earlier encounter could not be dismissed, and kept intruding. Awkwardness lay between them, the knowledge of a forbidden indulgence not to be repeated. Guilt and temptation were not a mixture of emotions conducive to the enjoyment of an easy relationship. She wished it had never happened. Then wished it could be repeated.

John Smith left her side as soon as politeness allowed, drawn to the shelves containing books on military subjects. She frowned a little anxiously as she searched for new novels by her favourite authors, attempting to keep an eye on him the while. He was pursuing his recovery in his own way, no doubt, hoping that something on those shelves would jog his memory. The prospect of recalling military matters did not disturb him in the same way as that of discovering himself guilty of youthful follies at Oxford. But she was concerned for him, just the same.

With such a divided mind she did not succeed in finding much that she wanted, but came away with a copy of *Sense and Sensibility,* a novel much recommended but so far not read by her.

"You made a purchase," remarked Mr Smith as he politely relieved her of the parcel on leaving the premises.

"A novel," said Vinny brightly, feeling disinclined to apologise for having such low taste. She had felt more inclined to feel regret over being caught with Adam Smith! "I find many of them most entertaining. Look! There is Ellis!"

An enormous commotion had erupted some yards distant. Her carriage looked to be in the middle of it! Ellis must have become caught up in the trouble as he walked the horses while waiting. Carriages and animals filled the road in such disorder and so noisily that from their distance it was difficult to make out exactly what was amiss. It looked as though a curricle had come to conclusions with a heavy coach. No doubt the young exquisite who had been driving the fancy equipage, now waving his arms and shouting to little effect except to frighten his horses into a frenzy, had considered himself more the complete hand, better able to drive to an inch, than his skill with the reins warranted. The wheels of the vehicles had clashed and become entangled.

While the coachman and footmen accompanying the more stately outfit attempted to calm the neighing, prancing horses and lift the lighter carriage aside, the loud altercation between the gesticulating youth and the invisible occupant of the splendid coach continued in full spate.

Ellis could not turn the carriage or back up, and until

the blockage was cleared could most evidently not go forward.

"Shall we walk to the landau?" suggested Vinny. "We can sit in it while we wait for the road to clear."

"The wheels are already parted," observed Mr Smith, who had been observing events keenly. "We should not be held up for long."

They strolled slowly towards the obstruction, Vinny conscious as never before of the man at her side, of the untold pleasures his arms would offer if only she had the courage to defy convention! But she could not do that without courting social disaster.

All other thought, even of her companion and their predicament, fled as a crash of splintering wood and a wail of anguish from its owner greeted the overturning of the curricle, the expensive horses harnessed to it having decided to rear and bolt once the weight of the heavier vehicle was removed. A footman from the coach, rather than be trampled underfoot, let them go and beat a hasty retreat. In another moment the pair of chestnuts reared again, brought to another unwanted halt by the drag of the smashed curricle, which caught up against a drinking trough. Should their traces snap the animals would create fresh havoc with their hoofs.

With a hurried word of apology John Smith thrust her parcel into her hand and ran across to catch the headstall of the nearest animal. Vinny watched breathlessly, fear clutching at her heart, for both horses were lashing out with their hoofs—but John Smith managed to gain a hold as another man limped from the throng of bystanders to catch the other bridle.

Smith spoke softly to the crazed horse in an effort to calm it. The man who had rushed to his assistance, despite a roughness of dress and deficiency of form, seemed familiar with horses too, and between them they soon had the quivering, sweating creatures under control. The four animals drawing the heavy coach were less spirited and, although uneasy, had not caught the panic. The coachman, aided by both the footmen, had them well in hand.

Knowing she should stay clear, Vinny crept nearer, her heart slowing down as she realised that the immediate danger was over. She was almost at John Smith's side when a hoarse cry stopped her in her tracks. The man holding the other animal was staring at him with an expression of glad surprise on his weathered face.

"Captain Pelham, sir! You're back from the Peninsula, then? Are you on leave, sir?"

John Smith stared back. Vinny caught her breath as she waited for his response. He gave a little shake of his head, and the other man shifted uncomfortably; his somewhat thin cheeks, from being pallid under the weathering, suddenly became stained with red.

"You don't remember me, your honour?" he asked in a hesitating manner. "Sergeant Gill, sir; I was in your honour's regiment…"

Vinny sucked in a deep breath of excitement. Her heart was hammering again, making her tremble, but she rushed forward to touch John Smith's arm and smile warmly at the older man.

"He knows you!" she whispered urgently into her silent companion's ear, then addressed the sergeant.

"Captain… Pelham…" She swallowed, for the name felt strange yet wonderful on her tongue. "Captain Pelham," she went on with more assurance, "was wounded at Badajoz. He has no memory of his life before regaining consciousness after the battle. Otherwise I am certain he would remember you, Sergeant."

Others had freed the horses from their traces, and now took charge of the animals. Sergeant Gill released his hold and stepped back, giving his erstwhile captain an uncertain glance as he made the lady an awkward bow.

"I'm powerful sorry to hear it, my lady," he muttered.

"Being greeted by his name—of which he had no idea—has been a shock, as you may imagine. I am Mrs Charles Darling," she introduced herself. "My carriage is here—the road is almost clear now. Will you accompany us home, that Captain Pelham may speak to you at leisure?"

"An excellent idea," said John Smith—or rather, Captain Pelham—firmly, having recovered quickly from his initial shock. "Forgive my stupidity, Gill, but I protest, your greeting took me unawares! I had not thought to meet someone who knew me in so fortuitous a manner! Mrs Darling's invitation to you is one I appreciate vastly, since I am merely a guest in her house." He smiled, extending a hand to shake the other man's. "Pray come with us and grant me the benefit of your knowledge of my history."

The man returned the handshake with fervour. "It isn't that much, sir, your honour, but we were together under Sir John—God rest his soul—and under Sir Arthur himself until I lost me foot in Cuidad Rodrigo earlier in the year. Shot off, it was," he said, looking down at the wooden stump protruding below his tattered trousers, "and lucky I am to be here. You saw I was treated right, Captain, and if there's anything I can do for you now, you're more than welcome."

Gill insisted on riding on the box with Ellis, although Vinny would have welcomed him into the landau in order to question him.

"No, madam," he said stiffly. "I won't dirty your cushions with my old clothes."

"Don't embarrass him," murmured Captain Pelham as he handed her into the carriage. "He'll be happier up front."

Captain Pelham! Well, it was better than John Smith, but Vinny wondered what his forename would be. And whether Gill knew it. She could hardly contain her excitement, but Pelham himself appeared to be taking the revelation calmly. In fact, as she gave Ellis a nod and said, "Home, if you please," he closed his eyes and did not open them again until the carriage drew up before the house in Portman Square.

Sergeant Gill thought the front entrance too grand for him and passed through its portals reluctantly, gazing in awe at the splendour inside. Spotting a large, gilt-edged invitation lying on a table in the hall addressed to The Honourable Mrs Charles Darling, he eyed it apprehensively.

"She's an Honourable?" he questioned hoarsely, beneath his breath.

"Her father is Viscount Marldon," the captain told him with a smile. "Just continue to call her madam."

Vinny ordered refreshments to be served in the morning-room. "We shall be snug in here, and remain undisturbed," she told her guests. "Sit down, Sergeant. I'm certain you will relish a tankard of ale, though I can offer you tea if you prefer?"

Sitting reluctantly on the edge of the least comfortable chair, Gill took a deep draught of his ale and wiped his lips with the back of his hand.

"What can I tell your honours?" he demanded.

"My full name, rank and regiment, for a start," urged Pelham.

"Justin Pelham, Captain, sir. In the Rifles, best regiment in the Light Division."

"Ah! A foot regiment, as we had supposed."

"The Ninety-fifth, sir," put in Gill proudly.

"And my name is Justin Pelham, eh? I cannot say it

sounds particularly familiar,'' observed Pelham with a frown.

"Have you remembered nothing?'' whispered Vinny anxiously, sipping at her tea. "Will you take a slice of cake, Sergeant?'' she added, remembering her duties as hostess.

"Thank you, ma'am.'' Gill bit into the substantial fruit cake with obvious relish. Vinny suspected him of being extremely hungry.

"No, nothing.'' Pelham shrugged, answering her question casually, but his eyes were keen. "Another visit to the Horse Guards should reveal more of my personal history. Meanwhile, I am certain Sergeant Gill will not mind telling me all he knows.''

Gill looked from one expectant face to the other and, having finished his cake and ale, he relaxed slightly, sitting further back in the chair, though his spine remained stiff as a ramrod.

"We first met at Horsham, in '99, sir. We were both detailed to attend a course of instruction to become part of the Experimental Rifle Corps, set up by His Highness the Duke of York, if you remember. I was a private then, and you a raw young ensign without two pennies to rub together apart from your pay, if you'll forgive me the liberty of saying so, sir, and what you won at cards, though you was always modest in your gaming.''

"Horsham,'' mused Pelham, looking blank. "What then?''

"Windsor,'' said Gill succinctly. "Trained in Windsor Forest under Colonel Manningham and Lieutenant-Colonel Stewart, learnt all the tricks of advancing under cover and sniping at the enemy. They gave us green uniforms with dark buttons to blend in with the trees. In the Peninsula they called us grasshoppers, sir.''

"Ah! Green. Yes. Felt deuced uncomfortable when they put me in a red coat…"

"We landed at Ferrol in October 1800 and fought with Nelson at Copenhagen. They made us the Ninety-fifth regiment of the line in the spring of 1801."

"The Ninety-fifth," repeated Vinny, recalling things her mother and brother had said. "Wasn't that the regiment that lost so many officers at Badajoz?"

"Quite correct, ma'am. I heard it was twenty-two. But no doubt you were counted in that number, sir."

"No doubt," agreed Pelham drily. "But go on, man!"

"Well, sir, we were disbanded at the end of the Frenchies' revolutionary war, but they got us together again shortly after and armed us with the new Baker rifle."

"That explains why I did not feel at home with a musket in my hand," interjected Pelham with a wry smile.

"That's as may be, sir, but anyway, late in the year 1802 we were off to Shorncliffe Camp to train under General Sir John Moore—God rest his soul," added Gill piously once again. "Three years we trained under him, and it was him as picked you out, sir. Couldn't afford a promotion yourself, so he bought it for you. Did that for several promising young sparks, though he wasn't a rich man himself. We all knew what he did, and honoured him for it. You should've been a major, sir, only he died afore that could be bought."

Pelham eyed Gill keenly. "At Corunna." He'd learned that since he'd been back.

"Yes, but that's a bit ahead, sir, after we were joined up with the Fourteenth Light Dragoons and the Fifty-second and Forty-third regiments to form the Light Brigade. We were different from every other brigade in the Army," Gill added proudly.

Pelham smiled suddenly. "We were supposed to be

thinking soldiers, highly trained physically, able to act on our own initiative.''

Gill chuckled. "Aye, and instead of competing to see who could drink the most bumpers in the mess, *our* officers raced the commander up the hill from Sandgate back to camp!''

"They were great days," remarked Pelham quietly.

"You remember?" demanded Vinny eagerly.

"Not precisely. No details, but I feel as though I was there…''

"Thank God! At least it is a beginning!''

"Shall I go on, sir?" asked the sergeant.

"If you please.''

"Well, sir, to cut a long story short, we went to the Peninsula to fight under Sir Arthur Wellesley—Lord Wellington as he now is—and then under our own Sir John. We won some famous battles, but it all ended in the terrible retreat to Corunna and what seemed like disaster. We sailed back to England battened down in vermin-infested holds and emerged at Plymouth more dead than alive. People saw us in all our filth and rags and took pity on a grand army of scarecrows!'' He chuckled reminiscently.

Pelham frowned, searching his memory. Gill waited for a moment, but when the captain made no comment he continued. "The campaign was put down as a disgrace, but it wasn't. Sir John knew what he was doing was dangerous—I discovered that much from listening to Black Bob—but despite the dangers the commander marched us out in December to cut old Boney's winter supply lines. He knew Boney would have to change his plans and chase him, that the British Army would have to run for its life, but it was worth the risk because it would give the Spanish a bit of time. And Boney fell for it! He gave up his conquest of the Peninsula for that year and came after us instead!''

Gill paused to quaff more ale from his refilled tankard. Vinny, sitting silently watching the two men, thought she saw dawning comprehension on Justin Pelham's face.

"Brilliant!" he breathed. "It stopped his campaign dead in its tracks!"

"Aye, sir. And we were in the van of the army, led by General Craufurd—Black Bob—you do remember, sir?" Pelham shook his head slightly, and Gill went on, looking disappointed. "Well, we were at the head of the column, marching on Soult's army guarding the supply lines. The weather was that dreadful, the pace killing, but we pressed on to battle—or so we thought. Then came the order to retreat. All that hardship seemed to be for nothing!"

"And discipline broke down," muttered Justin Pelham. He sat with his eyes closed, a pained expression on his face.

"That *was* a disgrace, sir. But there you are—we were in the mountains, freezing, suffering from frostbite and starving, for the commissariat let us down and supplies failed, and the weather got worse than anyone had expected. More than two hundred miles to retreat, with all those *parlez-vous* after us! A fine Christmas and New Year that was, sir!"

"They asked where the devil we were taking them," remembered Pelham in an anguished tone. "'To England,' we replied, 'if we get there.'"

"Aye, Captain, you'd remember that, for certain. But the commander, he got us out of the scrape all right, those of us with the stamina and guts," insisted Gill loyally.

"I lost my horse at Corunna," remembered Pelham suddenly in a strange, harsh voice.

"That you did, sir! Real fond of that animal you were; it fair broke your heart to see it shot! But, like so many other horses, its hoofs had been ruined in the mountains from lack of shoes and there wasn't room for any but the fittest animals aboard the transports—"

"A big, raw-boned roan. I'd had him since I joined. Full of heart, up to anything."

Vinny sat enthralled, not only with Gill's story, but by Justin Pelham's reaction to it. Despite the obvious pain of his memories his eyes were alert, wry smiles touched his lips from time to time, and now he had remembered his horse!

"What was he called?" she asked.

For an instant, the captain looked lost. Then he grinned. "Vertigo!" he pronounced in triumph. "Had a habit of twisting round in circles when he was a youngster!"

"Where did you get him?"

Now confusion descended again. "I don't remember," he admitted, frowning.

His discomfort alerted Vinny to the exhaustion taking hold of him. Gill's revelations, however welcome, were proving a strain. The clock on the mantel gave her an excuse to end the session.

"It is time we dressed for dinner," she reminded Captain Pelham gently. "I am sure Sergeant Gill will not mind returning tomorrow to finish his story—and to accompany you to the Horse Guards, if that is your intention. Meanwhile, I will instruct the kitchen to give him a meal before he leaves."

"Of course!" Pelham was suddenly all brisk efficiency. "Can you be here by eight, Sergeant? Then you can eat breakfast here too, if Mrs Darling agrees."

Vinny nodded and the matter was settled. Pelham accompanied Gill to the hall and left a footman to show him the way to the kitchen, a thoughtfulness which seemed to fill the erstwhile soldier with gratitude.

"He has not eaten well for a long time," observed Vinny upon Pelham's return to the morning-room. "We do not treat our wounded and retired soldiers well, I think.''

''Were he sixty years old he might hope for lodgings in a hospital. But I doubt he has seen many more than forty summers yet.''

''Poor man! How glad I am we met him! You are beginning to remember, are you not, Captain?''

He made a dismissive motion of his hand and gave her a somewhat deprecating smile. ''Pray do not feel obliged to address me as 'Captain', ma'am. Pelham will do well enough. I wish it could be Justin,'' he added softly.

''That would be too familiar, sir,'' replied Vinny, blushing, wishing it were not. ''I shall not mind calling you Mr Pelham! But I could scarcely bring myself to address you as Mr Smith!''

He bowed, smiling with engaging amusement. ''So I apprehended, ma'am.''

''What will Percy say, I wonder? And where can he be? He has been absent the entire day!''

''I am sure he has much to engage his attention in London, Mrs Darling. Do not begin to distress yourself on his behalf again, I beg!''

''I will not, I can assure you! And I shall wait with bated breath to hear him address you as Pelham—without feeling the need for any hesitation!''

He laughed. ''Justin Pelham,'' he said, musing over the name. ''I protest, it sounds familiar—and yet...'' He shook his head.

''It must be right!'' exclaimed Vinny indignantly. ''Gill is so certain, and he cannot be bamming us with a Banbury story! I am quite certain he is far too honest a man! In any case, he speaks with too much authority.''

''I am quite certain his story is the absolute truth. And yet... I cannot quite feel... I do not know,'' he ended abruptly.

Vinny had risen from her chair when he re-entered the room. She took the few steps that would bring her close enough to touch him and laid a soothing hand on his arm.

"Tomorrow the Horse Guards will be able to look up your records and tell you more," she reminded him gently. "Now it is my turn to tell *you* not to worry! You have begun to remember, and soon everything will become clear!"

"That," said Justin Pelham bleakly, "is what I am rather disposed to fear."

Chapter Eight

"Percy!" exclaimed Vinny when her brother finally appeared, already dressed for dinner. "Wherever have you been?"

He grinned rather shamefacedly. "Went to call on Miss Rosedale first and deuced awkward it was too. Miss Hartwood refused to leave my side the entire time I was there. Didn't stay long. But I was not refused admittance to the presence of the ladies—I had feared I might be, after last evenin'."

"But where have you been since?" demanded his sister, barely able to suppress her excitement. "You have missed the most astounding thing—"

"Met a fellow I know. Took me to a deuced good mill," confessed Percy. "Lasted over twenty rounds, and I backed the winner. Made more blunt on one wager than I ever manage at cards." Grinning complacently, he noticed her state of ferment for the first time and enquired lazily, "But what's this astoundin' thing I missed here?"

"You'll never believe—but here he is!" cried Vinny, leaping to her feet to greet Pelham, who entered the room at that moment, looking as devastating as ever in his evening clothes. She thought she might swoon if she should ever see him in his regimentals, but fortunately that was unlikely. "Percy, allow me to introduce you to—Captain Justin Pelham!"

"Justin Pelham will do," smiled the other man, bowing with ironic courtesy to the astonished Percy.

"I say," exclaimed the latter, "no wonder you looked all worked up, Vinny! How ever did you discover your identity, my dear fellow?"

Dinner was announced at that moment and Vinny took the opportunity of telling the butler to inform all the staff that in future the man they had known as Mr Smith must be addressed as Mr Pelham. And the entire meal was spent in bringing Percy up to date with what they knew.

"And Sergeant Gill is returning tomorrow morning to relate the rest of the history," Vinny informed her brother at the end. "I can scarcely wait to hear what he has to say!"

"Nor I! I may be present, I suppose?"

This point having been settled to his satisfaction and the party having no formal engagement for that evening, Percy proposed a visit to one of the clubs to spread the news.

Justin Pelham shook his head. "I would rather remain here this evening. I have experienced more than enough melodrama for one day!" A quick glance at Vinny assured him that she had not forgotten the drama with which the day had begun. The extreme consciousness of each other which had made communication so difficult earlier had been modified by the exhilaration of discovery. He did not want her to forget, but he did welcome a less strained atmosphere between them. "What I should enjoy above all else," he smiled, "is to sit and listen quietly to Mrs Darling, if she would be so obliging as to play on the pianoforte."

Vinny agreed readily, having been looking forward to a quiet evening at home, though preferably not alone, and she needed the practice. "It is some time since we had the pleasure of singing together," she reminded Pelham. "Perhaps you will join me in a song or two? And if Percy will remain with us I have no doubt we could accommodate him with a hand of cards!"

To Vinny's relief both gentlemen agreed to this plan, Percy's presence avoiding what could otherwise have been an embarrassing tête-à-tête.

Sergeant Gill presented himself promptly at eight the next morning and all three were up to greet him. Percy was introduced and subsequently listened with as keen an interest as the others to what the ex-soldier had to relate.

"Boney didn't plant his eagles on the towers of Lisbon and he was no nearer crossing the Straits of Gibraltar to stick them up in North Africa, either, which is why he invaded Spain in the first place," Gill reminded them, "and he didn't destroy the British Army, although we left thousands of dead behind. But it was touch-and-go, and mostly thanks to the Light Brigade, guarding the flanks and the rear, that so many managed to embark in safety."

"But not Sir John," observed Justin quietly.

"No, Captain. He was brought down by a cannon-ball during the final battle to defend the embarkation. He never left the Peninsula."

"And yet Sir John was vilified by the blockheads here!" exclaimed Percy indignantly. He had always admired Moore and been offended by the way his generalship had been criticised. "I always knew he must have the right of it!"

"Aye, that he did," confirmed Gill, pleased to have another sympathetic supporter of that most dedicated and misunderstood of leaders. "And we were back before summer to join Sir Arthur, on our way to Talavera and a new battle."

Pelham, who had spent a restless night chasing half-formed, elusive visions of his past, was suddenly transported back to a hot, dusty road where his weary regiment, in company with the Fifty-second and the Forty-third, the three finest regiments in the British line, were marching behind "Black Bob" Craufurd in insufferable heat to reinforce the hard-pressed army facing the French.

His horse pricked its ears at the sound of distant gunfire, heard faintly above the sound of drum and bugle, the tramp of hundreds of feet, the clip-clop of horses' hoofs—not only those of the officers' mounts, but also those of the Chestnut Troop, who were trotting in their midst. Every soldier in the file at his side straightened his tired shoulders, firmed up his steps and pressed on at his fast light-infantryman's pace towards the sound of battle.

"Gawd 'elp 'em! Will us get there in time?" wondered a rifleman aloud.

"Those of us as don't fall dead from the 'eat and 'unger!" joked the man at his side, and coughed the dust from his throat.

The joke was a black one, for more than one man had indeed dropped dead. Besides his rifle and ramrod, every soldier carried eighty rounds of ball and a pack weighing forty pounds. They'd eaten no more than a crust of mouldy bread that day, yet, as they marched, not a man had voluntarily left the column. Justin Pelham had never felt more proud of his men. Endurance was their pride, courage in battle their stock-in-trade.

They'd covered more than twenty miles and had as many more to go when the first faint-hearted Spaniards began to pass in the opposite direction, fleeing the battle with tales of a British Army facing frightening odds. Pelham felt all the scorn for the deserters expressed in succinct, unrepeatable language by his men. The pace increased, for far ahead they could now clearly hear the sounds of the British Army fighting for its life.

Night brought relief from the sun, a cessation of the noise of battle ahead, but little other comfort. Rest was essential, and they dropped to the ground and slept, cradling their rifles as though they were wives or lovers. Then up and on again, marching now towards an ominous orange glow.

At dawn, to the brave sound of drums and bugles, they marched upon the battlefield. Even Pelham gagged. An appalling sight met his weary eyes, a revolting stench assailed his nostrils. He sought the source of the evil reek and saw the charred bodies littering a still burning hillside, the parched grass set ablaze by the firing of the guns to consume killed and wounded alike. As his gaze swept round, the evidence of a bloody battle became clear. Heaps of dead and dying lay among shattered ammunition wagons and all the other terrible debris of war. Lifeless horses lay beside overturned guns, entangled with broken trappings. Yet as the bugles gave the command to halt, not a man flinched. They kept their ranks, grasped their rifles more firmly and awaited the order to advance.

"Sorry, ma'am," he heard Gill say at a horrified gasp from Vinny, and realised he had been re-living the events as the sergeant told them. "This is not a fit story for a lady's ears. But at the sound of our bugle-horns a cheer went up from the survivors, for, glad as they were to see us, the battle was already theirs. The French were in full retreat to the east."

"Thank God!" gasped Vinny.

"Aye, ma'am, and thank our Sir Arthur, too, and the fact that the French thought a Spanish army was advancing on Madrid from the south."

"The aftermath of that battle was terrible, but the campaign went on," murmured Pelham.

"Aye, sir. Fifteen or sixteen miles a day, we covered, marching through mud or ice and bivouacking on soaking hills and arctic sierras. In summer it was different—we sweated under a scorching sun! We spent most of the time on the move, but rested in cantonments now and again to regroup and recover, mostly in poor mountain villages so infested with vermin and stinking so high, we sometimes thought we'd arrived in hell. I never did scratch so much in all me life!" Gill grimaced wryly, and gave himself a reminiscent rub on his chest. "But we were hunting the French now, so mostly the men were in good spirits, and the officers treated it like a fox hunt; they were up to every lark—you among 'em, sir, if you'll forgive me saying so!"

Pelham smiled slightly. "Go on."

"The Light Division was Atty's eyes and ears. We weren't with the main army, but out ahead, and Black Bob had us so well disciplined that the whole division could be brought to battle order in fifteen minutes, even in the middle of the night. We were proud of that, sir. And our piquets never once got taken by surprise. The French couldn't get past us to find out how the main army was deployed. We harassed 'em and we fought 'em and, although he got us into some scrapes, Black Bob got us out again. 'The first in the field and last out of it' was the toast of the Rifles—the bloody, fighting Ninety-fifth!"

Percy stirred from a trance-like attention. "I vow I'd be willing to drink to that any day!" he cried.

"And despite our faded and ragged uniforms the Spanish ladies came out at nights for impromptu balls—we were their heroes. I think it was Johnny Kincaid—you must remember him, sir, you were real chums, went hunting together as well as chasing the ladies—"

"Yes," put in Pelham hurriedly, before Gill could reveal any more embarrassing information, "I do remember Johnny, and our escapades. A fine officer."

"Well," went on Gill, not to be diverted from his story, "it was him who claimed that even nuns were willing to elope with him, and unconditionally!"

Pelham directed a wicked smile in Vinny's direction. "Nuns, I collect, were not so strongly perfumed with garlic as the ordinary Spanish *señoritas!*"

"Really, sir, if that is how you all behaved—"

"The regiment—the entire division—had been welded together by the sharing of endless danger, discomfort and hunger. We were living hard and staring death in the face, my dear," he said quietly, a far-away look in his eyes. "The officers rode straight, spoke the truth and never showed fear. That was our creed. And we lived each day as though it were our last. But that nun thing was all a joke, you know," he added with a grin. "To see what answer we got. We never took 'em up on it."

Vinny instantly forgave him the quite unforgivable intimacy of his mode of address because it sounded so wonderful when he said it. Little tendrils of hope were beginning to unfurl in her breast. He spoke with authority. His memory was returning. They would soon know his whole history, and then...

"So I should hope!" she exclaimed, unable to stop herself from returning his smile.

"And I thought that day in January would be my last!" went on Gill, interrupting her pleasant visions of the future. "The order came to storm the fortress at Ciudad Rodrigo— death or glory, that's what we thought. Black Bob was killed, a tragedy for the division, other splendid officers lost their lives too and George Napier of the Forty-third lost an arm."

"And you lost a foot," prompted Vinny softly.

"Not in the storming, ma'am. Inside the walls, afterwards, the men went berserk, sacked the town and killed some Italian soldiers they found there. It was a real disgrace, though it was the result of snatching victory against the odds. Wellington attacked at night, took the defenders by surprise. The men got exhilarated, then enraged by some stupid Spaniards, and went about letting off muskets and rifles everywhere.''

"Impossible task, to keep order," muttered Pelham. "I asked one of my men what he was firing at, and he replied, 'I don't know, sir. I'm just joining in.'"

"And then some fool caught me in the foot," growled the sergeant.

"What bad luck!" exclaimed Vinny sympathetically. "After all you'd been through, to be shot by a comrade!"

"Exactly, ma'am. But I survived and was shipped home. And that's all I know, sir, from first-hand experience, but I heard that the Army marched south and stormed Badajoz in March."

"Of which action I can still remember absolutely nothing," Pelham told them ruefully. "Perhaps I never shall."

"You'll have been leading a storming party, no doubt of that, sir, and been met with explosions and fireballs, grape-shot and canister. The wondrous thing is that when you fell you weren't trampled to death by those coming on behind..."

"In that ditch I've heard so much of since I've been home... But forget that. Your tale has brought some glimpses of memory back to me, Gill, and I am eternally grateful to you. I rather fancy I am beginning to remember the best years of my life! After breakfast, we will depart for the Horse Guards, where we should discover the whole of my history from the records."

Vinny, of course, did not go with them and sat on pins awaiting their return. The advent of a number of callers did nothing to assuage her impatience. Only the announcement of Lady Hartwood and her two daughters caused any diminution of her abstraction. She almost refused to receive them, but inbred courtesy and concern for Jane and Percy's fortunes forbade such a rebuff.

She greeted them coolly. They could not possibly have heard of John Smith's identification as Justin Pelham—unless there was communication between the servants...

But no. Lady Hartwood had come to discover why Percy had defaulted that morning.

"We have become so used to your dear brother waiting upon Mary that we felt sure he must be indisposed," she excused their visit, inclining her turbanned head in gracious greeting. "We came to leave him our card, that he should be aware of our concern."

"That is most civil of you, my lady, but I can assure you there is no cause for it. He has another call upon his time this morning."

"Then we may hope for the pleasure of his company tomorrow! Mary was really most anxious—were you not, Mary?—for she daily expects—well, it would be indelicate of me to put her expectations into words, but nevertheless I am certain you will understand her anxiety—such a suitable match—she would make a splendid viscountess one day—"

Vinny had had enough. "I have no doubt of it, madam," she retorted frigidly, "but I cannot hold you out any hope that Mr Sinclair intends to honour Miss Hartwood with a proposal. In fact, I can promise you that he does not."

Lady Hartwood rose to her feet, quivering with outrage. "If you are privy to his intentions, ma'am, then I have nothing more to say, except to register my deepest displeasure. He has been most assiduous in his attentions to my daughter; why, everyone has been linking their names—Society will think her very ill-used—"

Vinny could see the extreme discomfort her mother's indelicacy was causing Mary and immediately felt in charity with the girl, convinced that her more recent pursuit of Percy had been forced by Lady Hartwood. She did not believe Mary loved Percy. She would suffer nothing but mortification.

"I doubt it, my lady. I admit he did show a certain partiality for your daughter earlier in the year, but not in so strong a manner as to occasion serious remark. Since our return to London he has not stood up with Miss Hartwood above once at any ball, nor sat with her, I believe. Society cannot share your expectations. My brother's interest is now fixed elsewhere, on a young lady whose superior understanding and gentleness of manner have quite won his heart."

"I told you, Mary," spat that young lady's mother. "While you wasted your time and smiles on that Smith man, that sly puss, your cousin Jane, was stealing your beau! That is how she shows her gratitude to me!"

"You encouraged us, Mama, with all your questions and speculation," protested Miss Hartwood with spirit. "He is a most interesting and entertaining gentleman, you must agree; everyone has been quite in raptures over him. And he might still be a person of consequence."

"His name is Justin Pelham," Vinny informed them, casually smug. "A captain in the Ninety-fifth Regiment— the Rifles. He is even yet at the Horse Guards attempting to discover more of his history. My brother is with him."

Lady Hartwood sat down abruptly. The loose skin under her chin wobbled. "Well, I declare!" she exclaimed. "He has recollected his name? And his family? Has he admitted to being that disgraceful student?"

"I am sorry to disappoint your hopes, madam, but he remains in ignorance of his personal history. I still do not know his connections, or whether he was indeed that foolish youth spoken of the other night. But no doubt all will be revealed in short order. And now, madam, I scarcely think there can be any merit in your remaining longer.'' She reached for the bell-pull. A footman entered immediately. ''Good day to you, my lady. Miss Hartwood, Miss Arabella.''

''I am sorry, ma'am,'' whispered Mary as she made her curtsy.

The girl was showing such delicacy of feeling that Vinny felt able to offer her comfort. ''You will find a true suitor, Miss Hartwood, never fear. But do not depend upon Mr Pelham. And when you do enter into an engagement I shall be the first to wish you the happiness you deserve.''

Percy returned within a quarter of an hour of the Hartwoods' departure. He immediately sought Vinny and, finding her in the morning-room, gave her a triumphant smile.

''I have done it!'' he announced. ''Congratulate me on my good fortune, Vinny! I am become the happiest of men!''

''What can you mean?'' demanded his sister, baffled. Why congratulate him? Surely any news he had to impart must concern Pelham. ''Where is Mr Pelham?''

''Pelham? Oh, he went off with Gill to visit his old address. Lookin' for his roots. I trotted round to Portman Square. Had the deuced good luck to find Jane alone. Told her she was the first object of my affections. Asked for her hand. She accepted.''

''Percy! Such news! And how strange! Lady Hartwood and daughters were here, looking for you!''

''Serves 'em right, then, that I caught Jane alone!''

''But it was quite improper for her to receive you without a chaperon present! I should not have thought her so indifferent to propriety—''

''Oh, don't concern yourself over that! Did it all in form. Applied to Sir Jonas for permission to address his niece in private. He made no great work of the matter,'' said Percy airily. ''Shall have to write to her father, ask his permission, and let our parents know. But it is all settled between us. Lady Hartwood may do her worst!''

''How glad I am that you did not place Jane in an embarrassing dilemma!''

''Not quite demented yet, Vinny. Knew I couldn't expect her to receive me without permission. But the opportunity was too good to miss!''

''And I heartily congratulate you on seizing it, and winning Jane's hand! She may suffer some unpleasantness, I fear. But she is strong enough to withstand it. I really am delighted, Percy. But—'' she could disregard her own preoccupation no longer ''—you must tell me, what happened at the Horse Guards?''

''Wait for Pelham. He'll reveal all. Shouldn't be long now.''

''Oh, Percy, don't be such a tease! You know I must be dying for information!''

''You know his name, rank and regiment. Nothing else of much importance came up, except this address he's gone to.''

''Where is it?''

''Chelsea, Sloane Street. But really, Vinny, you'll have to wait. He'd rather tell you himself, I'll be bound.''

''And he discovered nothing much else of consequence?'' she persisted. Anything and everything about him was of importance to her. But although she could not conceal her eagerness she must not give Percy reason to suspect how deep her interest really ran. He had already shown more perception in that direction than she previously would have given him credit for.

Percy was in his room composing a letter to Jane's father when Pelham returned.

''I left Gill with your housekeeper,'' the captain told Vinny rather apologetically. ''I should have spoken to you first, but I felt secure in your approval. Gill is in poor circumstances, and on his own. He is a man of some education and has many superior qualities. I offered him a position as my personal servant, which he gladly accepted. My only doubt, and it was slight, concerned your readiness to accept a servant of mine into your household.''

''How could you imagine for one moment that I would refuse such a request? You are the first guest I can remember entertaining who has not been accompanied by at least one person in his service! I have thought you should have a valet, and Gill will do splendidly, I am sure, once he is trained. But what of your news, sir? Did you find the house where you were used to live? Did you meet your family?''

''Ah.'' He looked slightly crestfallen. ''The house, I regret to say, does not exist and never did. I infer that I gave false information when I answered the call to the colours and purchased a commission.''

Vinny, who had risen eagerly on his entrance, sat down again abruptly. Disappointment made her voice flat. ''So your name is not Justin Pelham?''

He shrugged, and smiled his most impudent smile. She could immediately see the young, dashing, devil-may-care officer revealed by Sergeant Gill that morning, and felt the trembling in her limbs again.

''Who knows?'' he wondered. ''Could I have made it up?''

''Doubtless, sir!'' she controlled her senseless reactions with rigid determination. ''But this means that you still have no idea of who your family or connections are—unless your memory has extended back beyond your days in the Peninsula?''

''It has not, and you infer correctly.''

''Then you have little alternative. You must travel to Oxford.''

His expression darkened. His features, uncompromising at any time, became cast in iron. ''No. People must be prepared to forget the first eighteen years of my life. I have discovered a satisfactory identity in which I have lived for the past fourteen. I can offer a detailed account of those years, and that must suffice, unless my memory returns of its own accord.''

"If that is your last word, I must accept it, though I believe you to be wrong. But come, Mr Pelham," she cajoled, "you must have discovered something more of your history! Have you...a wife?'' It almost choked her to ask, but she had to know.

"Not according to army records. Of course, I may have been running away from a shrew...''

The devilish light in his eyes told her he did not believe it for a moment. He was teasing her. She rejoiced in his change of mood and relaxed, though not completely, for she found it impossible to laugh other than half-consciously under the mortifying conviction that he had detected her particular interest in that answer.

"Who did you name as next of kin?'' she asked hurriedly.

He shrugged a little too casually. "My commanding officer at the time. I joined a county regiment—the Glosters—but that could mean anything or nothing.''

"It fits your southern accent," she observed.

"True. So there you are. I am an ex-captain of the Ninety-fifth Regiment, name Justin Pelham, aged thirty-two, no known relatives, and of no traceable address. I have no fixed source of income, though I am now entitled to additional back pay, and am able to sell my commission. So I am not completely without funds. But neither am I in any position to promise—to ask anyone to share my future.'' He seemed to realise that he was speaking too earnestly. His face broke into a roguish smile. "Would you elope with me, Mrs Darling?''

He was joking—he must be joking!

"Unconditionally?" she enquired archly.

"Naturally."

"How can I refuse?"

At her words his expression changed. "Vinny," he muttered, "oh, my dear! Would you?"

The ground seemed to tremble under Vinny's chair. She gasped a little for breath. How could she respond to such a sudden, painful, impossible plea without giving offence, without hurt…?

"I think you mistake me for a nun, Captain!" she retorted lightly, resurrecting a joke that was no longer funny.

He stiffened immediately. The softened, tender expression on his face hardened again, though he kept a slight, mocking smile upon his lips. It did not reach his eyes.

"How could I possibly mistake *you* for a nun, my dear Vinny?" he enquired.

He excused himself and departed to change for dinner. Vinny sat on, afraid to move lest her legs refused to support her.

Chapter Nine

A week or so passed in comparative calm while Justin Pelham became used to his newly discovered identity and Percy awaited a response to his letter to the Reverend Mr Rosedale.

Meanwhile Percy suffered all the frustrations normally experienced by an eager lover denied access to his beloved.

"Lady Hartwood refused to receive me," he gloomed, after his first visit to Harley Street after the betrothal.

"You will see Jane at the opera tonight; I know the family has a box booked," Vinny consoled him. "I am certain you will be able to snatch a few words."

But Jane did not appear in public, that evening or on any other.

"The old tabby is keeping her indoors, confinin' her to Harley Street," grumbled Percy, "and even Sir Jonas has withdrawn his permission for me to see her."

"He's back under his wife's thumb," guessed Vinny. "I'll see if I can snatch a word with Mary or Arabella tonight. There should be plenty of opportunity at the squeeze we are attending."

"If they are present," muttered Percy, steeped in pessimism.

Vinny did manage to catch Arabella and, since Percy was at her side, all three enjoyed what they felt to be an excitingly furtive conversation, while Pelham stood guard. Rather surprisingly, in Vinny's view, Arabella offered to act as the lovers' intermediary.

"Mama is in a miff," she explained with a grin. "But Jane is well," she went on reassuringly, "although she is naturally mortified at being denied the opportunity to leave Harley Street or to receive calls, and prodigiously upset at not being allowed to see you, Mr Sinclair. But I'll tell her I've spoken with you," she assured Percy in a conspiratorial whisper, "and say you are pining away with love!"

"No need to go that far," muttered Percy, flushing, "just let her know I still consider myself engaged, and have not yet received a reply to my letter to her father."

"I'll bring you a message from her tomorrow," promised Arabella, who appeared to be thoroughly enjoying her role of emissary between the lovers.

So Percy and Jane survived the ordeal of separation and renewed their vows of love in clandestine fashion. For Percy, at least, Vinny suspected that this added an extra and probably beneficial spice of excitement to the affair.

September drifted into October. Justin and Percy were full of the situation in Spain, discussing it endlessly, for the news was creating great excitement at home. The tide had turned at last, Napoleon's armies were on the run all over Europe. Madrid had been taken in the middle of August, Wellington had marched north to invest the fortress of Burgos, and they daily expected to hear that it, too, had fallen.

Vinny went about her duties and attended entertainments with apparent pleasure, but beneath the surface her emotions seethed.

Justin behaved as though his proposal had never been made. He evinced no sign at all of any wish to deepen the relationship between them, maintaining a uniformly courteous but distant manner, reserving his enthusiasm for pursuing news of the war. With painful determination Vinny matched his attitude, hiding her true feelings behind the cool façade of hostess.

She might declare her disdain of others' opinions in the heat of the moment and when her position was not seriously threatened, but she had been brought up to value her consequence, without allowing it to result in undue pride. For her to contemplate marriage to someone with so dubious a background and so small a fortune without considering the damage it would do to her position in Society was impossible. Marriage was a most grave step, and she had already made one mistake. Charles Darling's early death had rescued her from a lifetime of regret.

Not that she could imagine regretting union with Justin Pelham on any personal level. The very thought brought desperate longing and an anticipatory glow of excitement. In him lay all her hopes of happiness. Yet she had more than once seen rash alliances, made in the name of love, perish on the rocks of penury and disapproval. Everything in her experience counselled caution.

All she could do was to pray for some miracle to restore Pelham's memory and prove him eligible, and yet another to dispose him to overlook her rebuff and renew his offer in form…not just as a joking invitation to run away with him…

Meanwhile, moving in Society sometimes made it difficult to keep as cool a distance between them as she would have liked.

"Suggest you ask Mrs Darling and Mr Pelham to sing a song," cried Percy one evening, having just suffered an excruciatingly inept recital given by a young lady of great fortune but little talent.

"Oh, yes!" gushed Lady Chandos, a younger and rather

silly matron still attempting to make her mark as a hostess. "Do, please! A duet! How delightful! You sing, then, Mr Pelham?"

Pelham, with a perfectly sober face, admitted that he did.

"Really, Percy," remonstrated Vinny, her cheeks hot with embarrassment. They had never performed together in public, and seldom in private! Singing with Pelham caused agitation enough—how could she support doing so before all these curious people?

"Go on," whispered her brother unfeelingly, "or I declare I shall disgrace myself. If Jane were here—but she ain't, and listenin' to the pair of you singin' together has less power than anythin' to bore me to distraction!" He spoke across her to the other man, who sat following the exchange with a show of languid interest. "What do you say, Pelham?"

"I have no objection, if Mrs Darling agrees," he replied, accompanying his words with a small shrug and deprecating smile.

Vinny had little choice but to give in gracefully, if apprehensively, to the importunate demands of the company.

Although Vinny was well known as a pleasing accompanist to her own singing, Justin Pelham's talents were until then an unknown quantity. They began with a ballad in French. The normal chatter indulged in by those present largely died away as the piece progressed, their audience, almost against its will, becoming enthralled by the liquid blending of the two voices. But too many, including their hostess and a hostile Lady Hartwood, continued to make loud asides throughout the song.

"*Bravo!*" cried Lady Chandos, clapping loudly as they finished despite the fact that she had not been listening. "I do declare, Captain Pelham, you have been cheating us all these weeks! We did not know you sang so splendidly!"

He bowed an acknowledgement. "I sing a little ma'am,

that is all. Without Mrs Darling's skill on the pianoforte and her charming voice, mine would be nothing.''

Lady Chandos had by now walked over to lay a familiar hand on his arm. She tapped him lightly with her fan and smiled archly. ''You are too modest, sir! Such a superior voice! You must both sing for us again!''

''Willingly, ma'am, if you are ready to listen. Which song would you prefer? And in what language?''

Lady Chandos looked blank, then laughed. ''Anything! But in English! Something we can all understand!''

Vinny, more tolerant than Pelham of the rudeness of audiences, but nevertheless appreciating his baiting of a pretentious woman completely ignorant of music, played a few introductory notes on the keyboard. Pelham smiled, and bowed acquiescence to his hostess.

''A selection of nursery rhymes should not be beyond anyone's understanding, I vow.''

Lady Chandos blinked, not certain whether to take him seriously. ''If that is your wish,'' she responded uncertainly.

''An inspired notion,'' murmured Pelham as he resumed his place behind Vinny. They had sung the medley the other evening, for their own amusement, and he quite relished the thought of regaling the company with such tunes as ''Baa Baa Black Sheep'', ''Ring a Ring of Roses'', and ''Humpty Dumpty''. To finish the recital, Vinny slipped straight into ''Greensleeves'', all of which earned them a sincere round of applause.

After that evening they were called upon to perform at every informal gathering they attended. Four times in twice as many days they provided novelty in the evening's entertainment. Nursery rhymes became quite the thing in their circle.

These performances caused Vinny agonies of pleasurable confusion, since Justin stood close by. But, to compensate, the music permitted more intimate communion than that offered by any other activity. How he felt about it she had no notion.

They had never yet deliberately practised together; it had not seemed necessary. So, as she sat at the pianoforte one morning before breakfast going through her scales, his voice behind her made her start.

"Mr Pelham! I had not realised you were come in!"

Smiling, he bowed. "You were absorbed in your practice, ma'am. I heard the sound of the pianoforte, and took the liberty of coming to express my opinion that the new song we attempted last evening requires some rehearsal." He gave a slight laugh. "I do not consider our rendering did the piece justice, and although we are largely singing to ignorant fools we should seek to improve our performance for our own satisfaction."

All the familiar sensations raced through Vinny's body. How bittersweet was his presence!

"Which piece?" she asked brightly, controlling her agitation as he moved to stand beside her, while trusting he remained unaware of it. "The new Italian song?"

She turned her head to look up into his face, soliciting his answer. He drew in a sharp breath. At this early hour her skin looked fresh as the dew, her eyes bright, dark jewels framed by long, sweeping lashes. Her wide cheekbones, softly caressed by dancing black curls, held a slight flush. Standing close to her to sing was invariably a torment. All he could do was look, when he longed to touch.

The colour in her face deepened as she saw the arrested look in his eyes. She couldn't tear her own away. Something in his gaze held her spellbound. He was impeccably turned out, as usual, but since the advent of Gill his hair tended to be less restrained. It tumbled over his brow, giving him a rakish appearance which nothing in his changing expression denied. Dashing, reckless, he looked as she imagined he might have done leading an attack against insurmountable odds, or risking all on the turn of a card.

He made a quick movement and reached for her hand. She felt his touch in her breast, and suspended her breathing. Something was coming...not a kiss...but his eyes shone brilliantly, eager, intent...

"Vinny! My dearest Vinny," he uttered, his voice vibrant with emotion. "You must know I hold you in regard above all other women...will you honour me by trusting me to care for you? It is the dearest wish of my heart to make you mine...will you consent to marry me?"

Vinny heart leapt in delight—but she had been convincing herself for so long that marriage to him was impossible that she believed it. Her pent-up breath escaped in a distressed gasp.

"Oh, no!" she cried. "No! You must know it is impossible! How can you ask such a thing?"

He let go of her hand slowly, reluctantly, and straightened up. The eagerness had left him. Any expression in his eyes was hidden behind a greeny glaze.

"Forgive me, ma'am. I have obviously mistaken your sentiments."

"Oh, dear!" wailed Vinny. She knew she was not saying anything right; she could not think with so much pain tearing at her raw emotions. "Justin!" Her voice quivered on his name; she had never so addressed him before. "Justin," she repeated more firmly, "you know I have grown to admire you greatly, and I am sensible of the honour you have done me—"

"I have no wish to hear all the usual platitudes," he broke in forcefully. Hearing his name so sweetly on her lips, he had thought— But he had been wrong. "I am sensible that I do you small honour by asking for your hand in marriage, since I have little to offer of either fortune or consequence."

Vinny made a small sound of dissent, which he ignored. "I do not as yet possess even a competence upon which to live," he admitted painfully. "But I am persuaded that such a situation will not endure. I protest I am not a man to depend upon his wife's fortune," he stated proudly, "and had not planned to speak until I was able to offer you adequate means... But my feelings overcame both pride and good sense, and in my eagerness I spoke rashly—trusting, in my arrogance, that if your sentiments were as strong as mine you would take the risk of committing yourself to so worthless a fellow."

"Oh, Justin, you must not believe that I think you worthless," cried Vinny in distress, "that I do not value your regard above everything, but—"

He held up a hand, staying her speech. "It is too much to ask. I am aware that I have only my rash proposal to blame for your refusal. The error was mine; I should not have spoken."

"I am flattered that you did," murmured Vinny, feeling some sort of response necessary but not knowing what to say. But this protestation served only to distance him further.

"Feeling as I do, to remain any longer under your roof would be intolerable," he went on, as though she had not spoken. "I shall therefore seek lodgings for myself and Gill. You may expect us to depart within the week."

He made a brief bow and, before she could protest against his decision, had left.

He arranged his removal within two days, and in the intervening time barely entered the house except to retire to his room. He did not appear at meals until his last morning, when he entered the dining-parlour at breakfast-time in the hope of finding her alone. The sight of her lonely, disconsolate figure sipping abstractedly at a cup of chocolate almost overset his resolution.

"Mrs Darling." He bowed with perfect formality. "I am come to take my leave."

Vinny dismissed a servant with an abrupt motion of her hand. As the fellow withdrew she rose and approached Pelham.

"I wish you would change your mind, sir. I have no desire for you to leave my house—"

"But it *is* your house, ma'am. I could not remain as your guest indefinitely. I must seek to make an independent life for myself."

"You will not re-join to the Army?" she asked as the knot in her stomach tightened. He had escaped death so many times already, it would surely be tempting fate for him to return to the Peninsula...

"No, ma'am. I believe I have served His Majesty long enough, and the war appears to be almost won. It is time I settled down."

"Then—" she swallowed "—then I must wish you well, sir. But—oh, Justin! Must you go?" she cried piteously.

He lifted his brows. Otherwise his austere expression did not change. "I fear that, since you will not honour me with your hand, I must, ma'am."

"I wish—but I cannot!" she cried in desperation. "Go, then if you must! I do not care!"

"Vinny! I know that you do!" he exclaimed, his voice raw with sudden emotion. His eyes blazed into hers, scorching into her soul. "And why should you not, you, to whom I owe so much? You have helped me to discover what memory I now possess! But you are right; without the whole I cannot hope to attach a woman of your consequence and worth."

"And you will not seek to discover more," she accused,

the tears running unchecked down her cheeks. "Why not, Justin?"

"You once termed my quest exceptional," he answered her tightly. "It is, and in more ways than one. No other man, I imagine, has ever chased his memory quite so hard as I have mine! Yet there is something hidden in my mind which will not allow me to continue the pursuit." He flared his nostrils, inhaling a deep breath which enabled him to carry on calmly. "I must be content with what I have. Which, though not inconsiderable, is not enough to bring me the happiness of winning your hand. So—farewell, my dear. Accept my deepest thanks for all your concern, your inestimable help. Without it I should have been in poor case."

"You would have managed," quavered Vinny. "You have no need of anyone but yourself."

"So I have always believed. Perhaps it is still true. But I have learned the value of—well, of having someone to care," he finished awkwardly.

She looked into his eyes, hers still brimming with tears. "Justin, you know I do care. May we part friends?"

He took her hand and lifted it to his lips. "That is my fondest hope."

"Then—we shall continue to meet in Society—your rooms are off Jermyn Street, I believe?"

"They are." He told her the address, although she already knew it, having received the information from Percy. However, she wrote it down at his dictation. When she had finished he added softly, "If ever you are in need of assistance, I shall be honoured to be of service."

Shortly after, he made his formal bow and left. Vinny had never felt anyone's departure so keenly. She watched from the window until the hackney he had insisted upon hiring moved off and, splashing through muddy puddles and a dreary, lashing rain, passed out of sight. Only then did she turn back into the empty room, giving a dispirited sigh. Her tears had dried and she had no more to weep. All she could do was sit and consider what she had lost.

She had come to depend upon his society, to value his good sense, to rely upon his instant compliance with all her plans—well, not quite all her plans, she acknowledged with a wry twist of her lips. On some things he maintained a rock-like firmness it was impossible to shift. But, above all, the sight and sound of him had lifted her spirits, brought confusion and animation and all that was desirable to her life.

Shortly after his departure she discovered that Pelham was not the only person in Town making a move. News quickly spread that Jane Rosedale had been dispatched home and that Sir Jonas and Lady Hartwood were returning to their country seat, taking their daughters with them.

This intelligence, combined with the receipt of an encouraging letter from Jane's father, prompted Percy to propose a visit to the vicarage in Hertfordshire to see his love and to press his suit in person.

"You don't mind, do you, Vinny?" he asked, though it was a question to which he did not expect an answer. "Now Pelham is set up in his own establishment I do not have to remain as chaperon," he grinned. Percy did not know the true reason for his friend's departure, hailing it as the best possible thing—Pelham would be near the gentlemen's clubs where he exercised his skill at cards to such advantage. "And you will be returnin' to Preston Grange, no doubt, to finish your visit there," he guessed.

"I don't know." Vinny felt disinclined to commit herself to any particular course of action at that moment. "The roads will be so dirty after all this rain. In any case, I shall be perfectly all right here on my own. This is, after all, my home!"

Home it might be, but after a bleak couple of weeks

when she had caught but the briefest of glimpses of Justin Pelham, who had largely withdrawn from Society, she knew that nowhere would truly be home in future were he not part of the household. Hope still flickered in her heart, but with each day that passed the flame burnt a little lower.

That year the equinox had been followed by fierce gales and storms all over Europe.

"Did you hear, ma'am," cried Flora excitedly one morning as she delivered her mistress's chocolate, "the Thames has overflowed into Westminster Hall?"

"I'm not surprised," retorted Vinny sourly. "It has hardly stopped raining this age!"

"But this morning is fine! Just look, ma'am! Hardly a cloud in sight!"

Vinny sat up with more enthusiasm and eyed the patch of greyish-blue beyond the window. The wind no longer howled about the chimney and the rain had stopped lashing the glass. Desperate for diversion, she decided to seek it in Hyde Park. The crowds would not be so great as in the Season, or when an exceptional spell of warm weather brought everyone out for a breath of air. But that morning plenty of people were likely to take advantage of a break in the dreary weather to promenade.

The day was surprisingly mild for late October. Vinny donned a becoming silk bonnet covered with crape and trimmed with coquelicot ribbons, which matched the red spot on her pretty coloured muslin gown and its matching pelisse, and set forth under the protection of the rear section of the landau roof. To close the carriage completely would isolate her inside and defeat the object of her excursion.

She bade Ellis stop several times in order to exchange greetings and was still engaged with Lady Chandos, riding in a partly open barouche, when that lady's attention was caught by one of the many approaching vehicles.

"Why," she exclaimed. "I do declare! That is Mr Pelham, is it not? I heard he'd departed your roof, my dear Mrs Darling. We have seen little of him since."

"Indeed he has, Lady Chandos, and appears to prefer the gaming clubs to Society."

Lady Chandos scarcely heard Vinny's hard-won reply, being too engaged in assessing the approaching equipage. "What a splendid carriage!" she cried. "And drawn by what my spouse would call two prime pieces of horseflesh! I declare he must have become quite rich to afford such an expensive turn-out!"

"It may not be his, ma'am."

Vinny managed to speak casually with considerable difficulty, for he was almost upon them. She doubted his ownership, because, from what she could see between the liveried figures of Ellis and a footman sitting up on the box and obscuring her view, such a pretentious outfit did not suit the image of the man she knew.

As the extravagantly appointed curricle, drawn by a pair of showy light greys, drew near, she saw that Pelham, looking positively devastating in his new blue superfine coat and buff pantaloons, was acting gentleman-coachman to a young lady of quite outstanding beauty.

The meeting could not be avoided. Pelham halted his horses and Vinny greeted him with as much sang-froid as she could muster.

He made his duties to both ladies and introduced his youthful companion as Miss Isabella Day, the daughter of his landlord.

"Papa allowed Mr Pelham to drive me out in our curricle," said that young lady breathlessly. "He is so splendid with the reins, has such safe hands, Papa is quite persuaded of my safety." She gazed up at Pelham from soulful blue eyes. "I do so adore driving in the Park. Papa says I may come whenever Mr Pelham has the time to bring me.''

Driving in the Park was not the only thing she adored, thought Vinny in disgust. The chit could not be much above sixteen, and should not be allowed so much liberty, or such expensive, becoming apparel. But she could not blame a man like Pelham, looking to settle down, for being tempted by her youth and fair attractions. He would have a doting young wife he could educate to his ways...rather than putting up with an opinionated widow...and Mr Day, a rich City merchant as far as she knew, would not see his daughter want, and could entertain no scruples about Pelham's background, or he would not allow...

She dared a glance at Pelham and discovered him to be studying her with an inscrutable expression which changed to amusement as he noticed her fulminating glare.

''Mr Day is most generous in allowing me to indulge the undoubted pleasure of driving such a prime pair, and in such charming company,'' he said, with a smile for the girl at his side which made Vinny's toes curl. ''But I believe we should proceed, or the horses will become chilled.''

''We have been going at such a pace!'' cried Miss Day with enthusiasm. ''I adore speed above everything!''

''Good day, ladies.'' Pelham doffed his top hat, sharing his wonderful smile between the two women in their separate carriages. But his eyes lingered on Vinny, a thoughtful expression in their brown depths, as he gave his horses the office to proceed.

Vinny made her polite adieus to Lady Chandos while her mind followed the curricle. Undoubtedly she wished most strongly that *she* had been seated by his side. Percy had often driven her in his, but the opportunity for Pelham to do so had never arisen, even on the journey to London. Percy had positively refused to enter her chaise. Not for the first time, she wished she possessed a light carriage herself...she could drive, had done so since a child...what could be more natural than to purchase a smart but unostentatious curricle—or perhaps a phaeton—and use it to drive herself about Town with a groom in attendance? Then if she should see Pelham she could invite him...

The daydream shattered into fragments as she was hailed by another acquaintance. But it persisted in the back of her mind.

It seemed more than an omen therefore when, a couple of days later, a young lord called to make his adieus, since he was due to depart for his ancestral home in Yorkshire, from whence he would be travelling to India in the spring, and mentioned that he would be forced to part with his curricle and matched pair of bays before he left Town.

"Deuced fine outfit," he told her sorrowfully. "But no sense in holdin' on to it. Shall be overseas for years, I don't doubt, and the cattle will be too old to be of use by the time I return. Must sell 'em."

"What price are you asking?" said Vinny, before she could think better of it.

He named a modest sum.

"I'm interested," she informed him. "I'll have Ellis, my coachman, look the curricle over and inspect the horses, if you've no objection? Do you have them here?"

"My groom is walkin' the cattle, ma'am. If you are serious, I'll have him take 'em round to your stables."

Vinny assured him that she was serious and within the half-hour a deal was struck. The curricle and a pair of dark bay horses were hers.

Although the acquisition had appeared fortuitous, the weather did not at all advance her cause. To purchase an open carriage at the end of October, even at a bargain price, was not the most sensible thing Vinny had ever done.

Between bouts of rain, Ellis escorted her on a couple of

outings round Portman Square and along the nearby roads. "They're splendid animals for you to drive, ma'am," he gave his verdict. "Spirited but easily managed. And you're a fine whip. I'd not be anxious if you took them out alone."

"Thank you, Ellis," she smiled, gratified. "Your recommendation to purchase was well justified. Ask the housekeeper to provide a livery for the best of your young grooms. He shall accompany me. Teach him his duties and have him ready for the first fine day."

She awoke one morning to see a wintry sun breaking through a misty sky. If the weather held, this would be the chance she awaited. By one o'clock she was ready. The sun still shone, if rather weakly, and although later there would most likely be a blanketing fog, at the moment there was nothing to stop her. She had donned her thickest pelisse and in addition folded a shawl around her shoulders. The groom carried a rug to be tucked about her feet.

Vinny's spirits lifted as she flicked her whip and set the horses in motion. As the curricle started forward the young groom, resplendent in his new uniform, let go their heads and scrambled up on his perch behind, there to cling on proudly as the carriage gathered speed.

Orchard Street was comparatively clear but Oxford Street was, as usual, full of traffic, heavy drays and wagons competing for space with carts, coaches, chaises, gigs and horseback riders, with hand-carts and pedestrians dodging everywhere, risking injury from the horses' hoofs and getting splattered with mud and filth from the road. But the distance was short to the first gate into the Park and before long she was bowling merrily along towards the throng of equestrians and carriages promenading by the Serpentine.

Her fingers froze on the reins, for her kid gloves did scarcely anything to keep out the November chill. But on the occasions when she stopped to greet an acquaintance and her groom jumped down to hold the horses' heads she was able to glean a few moments' warmth from her large and comforting muff. Excitement kept her tolerably warm otherwise, and when she glimpsed the object of her excursion approaching her skin positively glowed.

She reined in as Pelham, booted and wearing a much caped greatcoat, brought his mount to a halt and lifted his hat. As they exchanged civilities he eyed the curricle and pair with appreciative eyes.

"You have a new carriage, I see, ma'am. And added a fine pair of horses to your stable."

"I had a fancy to drive myself—I was always used to, before my marriage, you know," she explained rapidly. Embarrassment threatened to overwhelm her. Surely he must guess! "Perhaps I can persuade you to give your opinion of my purchase, sir," she rushed on breathily. "Will you take a turn at the ribbons in order to form it?"

She awaited his response with nerves taut as bowstrings. If he refused—or laughed at her...

But, "With pleasure, ma'am," he replied, dismounting immediately. "Only allow me to tie my horse behind your vehicle."

Vinny wanted no eager long ears overhearing what passed between her and Pelham. "My groom can walk it while we take a turn about the Park," she suggested, feeling weak with relief.

He agreed at once, handing over the reins of his rather bony but large, muscular piebald to the proudly liveried boy, who was already engaged in holding the bays. Fortunately all three horses were well-behaved and he had no trouble.

Pelham mounted the step and settled at her side. Every nerve in Vinny's body was conscious of his nearness. He would be warm in that greatcoat and those thick leather gloves, she thought enviously, shifting her prudently carried umbrella to accommodate him and tucking the rug more firmly about her knees.

As soon as he was ready she handed over the reins and whip. "You will find them quite biddable, sir," she remarked, tucking her hands back into her muff, not only for warmth, but also to hide their trembling.

"I am persuaded they are fine cattle, ma'am. Not showy, but of excellent quality."

The groom released their heads and stood aside, holding the huge piebald. The bays obeyed Pelham's light flick of the whip and trotted forward.

"Was that your own horse?" asked Vinny after several moments of uncomfortable silence.

"The piebald? Yes. Not the best-looking of animals, but an excellent piece of horseflesh just the same. We have come to understand each other well in the week I have had him."

"Where did you buy him?" asked Vinny, to keep the conversation going. He must have paid a respectable price for such a strong, healthy animal, despite its lack of beauty.

"I won him at piquet."

This announcement rather took Vinny's breath. "You have abandoned your scruples, sir?" she enquired, rather acidly, and frowned across at her companion, feeling peculiarly let down.

His mouth tightened at her censure. "No, ma'am," he rejoined in an icy voice, "I have not, but my opponent in the game will not miss the price of that animal. He is unlikely to feel its loss sufficient reason to commit suicide."

Vinny caught her breath. "You believe you *were* that student," she declared.

"No!" he exclaimed violently. "I do not! But, whatever the truth of it, that story was warning enough to all who heard. And echoed the opinion I have long held with regard to excessive gambling.''

Not entirely convinced of the honesty of his denial, Vinny relapsed into silence. He concentrated on his driving, staring ahead with an expressionless face, taking the curricle away from the main throng to less busy rides where he could allow the horses their heads.

They had become different animals, more spirited. In fact, in his hands, Vinny thought resignedly, they could be categorised as prime goers. A description she had never previously imagined applying to them.

''They go well for you,'' she remarked at last, breaking the long silence with difficulty. And once started could not resist adding, ''Are they as good as those of your landlord?''

She felt him relax as she spoke. The horses slowed. A slight smile lurked at the corner of his mouth.

''Better, Mrs Darling. Much better. Those light greys were all show and no stamina. By the time I returned them to their stable they had scarce another mile left in them.''

''Where is their stable?'' she asked, delighted with his praise. ''Not in Jermyn Street?''

''Oh, no.'' He nursed the bays round into a crossing path. ''The family lives out beyond St Paul's. Day merely owns the building in Jermyn Street, as an investment.''

''Of course,'' said Vinny, relieved that Miss Isabella Day lived at some distance from Pelham. ''He would not wish to reside among the nobility and gentry, where he would feel an outsider.''

''I do not see why he should,'' retorted Pelham shortly. ''He is an eminently respectable and pleasant gentleman. His daughters are all well-versed in the social graces, his son is at Cambridge. His family would not appear out of place in Jermyn Street should they desire to live there. Any more than I do.''

"But you *are* a gentleman," protested Vinny. "No doubt he feels his place is among others who have made their money by commerce."

"Is making a fortune by gambling preferable?" enquired Pelham distantly.

"No, and you know that is not what I meant! Some of the rich cits are splendid people, I have no doubt, but they will never be received in the first circles of Society—"

"Then Society is the poorer for their absence!"

"Are you in love with Isabella?" asked Vinny. And then could have died from mortification. What had possessed her? Her suffering was made worse by the sudden softening of the hard face beside her. He could not look so unless the answer was yes!

"I'm sorry," she gulped. "You have no need to answer that; it was a most impertinent question! But here we are! Back to your horse! Thank you for driving me; I am most grateful…" She tailed off, her fund of nonsensical chatter drying up. The curricle came to a halt. Pelham turned to address her.

"Yes, ma'am, it was an impertinent question. But if you will give me leave to call on you tomorrow I will provide you with an answer. Will you receive me in Portman Square—at about eleven?"

"Eleven," whispered Vinny as she took the reins in her warmed but nerveless fingers. "Yes, of course. I shall look forward to your coming, sir."

He got down from the curricle, made his bow and mounted his horse. His parting smile seemed a little austere, but it held no hint of disdain. "The pleasure will be mine."

He wheeled the patchy black and grey horse and cantered off. Vinny shook the reins, flicked her whip and turned the curricle for home. It had proved a most disturbing encounter. Yet her gamble had paid off.

He would be in Portman Square on the morrow.

Chapter Ten

Eleven struck as Pelham was announced. Vinny had spent an anguished night rehearsing what she should say, but the moment he entered the morning-room all power of speech left her. She received him with what she hoped was not a quivering smile, and cleared her throat.

Pelham himself appeared quite at ease, though she detected a tension in him she had not expected. All he had to do was to announce whether he intended to marry Miss Isabella Day or not, and that should be easy enough for him.

"You are well, Mrs Darling?" he enquired, searching her face with eyes bound to notice the dark rings beneath her own.

She nodded, still unable to find her voice. She could hear her pulse pounding in her ears and knew her ragged breathing must betray her even if her eyes did not.

"I have never known such a fog as there is today," he went on calmly, as though he had nothing more important to speak of than the weather. "Every chimney in London must be conspiring to thicken it. Quite choking. As I rode here I found it necessary to hold a handkerchief before my face in order to breathe."

Vinny felt as though she were teetering on the edge of a cliff with her entire future hanging in the balance. "I thought you might not come," she blurted.

He lifted a nonchalant eyebrow. "Nothing so paltry as a mere fog could prevent me, Mrs Darling, when I had engaged to call."

Having once spoken it did not seem impossible to do so again. Besides, she simply had to know, and the question burst from her. "Why *did* you engage to call on me?"

That was not what she had planned to say, in the silent reaches of the night. She had determined to bid him welcome, offer him refreshment, remind him, by behaving as though he had never left, of how well they could deal together. If possible to hint that if he should choose to renew his offer he would receive a different answer—as her gambling spirit had at last overcome the excessive prudence dictated by upbringing and convention.

But on the other hand, in the face of an avowal of his love for Miss Day, she must force herself to congratulate him upon his conquest with cool and dignified courtesy.

"Do you not remember?" he enquired. His eyes gleamed with humour at sight of her raised colour. She sometimes wore a cap in the morning and sometimes not, as though she could not make up her mind whether she wished to be considered a lively young woman or a mature widow. Today she was bareheaded, and showing every sign of being an anxious, jealous girl. His smile deepened. "You asked me whether I was in love with Miss Day. I have come to give you my answer."

That smug smile destroyed her last remnants of control. "Then stop teasing me and give it!" she flared.

"What would you say if I said I did?" he retorted mildly.

All the spine suddenly left her. She slumped slightly, breathed heavily and closed her eyes.

"Congratulations on your conquest," she croaked unsteadily. "I wish you happy."

So much for all that coolness and dignity she had been determined to display! He must be enjoying his revenge, she thought, as the colour fluctuated in her face. She took a quick glance through her lashes, for she would leave the room rather than endure his mockery.

But he sat still, his eyes on hers, all trace of amusement gone.

"I do not," he said with deliberation.

Vinny felt a new rush of blood flood her cheeks. "But you will marry her!" she choked.

"Will I? Are you a fortune-teller, then, Mrs Darling, that you know my intentions before I do myself?"

"Mr Pelham," she cried in frustration, "you are the most aggravating creature! Can you not tell me plainly? What are your intentions?"

His steady gaze rested on her agitated face as he told her. "My intention, ma'am, is to solicit your hand in marriage—the moment I am possessed of a sufficient competence."

"Oh!" Now the blood drained from her face, leaving her chalk-white. For a moment the room spun. She put a hand to her breast, hoping to still the erratic pounding of her heart. "Do you mean that, sir?" she whispered.

"I was never more serious in my life."

He looked completely so. But he made no move towards her. Fighting down the attack of dizzying relief sweeping over her, she straightened her shoulders and renewed her breath. If only he had made his declaration with more lover-like ardour her next task would have been so much easier.

"Then there is something I should tell you, Mr Pelham," she informed him as calmly as she was able. Her hands twisted and clenched in her lap, for what she had to say might well close the door on all her hopes of happiness.

"Really?" he drawled. Yet his eyes were alert, questioning.

"Yes. About my widow's portion." She paused to renew her courage. He looked a question but said nothing, so she had no choice but to go on. "My income would cease should I marry again. I should keep the lease on this house for life, but would not command the means to maintain it. My dower estate of Ashlea in Kent would remain mine, but the income from that would scarcely be adequate."

"Mrs Davinia—*darling!*" He smiled at her startled, exasperated expression, his own gently teasing. "No, I have not forgotten how I offended you with my misplaced humour over your name! But I have longed to call you my darling, meaning it, for many weeks past."

"You have?" She quavered. Her heart began a heavy, slow beat.

"Can you doubt it?" His voice deepened to a thrilling huskiness. "I love you, Mrs Darling."

"Oh!" Her face broke into a radiant smile. Happiness filled every corner of her being. "Oh, Mr Pelham! I love you, too!"

His smile made her heart quiver anew, and speed up its beat. So brilliant, so tender, so...so passionate, her nerves whispered, and tensed in remembered response. That passion promised so much...and yet...

She pushed the wayward, dispiriting thought aside. Pelham was like no other man she had ever known! After all that had passed between them, how could she imagine the promise would not be fulfilled?

"Then..." he paused now, as though afraid to pose his question "...may I hope that, when I do press my suit, you will not reject my hand?"

She nodded and shook her head, lowering her lashes in demure confusion like a silly young miss! Yet inside her breast her heart was bursting with joy!

"Mr Pelham—" she began, only to be cut off short by an imperious gesture of his hand.

"No! No," he repeated, smiling slightly at her anxious glance. "You once called me Justin. Can you not find it in your heart to do so again, when we are in private? For I declare I cannot tolerate being compelled to address you as Mrs Darling when there is no one else to hear. To me," he told her deeply, "you are simply my dearest Vinny."

"Justin!" She said his name softly, unconscious tenderness underlying her tone. "That is how I have longed to address you, though I have never dared to even think of you so! But—we are not even engaged—are we?" she asked uncertainly.

"Not officially, my love, for I cannot ask you to share my present penury—"

"Oh, but you can!" she cut in eagerly. "You cannot imagine how I have regretted my caution when you addressed me before! I have discovered that nothing is worthwhile without you to share it! I have been so lonely!" she admitted with unconscious pathos. "What do money and position matter? I would rather live in a cottage with you than in solitary elegance here!"

He was on his feet, and had drawn her up to stand close before him. As his arms enfolded her, Vinny knew that her decision had been right. Happiness did not depend on money or status. She would gladly relinquish them all for the joy of being loved by Justin Pelham. Whoever he was. She still did not know exactly whom she was promising to marry.

He felt the slight withdrawal and lifted his mouth from hers to gaze questioningly into her eyes.

"Regrets already?" he murmured.

She shook her head, denying the traitorous thought.

"No. But you still have not repeated your proposal—"

She broke off as he gave a great shout of joyous laughter. "Do you want me on my knees again, you little tease? If so, I shall be forced to stop kissing you!"

"I'm sure there is no necessity for that!" she rejoined pertly. "Just say 'will you?' so that I can say 'yes'!"

"Will you?" he murmured huskily.

"Oh, yes!" she breathed.

It was a long time before they sat down again, together, on the settee. Held securely in the circle of Justin's arms, her head on his broad shoulder, she felt disinclined to move to order refreshment. She had already told the footman that she was not at home to callers. They should not be disturbed until her tea was served. The impropriety of their behaviour she dismissed as irrelevant.

"How long must we wait?" she murmured in a pause between kisses.

His approach today was so different from that other time he had held her in his arms. Then he had been all arrogant, angry demand. Now he was showing how tenderly passionate he could be. She could not doubt the intensity of his desire but he had it well under control—his hands roved so far and no further, his lips teased and tempted but did not plunder. She loved him, loved his gentleness, but knew she would welcome the full force of his passion in the marriage bed.

"I could obtain a special licence," he mused, "but if we ask for the banns to be called immediately...let me see... Sunday is the fifteenth...we could be married on the last day of November. That would be in two and half weeks' time, on a Monday. Would that be too soon for you?"

"Too soon?" she exclaimed. "No! Tomorrow would be preferable!"

"Such eagerness!" He grinned, tracing the line of her delicately boned chin with a tender finger. "You flatter me, my darling! But do you not have things to arrange? Lord and Lady Marldon to inform? A new gown to order?"

"I will write to Mama and Papa today! As for my wardrobe, it is crammed with suitable gowns! And I must learn not to be extravagant, for otherwise how shall we live?"

He kissed her nose and then tucked her black curls under his chin. The arm about her shoulder tightened slightly.

"I have had considerable luck at the tables recently. With the sale of my commission—"

"Justin!" She jerked her head up, knocking his chin, in an effort to meet his eyes. "You did not gamble with that!"

He smiled rather bleakly. "I had little other choice. I was desperate. Even now, although I have increased it substantially, I did not—do not—consider my fortune large enough—but, my love, you were so deliciously jealous when you saw me with Miss Day—"

She made a sound of protest, at the same time blushing furiously. He laughed at her confusion and went on tenderly, "Do not regret showing your feelings, my love; they gave me reason to hope again. I confess to riding in the Park yesterday in the hope of seeing you, and when you invited me up into your carriage I could no longer deny my desire to address you again—though I confess I had not anticipated being made the happiest of men quite so immediately!"

He stopped to kiss her. "But together," he went on at length, "if you are willing, we could manage to live quite comfortably in the country, though not, I fear, in London. I am now in possession of ten thousand pounds, which, invested, will bring in five hundred a year." He ignored her gasp of surprise and continued with his assessment of their financial situation. "This house would command a similar sum in rent. And could we not live at Ashlea? Perhaps, with a resident landlord, the estate could be made to yield more…and I believe I should enjoy bringing the land back into profitable production.''

Her eyes did not leave his face during this speech. He saw dark concern where there should have been dawning content, and waited with sinking spirits for her to change her mind.

''Justin!'' She shivered. ''You risked so much! And went against your own declared principles! Your horse was only a small part of your winnings, was it not?''

He nodded.

''And—all those who gambled against you could afford to lose?''

''To the best of my knowledge,'' he returned grimly. ''They were all wealthy men, and would have lost to another had I not taken up their challenges.''

''Did they never win?'' she asked in wonder.

''Oh, yes!'' He grinned, partly in relief, for she had not thrown him over yet. ''My fortune would have been even greater without the losses I sustained. No one can win all the time, Vinny, I am only too well aware of that. But I know how much to stake, and when to stop. Unlike some other, compulsive gamblers—of which I am not one.''

''I know that, my dear. And you did what you did in order to feel able… Oh, Justin!''

She buried her face in his waistcoat, swallowing the sob in her throat. His arm tightened around her heaving shoulders.

''Hush, sweetheart! I confess your rejection plunged me into a fit of the dismals—I indulged in too much wine, and, finding I had the devil's own luck at cards that night, lacked the resolve to keep to my normal prudent play—and once having started on the forbidden path…''

''You gave way to temptation!'' She had herself in hand

again and looked up into his face with a wry smile. "Justin, how could you?"

"Very easily, my love," he assured her drily.

She shook her head at him in reproof, then flashed him a smile. "Yet I am so thankful that you did!" she admitted. "I do not truthfully care how you came by your fortune, as long as it was by honest means!"

"Quite honest," he put in solemnly.

"For it makes it possible for us to live in better style." She paused to kiss his cheek. "Though, truly, I would not have minded being poor provided we were together. But promise me not to behave in so reckless a fashion in future!"

"I promise." He chuckled, and kissed her. "Unless you do something to send me into the dismals again," he added wickedly, plucking at her lips with his mouth. "If you do that, I cannot answer for my actions."

She snuggled closer. "Mmm."

Her little sigh of satisfaction ended in a gasp as he swung her bodily on to his lap. At the same moment a discreet tap on the door heralded the entrance of a procession of servants bearing a tray of tea and various platters of cakes.

It could not possibly be two o'clock already! She shot a glance at the clock and saw that it was. The butler hesitated briefly on the threshold, his face set in an expression of pointed blandness. Vinny sprang up hurriedly, smoothing her rumpled skirts.

"Your tea, madam. Captain Pelham, sir."

"Thank you," muttered Vinny in confusion.

Pelham swung easily to his feet and tucked Vinny's hand under his arm.

"Jenkins," he addressed the butler gravely, "you may be the first to wish us happy. Mrs Darling has done me the honour of consenting to become my wife."

The man's expression relaxed into the slightest of smirks. A footman and two young housemaids behind him gasped in surprise and the girls' faces broke into knowing smiles.

Jenkins placed his tray on a table and bowed. "Congratulations, sir. The entire household will be delighted, madam, and wish you happy. Er—will you remain in residence here?"

"No, Jenkins, we shall be letting the house." She saw the fear flicker across his face and realised that all her staff would be worried for their jobs. "I have no doubt the tenants will glad of the services of most of you, and of course we shall require people in Kent—there will be positions for several…" She trailed off, her happiness somewhat marred by the thought of what might befall others because of it.

"We will see you all settled in good situations," put in Pelham decisively. "Either here, at Ashlea or with some other household—Mrs Darling has a wide acquaintance, and I vow there must be many in need of staff who will be delighted to engage those she recommends."

"In any case, you will all remain until everything is settled," put in Vinny cheerfully. "We shall not close the house for at least a month, possibly not until after Christmas. And inform the chef that Mr Pelham will be taking dinner with me this evening."

She sent a questioning glance in Justin's direction, and he nodded acquiescence.

"The chef, I fear, is one member of the staff we shall not be able to afford," Pelham remarked wryly after Jenkins and the others had gone. He accepted the cup of tea she poured. "A good plain cook will have to suffice!"

"Mrs Jenkins," said Vinny immediately. "Jenkins and Mrs Jenkins, between them, will run the household beautifully, I imagine. Flora must come, of course, and Gill and Ellis—''

"They may not wish to leave London," warned Pelham, "though I do not anticipate any objection from Gill. Or Ellis."

"Then the others must please themselves! Oh, Justin, I can scarcely believe it! I am so happy, I want to pinch myself to make sure I am awake!''

"You are awake, my love. The only thing asleep at this moment is part of my memory. Thanks to Gill I have almost complete recall of my army career, and I am happy to continue as Justin Pelham for the remainder of my life— but something may occur—we must be prepared.''

"Justin!" Vinny thrust aside her cup and saucer, flew across to where Justin sat and plumped down on his lap, flinging her arms about his neck. "Even if you turned out to be a murderer I should still love you!" she declared.

"Vinny! My darling!" he growled.

And that was the last either of them said for quite a while.

The arrangements for the wedding went ahead smoothly. Vinny wrote to her parents and received a cautious letter of approval in reply. There was also a note from Percy.

I warned you the match was impossible, and despite discovering Pelham's history I ain't really changed my mind. We still know nothing of him before he decided to follow the drum. But if you're determined to marry the fellow I shan't withhold my brotherly blessing—I can't bring myself to do it now I'm so happy myself! If the weather permits I'll post up to Town to arrive on the twenty-eighth, but Jane won't come, I shan't allow it, the journey would be too unpleasant and dangerous for her. She sends her best and teases me for not giving you my whole-hearted approval!

Jane Rosedale was staying at Preston Grange in order to become acquainted with her prospective new parents, and Vinny suspected her of being the moving spirit behind Percy's missive. His letters were normally more conspicuous for their lack than their frequency! But if Percy could tear himself away and attend at St George's Church off Hanover Square she would be vastly pleased. He would represent her family at the wedding, and the loss of family approval and blessing could not be as easily dismissed as wealth and position.

Since they were retiring from London Society, the notice of the intended marriage in the newspapers mentioned neither the place nor the time of the ceremony. Gill would support Pelham and Flora attend Vinny. No one else was invited. They wanted no display, nor did they wish to be the objects of endless speculation and curiosity.

Ashlea stood on the edge of the Kentish Downs, within fifteen miles of Royal Tunbridge Wells.

"I should have inspected the estate years ago," admitted Vinny, confessing that she had never yet visited her inheritance and had no idea what the manor house would be like.

"So you should, my love, but I collect that your late husband did? You have his description?"

"No, he did not. Neither of us thought the property worth much trouble. Neither did my father. I do not think he has visited it above twice, and that years ago."

"What splendid landlords you have been!" chided Pelham, only half joking. "Did you never consider the needs of your tenants?"

"Father appointed a land agent. He reports," retorted Vinny shortly. Justin was making her feel guilty.

"Things must change," announced Justin firmly. "What the place probably needs…" he said—and went on to give her a lecture of the proper management of an estate.

Vinny listened, partly resentful, partly enthralled. By the time he had finished, she was openly grinning. "Thus speaks one who comes from a long line of land-owners."

For the first time in some weeks he looked thoroughly confused. "I suppose so," he muttered uncomfortably.

"My dear love, you will be in your element," said Vinny softly.

"I believe I shall. I have not found moving in Society greatly to my liking. But you—you will miss the social life."

"If we feel the need of society we can attend the Assembly Rooms at Tunbridge Wells," said Vinny dismissively. "The house at Ashlea has stood empty for over a year, since the last people left. There seemed no urgency about letting it again. I am glad I did not press the agent and lawyers to find new tenants!"

Pelham laughed. "I am somewhat apprehensive over what we shall find! The house has been in the hands of caretakers for too long. I think it necessary for me to ride down and inspect its state. I will set out tomorrow."

Vinny did not want him to go, but saw the sense of his decision.

"I pray you have a safe journey, Justin," she said as she saw him off the following morning. He had called in at Portman Square especially to bid her farewell. "The weather is scarcely fit for such a journey!"

Pelham rubbed the nose of his piebald affectionately. "Marble will take me on the first stage, and post horses are used to difficult conditions. The fog should clear once we are out of Town. Do not fear for me, especially with Gill to look after me!"

She laughed, and shot an affectionate glance towards the

old soldier, standing ready to mount his hired horse. A special fitting had been attached to his stirrup to accommodate his peg. "I am persuaded that the two of you would be a match for any robbers or highwaymen you might encounter! God speed you, Justin."

Regardless of any watching servants and passers-by, he took her into his arms. Vinny responded as always, melting into his embrace as though she had no will of her own. She closed her eyes, savouring the delight of his kiss.

"I shall return with all speed, my love. Two nights should be sufficient for me to spend there. That will give me a whole day to look around and make my assessment."

"And no doubt you will come back with a list of things that need doing! Make sure there is enough furniture, Justin. I can take some from here if necessary. But don't bother with linen, or the cutlery or china or glasses or anything like that. I shall not leave those things here for tenants to destroy."

"I believe, my dear girl, that all your instructions are already firmly fixed in my head! I must go. Farewell."

Another quick kiss and she had to watch him mount and ride away. She knew she would know no peace of mind until he was safely back again.

She had wanted to go too, but Justin could make such better time on horseback. The conditions were not suitable for any lengthy journey by carriage. It was only fifty miles, but even a chaise and four needed good roads to achieve that distance in a day.

Justin returned safely, looking quite cheerful.

"A lot needs seeing to," he informed his promised bride after a suitable interval for a lengthy greeting. "But nothing we need worry about before we move in. The house is a fine place—"

"Built by my great-grandmother's father at the end of the seventeenth century—"

"So you informed me. It needs some repairs and redecoration, but the structure is sound. The estate is a different matter, I fear. It will require a lot of hard work to bring it back into profitability. The tenants were not inclined to be friendly or helpful. Their interests have been neglected for too long. We shall have to win them over."

"We will," she declared. If it pleased her husband to immerse himself in the running of the estate she would not attempt to stop him. She would have plenty to occupy herself with, arranging the interior of the house and making friends with neighbours and tenants alike. At least until such time as she began to breed. Her blood quickened at the thought. She and Justin must surely produce an heir.

Two weeks passed with incredible speed. That evening, with great solemnity followed by a burst of gaiety, they drank to the second anniversary of their engagement. They were in the morning-room when they heard a carriage draw up at the door.

Vinny peered from the window but could see little but the moons flaring from what looked like a hackney. Against their glow she saw the outline of a woman alight and hold the door for her companion, who immediately mounted the steps to her door.

"I wonder who it can be?" she exclaimed.

"No doubt we shall soon be informed," said Pelham drily, amused by her eager curiosity.

"I shall not be at home!" she declared. "I was so looking forward to an evening alone with you!"

A footman shortly appeared to present Vinny with a salver holding a crested card. She picked it up. "The Lady Harriet Shatton," she read, and frowned. "Do we know her?" It was a rhetorical question which Pelham did not answer. "Did she give a reason for her call?" Vinny asked the servant.

"No, madam. Except to say that it concerned Mr Pelham, madam."

"Oh." Vinny shot a glance in Justin's direction and was immediately arrested by the shocked look on his face. Her heart thumped. "Justin?"

"Ask her up."

His voice did not sound like his. Vinny began to panic. Suddenly her little world of happiness seemed under threat. But she could scarcely send the woman away.

"Very well, bring the lady up," she instructed the footman.

Justin sat quite still, staring into space. She walked across to stand behind his chair, pulled his head back against her body and stroked the black hair from his forehead with trembling fingers.

"What is it, my love?" she asked gently. "Is she someone from your past?"

He sprang to his feet, throwing off her touch, and began a furious pacing. Four steps one way, four back.

"How the Devil should I know?" he roared.

He had taken his disability so calmly until now that Vinny was shocked by such signs of violent disturbance. She laid an urgent hand upon his arm to stop his progress.

"Justin, my dear love, calm yourself! She will be here at any moment! Be still, my dear."

He did stop. He closed his eyes. And they were standing quietly together when the footman returned with their visitor.

"The Lady Harriet Shatton," he announced.

She made her formal curtsy. "Mrs Darling."

Tall and elegant despite a rather old-fashioned travelling dress and cloak, she gave the impression of having been on the road for some time. Tiny lines of weariness were etched round bright brown eyes which flew straight to the tall man at her hostess's side.

For a moment she frowned, then walked slowly forward to gaze deliberately into Pelham's eyes. "Henry!" she exclaimed. "I thought it must be you."

Chapter Eleven

Pelham stared back at the woman, his eyes glazed. Vinny could feel the tension emanating from him. It was as though he were electrified.

"Forgive me," he said at last, in that same strange voice he had used before. "You have the advantage. I am afraid I do not know you."

Lady Harriet Shatton glanced from one to the other of them, a rather grim expression on her face,

"Can you still not forget—or forgive?" she demanded.

An unfortunate question in the circumstances. But who was this woman? She must have know Justin intimately. Had they been attached, and quarrelled? Vinny pulled herself together. She could not stand the agony, the pressure on Justin, the entire, palpitating atmosphere, for one moment longer. She must intervene.

"Lady Harriet." Her own voice sounded forced and strange and she cleared her throat. "I believe an explanation is necessary," she went on grimly. Her hand tightened on Pelham's arm and she felt his muscles respond.

Harriet Shatton frowned. "What can possibly require explanation?" she demanded. She looked about to speak again, to accuse Justin of something worse than a stubborn memory and lack of charity. Vinny leapt in before she could add something more hurtful.

"Captain Pelham was injured in the Peninsula." Explaining this man's condition was becoming quite a habit, she thought ruefully, and wondered how many more times she would be called upon to do so. "He can remember nothing of his early life. He truly does not recognise you, my lady. Are you certain he is the man you think he is?"

The other woman's face cleared miraculously. "Oh, Henry! My dear! So you ran off to answer a call to the colours!" She held out both hands to the immobile man. "I am your sister, Harriet, and I cannot possibly be mistaken as to who you are—you have altered, of course, as have I." She gave a deprecating smile and a slight shrug. "We are both somewhat older now. But your eyes have not changed. I would know them anywhere."

"Harriet." He repeated the name like a child learning its lessons. But he took her proffered hands and allowed her to kiss his cheek.

"I grieved for you most sincerely at the time, my dear," said Harriet softly. "I was convinced there must have been some mistake."

Vinny wiped sweaty palms down her skirt, picked up her fan and began to flutter it in agitation.

"Won't you sit down, Lady Harriet?" she invited.

As his sister relinquished Pelham's hands to do so, Vinny thankfully seated herself. She doubted she could have remained standing much longer. Justin—or should she begin to think of him as Henry now? It was all too confusing!—moved to the fire and kicked it into new life, sending a shower of sparks flying up the chimney. His expression remained inscrutable while he executed this unnecessary chore. With the flames leaping up to his satisfaction he propped his arm on the mantel, keeping his face in shadow.

"I collect," he said tightly, "that I disgraced myself in some way before I took on a new identity to join the Army. Perhaps you will be good enough to tell me who I am, and what I did."

"You really do not know?" wondered Harriet, shaking her head in disbelief. "And yet you have engaged to marry Mrs Darling?"

Vinny broke in again. "I have come to hold your brother in great affection and regard; his past—even his family connections—seemed immaterial to our union. Army records showed him to be a most gallant officer and free to marry. I should have been honoured to become the wife of Captain Justin Pelham."

Harriet smiled, somewhat mirthlessly. "Instead, if the wedding goes ahead, you will find yourself the wife of Lord Henry Broxwood, Viscount Roxborough, heir to the Marquess of Hazelbourne."

Vinny's nerves contracted. She cast an anxious glance at her betrothed. At least now she knew exactly who he was, and found herself tolerably unsurprised and quite undisturbed by the disclosure of his noble birth. But his sister was already casting doubt on their forthcoming marriage and this *did* dismay her.

Pelham straightened and turned. "Heir?" he demanded thickly. "I was not the heir."

"You remember?" urged Vinny eagerly, her anxieties momentarily forgotten in a surge of hope.

He shook his head, sending her expectations plunging into gloom. "But instinct tells me that much."

"And you are correct," said Lady Harriet briskly. "Your elder brother, George, died last year, leaving no known male heir except some remote cousin in America. According to Mama's letters, Papa has been in fits ever since. When I read the announcement of a wedding in an out-of-date London paper and noticed the bridegroom's name, I immediately posted up to see the man who called himself Justin Pelham. I went to your rooms first. Your man sent me on here. You see, they are your middle names, Henry, family names,'' she explained. ''You were christened Henry Justin Pelham Broxwood.''

Pelham-Broxwood-Roxborough grinned. While she was speaking he had relaxed completely.

''So—I adopted my middle names, which I suppose were never normally used.

''You left Broxwood Hall in a resentful huff, feeling wronged, but the evidence was all against you, Henry dear. Father would do nothing to have you traced, but I did. We were close, Henry,'' she smiled, her whole rather austere face softening into lines of affection, ''and I could not bear for us to be estranged. But I was on the point of marrying Shatton and my resources were limited. All I could discover was that you had sold your curricle and your beautiful carriage and riding horses and purchased a half-broken nag in their place.''

''Vertigo,'' he smiled. ''He turned out to be a wonderful officer's mount. I suppose I needed the blunt to purchase a commission.''

''But what did you do with all the funds you won off that poor young fellow who did away with himself?''

A heavy silence fell at Harriet's question. Roxborough straightened and moved across to stand before his sister. Vinny watched his face anxiously, afraid for his damaged mind. But his eyes were clear and all the agitation had left his manner. He no longer feared to face the truth.

''I have been told part of that story by one who did not recognise me or remember the name of the culprit. Tell me exactly what happened, Harriet.''

''Then sit down,'' she ordered. ''For the tale is quite a long one, even though I do not know the whole.''

Roxborough sat with his head back, his eyes closed,

while Harriet recounted the events of that earlier year. Every now and again his eyes flew open, and Vinny knew something had struck a chord in his mind. Not until the end of her recital did he smile, rather grimly, and admit that Harriet had stirred great chunks of his memory into renewed life.

"I understand now why I did not wish to remember my murky past," he said ruefully. "I have been repressing the knowledge since that evening someone almost recognised me." He looked directly at Vinny. "I told you, my dear, that something in my mind prevented me from pursuing my past. Now I have been forced to face it and know exactly why I was so reluctant to remember." He lifted his brows and waved a hand in a gesture of regret. "You have engaged to marry a reprobate."

But he did not appear disturbed at having to make the admission.

"I agree with Lady Harriet," said Vinny stoutly. If he could remain unconcerned, then so could she. "There was some mistake. The man I know would not have behaved as you are supposed to have done! Not only taking the man's last penny, but stealing the woman he loved!"

"Thus driving the poor soul to suicide!" finished off Lady Harriet with a grimace. "Father stopped your allowance and turned you out of the house, but I suspected, and still believe, that there was more to the story than that. I knew you often returned some of your winnings when your opponent was in the suds. And as for women—you may have been a little wild in that direction, my dear Henry, but what young man is not?"

Roxborough shot Vinny a wry, embarrassed glance. "I dare say I did sow a few wild oats," he conceded.

"But I do not believe you set out to steal another man's intended," went on his sister firmly. "Mischievous flirtation of that kind was quite outside your character. There could have been no serious attachment intended, for you were already betrothed to our neighbour's daughter, Fanny Allingham. The contracts were all signed. Poor creature, you did not even bid her farewell. Do you not remember?''

Pelham-Roxboroug had gone pale. He drew a deep breath. "Yes, I do remember. What happened to Miss Allingham?"

"She remained single. She is still at Allingham Court, as its mistress. Both her parents are dead."

His hand clenched on the arm of his chair. This news did disturb him. Vinny watched his knuckles whiten and realised her own were in the same state, for her fingers were clenched tightly about her fan. Her thoughts were darting in every direction, asking questions, looking for answers. But she kept quiet. Roxborough had to sort out his mind and memory before he could calm her fears. Perhaps not even then. She had never been in such abject terror of what she might next hear.

"And the marriage settlement?" Despite his tension he kept his voice level enough.

"Cancelled." Harriet shrugged. "Father's dearest hopes of an alliance between the families were dashed again. George had refused to consider marrying her. He never did wed."

"Girls did not interest him," observed Roxborough. "But I," he went on grimly, "sought Father's favour by entering into an alliance for which I had little enthusiasm. I never loved her, Harriet. I wanted Papa's affection."

"We all knew that. But you were an honourable young man, Henry, and would not have deserted her for another woman, however fair. Neither would you have dallied with another's betrothed. So I did not believe the accusations against you." She shook her head sadly. "But you did nothing to defend yourself apart from protesting your innocence—which Lord Hazelbourne refused to accept."

"No." Roxborough's face had become quite inscrutable. "His affection was always fixed on George. He would have believed anything *he* protested."

"Perhaps, now, you can tell us the truth of it," suggested Harriet.

But Roxborough shook his head. "I am afraid that is beyond me."

Did he mean he could not remember, or that he still would not give a full account of himself? Vinny wished she knew. And wished she knew what he would decide to do.

"H-Henry," she began uncertainly.

He turned to her immediately and stretched out his hand. Their chairs were near enough for her to place her cold, trembling fingers in the warm strength of his.

"Friends and enemies alike have known me as Justin Pelham for the past fourteen years. If my family wishes to call me Henry, I shall not object. But I am used to being called Justin by my intimates. You, in particular, my dearest Vinny, must continue to call me so."

She smiled, reassured that she still held a special place in his life. "What will you do?" she whispered.

"I have little choice. I must go to Dorset, to Broxwood Hall, to see my parents, attempt to make my peace with them." He turned to Harriet. "Mother is still alive?"

"Yes, and in better health than Father. I will come with you—Justin." She answered his quick smile of approval with a wry one of her own. "It may soften the meeting with Father a little if I inform him of your presence first."

"You still live in Hertfordshire? Will Shatton not object?"

She ignored the frown with which his words were spoken. "He cannot, my dear. He died several years ago. I have two daughters and a son who is now the fourth baronet, for all his tender years! But I left them in good hands.

A fleeting expression of relief washed across Justin's face. Vinny wondered what had caused it.

"My condolences," he said.

"I will accompany you, too," Vinny declared firmly. She had no intention of being excluded from any of his affairs, especially those which so closely affected her own future happiness. "We can use the barouche-landau with post-horses. Your man, my maid and your sister's—I assume that was your maid with you?" she enquired of Lady Harriet.

"Yes. She is waiting downstairs."

"They can travel in the chaise."

Justin's face had become a cool mask. His voice held bite. "It is kind of you to offer, but it would be a deuced uncomfortable journey for you ladies. I certainly need no intermediary—I shall present myself before my father and plead my own cause. I am quite persuaded I should undertake the journey alone."

This statement was made in a tone which Vinny recognised. She swallowed down her quick response, love having given her greater understanding of his temper. A man of natural authority and used to command, he must react strongly against being deprived of his full powers and reduced to dependence upon others. She shot Lady Harriet a warning glance.

"Neither of us is in our dotage, Justin; we shall endure any hardship with immense fortitude," she insisted with an impish grin, and added, "I would welcome the opportunity to meet your parents."

Harriet was not slow to follow Vinny's lead. "I have been unable to afford the journey to Dorset since Shatton died. His affairs were in a parlous state," she admitted. "I vow I have not seen our parents this age, for they no longer travel. I am seizing the opportunity to visit Broxwood at someone else's expense, and had simply hoped to be of some service in return!''

Justin frowned. "That bad?" he enquired.

"Not good," admitted his sister.

"In that case, I shall be glad to have your company." He grinned ruefully at Vinny. "I know when I am being manipulated, ma'am, but find the result far from disagreeable. Perhaps you had better give orders for the morrow?"

Relieved, Vinny nodded. She glanced up at the clock. "Supper will be served in a few moments. Your sister would probably appreciate something more substantial after her journey." She turned to Lady Harriet. "And have you accommodation for the night?"

"You are most kind, Mrs Darling. A little cold meat would be welcome. And no, I have not yet arranged accommodation for tonight."

"Then you must stay here." Vinny reached out for the bell-pull. "I will give instructions immediately. Justin—''

He anticipated her question, his mossy eyes rueful. "I must return to my rooms after supper. Gill must be informed, and there will be packing to do."

"Then I suggest you come here for early breakfast, at eight," she returned with a little nod. Their eyes met and she knew that harmony had been restored between them, that he was as reluctant to leave as she was to see him go. But he had things to do. "From past experience I believe we should start at nine at the latest if we are to do the journey in two days. Were it summer we could hope to do it in one, but with the roads so dirty, and it getting dark early…" She hesitated. "This is Wednesday. We shall barely have time to return for the ceremony on Monday."

At her words he rose, moving to take possession of both her hands.

"I fear we shall have to postpone the date, my love." He squeezed her fingers reassuringly, his eyes demanding trust. "To attempt to keep that appointment after a double journey at this time of the year would be foolish. I do not know what I shall find at Broxwood, and the banns have been called here in the wrong name! I will send a message to the rector."

The colour drained from Vinny's face. For an instant the room rocked. Her grip on Justin tightened. "But we *shall* be married?" she whispered.

His face blazed into a wonderful, tender smile before he lifted her hands and kissed both palms, one after the other. "Can you doubt it, my darling? This is merely a postponement of the event to which I look forward with all my heart."

Vinny, trembling at his touch, did not doubt his sincerity—but the persistent worry at the back of her mind would not go away.

He went before his sister retired, which gave them no opportunity for private conversation. There were so many things she wanted to ask! So many things she wondered whether he remembered! Vinny longed for him to take her in his arms and kiss her lips instead of her hand on leaving. But that was impossible with Lady Harriet present.

Harriet Shatton seemed willing enough to speak of Justin's childhood at Broxwood Hall, of the strange coldness his father had always displayed in his dealings with his younger son and the terrible time when Justin had been told he was a disgrace to the family and warned never to darken the doors of Broxwood Hall again.

"Will his father, Lord Hazelbourne, receive him now?" Vinny wondered anxiously.

Harriet gave her a straight look. "I cannot say for certain. He has become rather an embittered old man. But Henry—Justin," she corrected herself with a smile, "is his only true heir. I believe he will relent. Henry's banishment hurt Mama as much as it did him. Perhaps more, for, unlike

her husband, she loved her younger son dearly. If only he
had explained himself! I am certain there was something
he was hiding!''

"Do you think he remembers now?" asked Vinny
doubtfully. "If he does, perhaps he will do so at last."

Harriet shook her head. "I do not know. We can only
hope."

She had removed her outer garments, revealing a grey
gown and a cambric cap which did not conceal the threads
of grey in her hair. She showed every sign of the genteel
poverty to which she had admitted. Vinny noted the tired
lines about her eyes and realised that Harriet was exhausted
after her journey. With another, longer one in prospect on
the morrow, Vinny dispatched her guest to her room soon
after Justin's departure.

Flora was not pleased at being obliged to venture into
the country so late in the year, and registered her displeasure by performing her duties in grim silence. Vinny
thought that she would not be too dismayed if the woman
refused to remain in her service when they moved to Kent.
Although even that plan must be held in abeyance now.
She had no idea what property Justin would inherit or what
income he might command as a viscount and heir to the
Marquess of Hazelbourne.

Despite her discontent, Flora packed their boxes with her
normal efficiency while Vinny scribbled a letter to Percy
telling him the news and their change of plan. It would be
sent to Devon by an express mail coach, and she could
only hope it would reach Preston Grange before he left.

Vinny expected to lie awake that night, her mind being
in such a turmoil, but she dropped off almost as soon as
Flora had pinched out the candles.

Justin arrived the following morning while Vinny was
still in her bedroom. She raced down to the dining-parlour

and flew into his arms. His kiss was entirely satisfactory, but cut short by the arrival of the breakfast dishes, closely followed by that of Harriet Shatton.

So there still had been no time for a private conversation.

Ellis had arranged for the hired horses to be brought to the house and, although he was not to accompany the party himself, had fussed about the carriages checking every last detail against breakdown.

"The wheels are sound enough, ma'am," he reported. "Those on the chaise were new this summer, as you know. The springs are in fine condition, and so are all the poles, and the harnesses needed only slight repair. You should have no trouble with the carriages, ma'am, just as long as the post boys drive them aright."

"They always go too fast," admitted Vinny, "but we are in a hurry so we shall not object to reasonable speed. I wish you could drive us, Ellis, I should feel much safer, but it would not be practicable in present circumstances. I am persuaded that we shall manage well enough. I trust you to care for my horses while I am away, and for Lord Roxborough's, too."

Justin was out in the stables overseeing the strapping on of the luggage. Harriet had retired to her room to don her outer garments. Ellis took the opportunity of being alone with his mistress to voice a more personal thought.

"Yes, ma'am. May I say how glad we all are that the captain has found out who he is at last? I always guessed he was Quality, ma'am. Could spot it a mile off. I'll be honoured to serve a viscountess, ma'am."

Ellis was assuming that the marriage would go ahead, and so must she. It seemed to Vinny that most people who had met her future husband had taken her coachman's view of his status, and she felt rather guilty for her own earlier doubts. But *they* had not been desperately attracted to the man and considering committing their future to him! Her caution had surely been justified. And in the end she had overcome her reservations. She smiled a little, thankful that she had agreed to marry him as Justin Pelham. He would never be able to accuse her of accepting him for his title!

The weather had turned cold, but they set off in bright sunshine, with plenty of rugs and bottles of hot water at their feet and the ladies' hands buried in huge muffs kept cosy by hand-warmers filled with hot coals.

The first stage took some time because of the congested state of the streets but once out of London the yellow-coated post boys riding postilion to drive the chaise cried a challenge to their comrade up on their box, and both vehicles raced at full gallop over the sticky, rutted roads until Vinny thought them certain to overturn and feared that if she survived the crash her bones would never stop rattling. She sat with Harriet, facing forwards, clinging to a strap, with Justin, braced against the motion, occupying the seat opposite. At any moment she expected to be pitched into his lap. Not that she would mind that.

Every now and again they exchanged a glance and a smile, though conversation was scant, the noise of horses and carriages rattling along making speech too difficult. Because both chaise and landau were hers, they were saved the discomfort and inconvenience of transporting the luggage and themselves to new and possibly stale-smelling vehicles at every stage. Only horses and post boys were changed. But while the new horses were put to they had a chance to stretch their legs and exchange a few words.

"I'll look after the mileage tickets," announced Justin at their first stop. "Do you wish to leave the carriage?"

"I should like to walk a little," said Vinny.

Harriet nodded her agreement and Justin assisted both ladies to alight before striding off to purchase the tickets from the posting master.

"Make certain they are correct," Vinny reminded him as he tucked the papers in his pocket.

"I already have," he replied drily. "They are quite in order and ready to hand to the toll-keeper at the next turn-pike."

Vinny recognised by his tone that she had done it again, though this time he had not retreated into icy arrogance. Perhaps he was beginning to realise that she had been used to seeing to things for herself these last few years and that the words had slipped out without thought! But now she had an autocratic, confident but highly sensitive man to look after her and her affairs. If that meant guarding her tongue and losing a little of her recent independence it was a price she was prepared to pay for the delight of becoming Justin's wife.

A fond smile touched her lips. He could not be driven— but he might be led!

The further south they travelled, the clearer the weather became. Sometimes they took refreshment as well as exercise while the horses were changed, sometimes not. Shivering in the yard of some posting inn, Vinny could not help but contrast this hurried gallop with that other, leisurely journey taken in the heat of summer. It had been then that her feelings had begun to soften towards Justin. She had fought those unwelcome sentiments long and hard, but in the end had been forced to admit defeat, such were their strength. Surely he could not be taken from her now? She dared not even contemplate the devastation such a loss would bring to her life.

Her gaze went across to where he was supervising the change of horses and drivers, a tall, commanding figure wearing a simple waistcoat under his impeccably tailored royal blue coat, his muscular thighs encased in the softest of doe-skin breeches tucked at the knees into shining hessians. Gill's efforts in that department were above reproach.

For some reason Justin's man was not travelling in the chaise, but had been detailed to follow on horseback as soon as he had completed some errand for his master. She missed the man's blunt good humour almost as much as Justin must miss his waiting upon him. Gill's skill with the comb and cravat could still be called into question, but he was leaning fast, and suited Justin admirably in every other respect, being a man of many skills with whom he could reminisce.

At the moment Justin's black hair was scarcely visible under his tall, curly-brimmed hat and his other garments were largely covered by his greatcoat. Her fur-lined pelisse had one cape, but how she envied Justin the warmth offered by the several layers of his!

By dusk they had arrived in Salisbury, the graceful spire of the cathedral outlined against the darkening sky. The posting inn reminded Vinny of those on the journey to London. Then they had played cards after dinner; now they simply talked. Justin and Harriet had so much to tell each other that Vinny listened in silence, learning more than she could have hoped of her future husband's early life.

"You loved that property," she broke in at last. "No wonder I could detect your descent from a long line of land- owners! Justin, you were born to inherit!"

Harriet nodded agreement. "I think so, too. George was not suited, though Papa would never admit as much. George loved his horses and his sport, but he did not love the land. Farming, even the administration of the estate, bored him. And he had no desire to provide an heir."

"While I," said Justin, casting a wicked smile in Vinny's direction, "have every intention of providing— several."

She blushed, wondering that he did not question her

ability to bear a child. She had been married to Charles Darling for eighteen months without any sign…and he was not to know…

Harriet laughed. "Stop teasing her, Justin! I am quite past being put to the blush!"

Justin sobered. "I am sincerely sorry for George's death. I never wished him ill, though we were never great friends, as you and I were, Harriet, and Father widened the gulf between us with his partiality. I had never looked to inherit. God knows, I came near enough to death myself on enough occasions over the years. And I tried not to remember…"

The thought of Justin's reckless, dangerous life while he followed the drum was enough to make Vinny blanch. "Oh, Justin!"

He grinned again, laughing at her fears. "I survived! And thanks to you, my love, I have become a whole man again!"

"Entirely whole?" she demanded eagerly. "Do you remember everything?"

A rather cautious look entered his eyes. "Not quite. There are still blank patches, but I might not recall some incidents at this distance in time, even without the blow to my head. So I am not concerned." He grinned again. "For the first time, today, I recognised a place! I must have seen the cathedral's spire many times in my youth. I knew this was Salisbury without having to be told."

"You did not say!" exclaimed Vinny accusingly.

"I hardly thought it necessary to make a great work of so simple a matter. I can visualise my parents, too, though I imagine they have altered somewhat from the pictures I hold in my mind. As you have, Harriet! I remember a young, beautiful and eager girl, deeply in love and looking forward to her wedding."

Harriet sighed. "I suppose I was in love. Or persuaded myself I was! He was a little like you in looks, Justin, and perhaps that helped! But unfortunately he did not resemble you in character. He gambled too heavily and when he died almost everything had gone.''

"But you were happy?'' asked Roxborough, a slight frown between his brows.

"At first, ideally! But then his gaming became a bone of contention between us. With three children to support he should have been more restrained—but by then the habit was too strong. He could not stop. The later years did not hold much contentment.''

Justin leaned forward to take her hand. "Harriet, I am sorry! Had I known I would have tried—''

"There was nothing anyone could do, my dear. He would not listen to reason.'' She shrugged, a helpless little shrug. "Had he not died of a fever when he did I would have been left a pauper, and little Hugo would have inherited nothing but an empty title. As it is, I do my best to make the estate prosperous, and to save for his future.''

"Does Father not help?'' The frown had deepened.

She gave a pitying little smile. "He most likely has little to give. He has been ailing for years and George did nothing but spend. The Roxborough estate of Fernhill, and Broxwood itself, are both in debt. Your inheritance has been mortgaged, Justin.''

Vinny saw the muscles in his jaw harden.

"Then it is time I remedied the situation!''

"What if your father refuses to recognise you?'' she whispered.

"He cannot disinherit me, the estates are entailed. And it seems there are no funds left for him to withhold.''

"Where is Fernhill?'' she asked.

"In East Devon. I suppose about halfway between Broxwood and Preston,'' Justin told her with a smile. Then asked, "Who is managing the estates, Harriet?''

She shook her head. "I do not know.''

"It is time," said Roxborough with all the authority inherent in his nature, "for me to take over. Father must agree."

Harriet rose to her feet. "I think so too, but do not expect too much from Papa." She smiled from one to the other. "I will wish you both a good night."

"I will not be long," promised Vinny. The two women were sharing a room.

"Do not hurry on my account," said Harriet. "You must have much to say to each other that is best said without another present."

"Even our chaperon?" taunted Justin.

"Particularly your chaperon!"

"I could come to love your sister," observed Vinny with a slight laugh as the door closed behind Lady Harriet. She felt strangely awkward and unsure in his presence. This would be their first few moments alone together since he had discovered his true identity.

He had risen to make his bow on Harriet's departure. He turned from closing the door of the private parlour behind his sibling and stood looking across at his betrothed. She looked tired, composed—and quite delectably lovely in her dark emerald travelling gown. He drew a deep breath and strode across to raise her to her feet.

The feel of her in his arms was balm after the travails of the last four and twenty hours. The touch of her lips, so responsive under his own, instead of rousing, soothed his troubled spirit. When the kiss ended he held her close, one hand holding her head against his shoulder where he could bury his face in her hair.

Vinny's arms were tightly clasped about his waist. She shut her eyes and rested where he held her, silently absorbing the delight of these few moments of shared need.

No show of passion could have reassured her half as much as this quiet exchange of loving contact and support.

And so, in the end, there was no need of words. When at last he let her go she rose to her toes to kiss his rather bristly cheek before bidding him a quiet goodnight and leaving the room.

Chapter Twelve

The landau crested a rise. Vinny caught her breath. Broxwood Hall!

Nestled against a backdrop of sparsely wooded hills at the end of the long drive, the ancient stonework of the sprawling edifice glowed with a creamy sheen in the bright, low-slung sun.

"How old is it?" was her breathless question as she thrust her head through the window of the carriage to get a better view.

"The first Marquess built the original in the fifteenth century. Subsequent holders of the title have added to it down the years." Justin laughed slightly, covering the nostalgia and pride in his voice. "I remember Father being in mortar when we were young—you cannot see the new wing from here—and we children thought the entire enterprise the greatest fun in the world."

Decorum forgotten, Vinny bounced across the swaying vehicle to change her seat, squeezing in beside Justin, who obligingly moved over to accommodate her. She took his hand and looked into his face her expression alight with love and happiness. "You remember," she breathed.

He smiled, his eyes shining back with new brilliance. "Yes, my love, I remember."

Regardless of Harriet's presence opposite, he bent his head to kiss her lightly on the lips. Vinny sank back with a contented sigh. Despite all the uncertainty and awkwardness ahead, she could not help but rejoice over Justin's accelerating recovery.

The carriages rumbled to a halt before the main entrance. No Palladian mansion this, but an attractive manor house of a previous age built on two floors, all angles and mullioned windows, with a deal of flaming creeper spreading along its walls.

After the final change of horses at Blandford Forum Vinny's nervousness had increased with every mile, for the moment of confrontation was drawing perilously close. Justin had already intimated that should he be turned from the door of Broxwood Hall there would be time to return to the posting inn at Blandford before darkness fell. He would not allow the post boys to leave with the horses until he knew.

"He cannot refuse me entry to Fernhill," Justin had pointed out grimly. "If necessary, we will travel on to there tomorrow."

The arrival of two strange carriages must be an unusual event, Vinny surmised, for several servants appeared as if from nowhere; some ran to the horses heads but others just stood and stared. The front door opened and an elderly manservant she took to be the butler emerged to received the new arrivals. Frilled caps and the sparkle of gold bobbed about in the dimness behind him as lesser household servants cautiously attempted to satisfy their curiosity.

Justin alighted first. Vinny, watching anxiously as he handed his sister from the landau, saw the butler's face change. After peering down to carefully negotiate the single step, he hurried to make his bow.

"Lady Harriet! Welcome home, my lady!"

Harriet smiled, accepting the old retainer's welcome with pleasure. "Good morning, Simpson. Are my parents home?"

"They are indeed, my lady, and pleased they will be to see you!"

"They are keeping well?"

"His lordship is as well as can be expected, my lady, allowing for the feebleness of his legs. Her ladyship still enjoys excellent health."

"His legs?" frowned Harriet. "I did not know— But no matter. I am glad to hear her ladyship is well. As you may see, I have brought others with me."

She indicated Justin and Vinny but did not announce who they were. Simpson bowed.

"His lordship will no doubt be pleased to receive your guests. Who may I say is here?"

Justin stepped forward, grinning. "It's a long time, Simpson, but you haven't changed in the slightest!"

The old man gazed at the clean-cut, uncompromising features toughened by experience, softened by a roguish smile, met the laughing eyes, and gasped. "Lord Henry! Oh, my lord, it's that thankful I am to see you safe and well after we had all given you up for dead! Her ladyship will be so relieved and delighted, sir!"

"But not, I imagine, his lordship!" retorted Justin drily. "I trust the shock will not be too much for them. You had better announce our arrival, Simpson—prepare them as best you can first—so that I may know what reception I am to receive from my father." He drew Vinny forward, "You may announce this lady as the Honourable Mrs Davinia Darling—a friend."

Vinny acknowledged the butler's bow and prepared to follow Harriet into the house. Justin detained her with a gesture as he paused a moment to speak to Simpson again.

"See that our servants and the post boys receive refreshment, and the horses are watered and given fodder. Men and horses will remain until I give the word for them to depart."

Simpson bowed. "Very well, my lord."

Justin turned to Vinny, bent his arm in invitation, and smiled. "Will you allow me the pleasure of escorting you inside?"

Vinny gave him a quick smile in return and tucked her hand under the proffered elbow, but none the less entered his ancestral home feeling as though her heart had been squeezed. She was not to be announced as his betrothed. She was just a *friend*.

As they entered the lofty, stone-walled entrance hall he seemed to sense her dismay. He patted the gloved fingers resting on his sleeve and gave her a reassuring smile. "It is best to leave all explanations until I know how—or even whether—I am to be received," he murmured.

She nodded, and some of the pain receded. But her underlying anxiety, forgotten in the first delight of seeing Broxwood Hall, returned. Her joy in accompanying her future husband into the seat of his inheritance, already dimmed by doubts over his reception, was further depressed by her own ambiguous position. For no marriage contract had been signed between them. Theirs had not been a match arranged between families, and any legal settlement could come at some future date. Or so they had decided, thinking nothing of immediate importance but their attachment to each other. She had only Justin's spoken promise to rely upon.

Two footmen, their blue coats frogged with the gold in evidence earlier, moved forward to relieve the visitors of overcoats and shawls. The maidservants wearing the white caps had disappeared.

Justin appeared perfectly calm. Yet Vinny knew tension

gripped the muscles beneath his immaculately tailored coat. She herself could scarcely compose her nerves enough to sit still while they waited. Harriet smiled reassuringly. She could have presented herself without introduction, but in deference to Justin's feelings was waiting with them.

"Do not be anxious, Vinny." They had come to Christian name terms while sharing the room last night. "Papa is of unpredictable and mulish temper, which I dare say has become worse with age and infirmity—I wonder what ails his legs?—but he is not an ogre. And you may be quite certain Mama will have something to say about it!"

Her optimism was justified, for before long Simpson returned to announce that his lordship would receive all the visitors.

Harriet led the way, hurrying across the small, cosy parlour to curtsy and kiss both her parents in turn. Vinny made her duties, first to the austere man ensconced in a large chair and grasping the arms with gnarled fingers, then to the tiny, plump lady who had risen to her feet to greet her daughter, but whose anxious eyes had gone beyond her to the tall young man bowing with exquisite formality to his parents.

"See who I have found!" cried Harriet. "Is it not capital? I had feared never to see my brother again!"

"Henry! Oh, my dear boy! You have returned to us! Wherever have you been all these years?"

Amelia Broxwood, the Marchioness of Hazelbourne, ran forward with outstretched arms. Tears rose to Vinny's eyes on seeing the emotion on both faces as mother and son clasped each other after so long a separation.

Justin attempted to conceal the shock he had received on seeing his parents. They had aged so much! His mother, soft and comfortable in his arms, had lines of suffering and anxiety etched on a face he would scarcely have recognised. From what remained visible under her mob cap, her hair had turned iron-grey. But then, he thought bleakly, she must be nearing her sixtieth year.

Vinny's attention was diverted by the sound of an impatient grunt of disgust. Lord Hazelbourne was gazing sourly on the exchange while his sharp eyes assessed the commanding figure of his son. Vinny watched them narrow on the broad shoulders and narrow hips, take in the lithe grace and lift to study Justin's arresting face. But his general air of disapproval did not alter.

Justin remained unaware of the scrutiny, being absorbed with his mother. He had both her hands in his firm grip when his father spoke.

"Come here, sir!"

Justin did not hurry. He released his mother's hands after a final squeeze and let his gaze turn towards his sire. The change in Lord Hazelbourne was even more surprising. Justin remembered a stiff, upright figure the picture of aristocratic propriety, whose dark features had so often been set in an expression of bored indifference or censure towards his younger son. Now he saw only an old man, his face crimped by deeply etched lines, his sparse hair white, his hands gnarled by rheumatism, unable to rise because of some unspecified ailment afflicting his legs. Something approaching pity stirred in his breast. He bowed again, with easy courtesy.

"I appreciate your receiving me, sir."

Lord Hazelbourne grunted. "Damned impertinence, presenting yourself here! Harriet's doin', I suppose."

"No, sir. The decision was mine. She accompanied me because she wished to see you again. She does not command the means to travel here at will. Not even," he added deliberately, "to attend her own brother's funeral."

Pain passed in a spasm across the elderly face. But only

scorn vibrated in the voice. "Huh!" he snorted. "Married a fool. But she would have him."

"You introduced us, Papa, and approved the match! You did not term him a fool then!" protested Harriet forcefully.

"Could've had that earl—what was his name?" grunted Hazelbourne.

"A hard-drinking, whoring man old enough to be her father!" exclaimed Justin in disgust.

"And I loved Shatton," added Harriet defensively.

"Love! What sense is there in love? A good settlement is what you should have sought, my girl, but no, you chose union with a handsome fool. And now you whine because you cannot manage on your widow's portion!"

"I have yet to hear my sister whine," observed Justin sharply.

Lord Hazelbourne eyed his son up and down. "You're rigged out in fine London style, I see. Not short of a bit of blunt yourself, it seems. Possess some fine carriages, too." The waiting vehicles could be seen through one of the damask-and-lace-draped windows. "Cattle to match, I don't doubt."

"The carriages belong to Mrs Darling, who kindly conveyed us here."

"Huh!" Hazelbourne snorted again. "Wondered what she was doin' here."

This unforgivable incivility brought a gasp to Vinny's lips. Justin's tightened.

"The Honourable Mrs Davinia Darling is the daughter of Viscount Marldon," he informed his father icily, pointedly repeating the full address to which she was entitled. "We are betrothed to be married." His voice softened as he turned to her and held out his hand. "Vinny, my love, let me present you to my father."

A black look descended upon his sire's countenance. Vinny held her head high and was immensely relieved to find that Justin made the formal presentation with evident pride. In that moment she had never loved him more.

Lady Hazelbourne greeted her with courtesy, her eyes guardedly approving, her manner anxious. In the next few moments, Vinny realised why.

"Engaged, eh?" grunted his lordship, the scowl still in place. "Contracts all signed and sealed?"

"No, my lord." Justin's voice held firm. "But we do not consider ourselves any the less engaged to be married. Any cancellation at this stage would cause a tremendous scandal. An announcement was made in all the London papers."

"Which is where I saw the name Justin was using!" exclaimed Harriet eagerly. "That is how I found him!"

"Justin?" scowled Lord Hazelbourne. "Who the deuce is Justin?"

"Henry, then!" cried Harriet impatiently. "You know very well his second name is Justin, Papa, so do not pretend you do not! He was using his two middle names, Justin Pelham. *Captain* Justin Pelham," she emphasised. "He has been in the Army all these years, and was in the Peninsula when George died, so did not see the announcement. And then he was wounded—"

A gasp of concern from Lady Hazelbourne brought further explanations.

"Lost your mind, eh?" sneered Lord Hazelbourne unsympathetically. "Kept enough of it to post down here to claim your inheritance the moment you heard."

"That is most unfair, Papa," cried Harriet. "Mama has written to tell me how distressed you were at the thought of that relative in America inheriting. I should have thought you'd rejoice to find you still had a son living—"

"I lost my memory, not my mind," Justin cut in tersely. "I came because I put family welfare before my own. I am now the heir, and intend to prove worthy of the Honour I shall inherit.''

"Impossible," grunted his sire.

"You are more than worthy," cried Vinny fiercely, springing to Justin's defence heedless of whether he either welcomed or needed her intervention. "Your son, my lord, gained respect and admiration at the highest level in the Army! Why, Sir John Moore even purchased a captain's commission for him because he could not afford to buy it for himself! His courage, his integrity are proven beyond doubt! You should be proud to own him your heir!"

"Moore was a bungler," snorted Hazelbourne.

"He forged the army with which Wellington is winning his battles!" intervened Justin sharply. "I beg you not to offer an opinion on something of which you know nothing, sir!"

"Please!" Lady Hazelbourne held out her hand to her husband. "Do not judge so harshly, Hazelbourne. We have yet to reacquaint ourselves with our son. They must all stay, of course." Seeing her spouse about to protest, she spoke with determination. "They *must* stay, husband!"

To Justin's surprise, his parent shrugged. Fifteen years ago his mother had not challenged her spouse over anything. She had stood by and allowed him, her favourite son, to be forbidden the house. But he had expected nothing different. She had been securely under her lord's heel. Another surprising change.

"As you wish, wife," said Hazelbourne sourly. "I desire to get to the bottom of that unsavoury business when Henry disgraced himself in Oxford, which he declined to explain at the time. If he is now willing—"

"Thank you, my lord! Henry, my dear, do let me tell Simpson to dismiss the post horses!"

"I will not remain where I am unwelcome." Justin's tone was as uncompromising as his features. "Lord Hazelbourne must understand that I have no intention of explaining anything of that affair. It is in the past, and I believe I have expiated any guilt by my prolonged absence. We begin anew, or I do not stay.''

"Hazelbourne?" pleaded his wife.

The lined face remained grim, the corners of the thin mouth turned down; but beneath the bushy brows Vinny detected a gleam of reluctant admiration in the sharp eyes. His lordship struggled to his feet, reaching for the sticks propped against his chair. "I shall expect to see you all at dinner," he growled, and hobbled to the door.

Justin watched his departure without expression.

"Thank God!" cried Lady Hazelbourne. "He agrees, although he would never admit it! You will remain, my dearest boy?"

Justin nodded. "The horses may be allowed to go. There is luggage to bring inside. And the carriages to be housed."

"I'll see to it all. And to your accommodation, and order more covers for supper! You'll have your own rooms, of course, and Mrs Darling the Chinese room. I cannot remember when I have been so happy!"

She stopped to reach up and kiss Justin's cheek in passing and bustled from the room, the lines of anxiety almost erased from her face.

Harriet gave a great sigh of relief. "That went much better than I'd expected!" she observed.

"They've changed," remarked Justin sadly.

"Even since I saw them last, five years since. I wonder when Papa's legs began to weaken…? George's death must have hit him hard. All his hopes rested on George."

"Aye," said Justin grimly. "The years did nothing to alter that!"

"But he has you," urged Vinny. "Surely now his attitude must change! The future of the Honour of Hazelbourne was naturally invested in his eldest son. I know how Papa regards Percy, although he does not dote on him and I do not believe he would shut a younger son from his affections…but now it is to *you* Lord Hazelbourne must look—he has no other choice!''

Justin grimaced. ''I no longer seek reluctant affection, neither do I desire it to be passed down, and second-hand,'' he told her grimly. But then his expression lightened. ''But what does it matter? We shall not reside here, but at Fernhill, with periods in London and Kent.''

''But there must be a peace between you,'' inserted Harriet decisively. ''Otherwise how are you to take over the administration of the Hazelbourne estates? And do not forget Mama!''

''I do not forget Mama. The change in her is most remarkable. She has learned to stand up to his lordship, at last. When did that begin?''

''Soon after your departure. She suffered so much guilt over not questioning his decision more decisively. She felt she had failed you, Justin, and although it was too late to do anything about that she swore never to be so feeble again.''

At that moment a couple of footmen appeared to escort them to their rooms. On the landing, Justin and Harriet went in one direction, while Vinny was taken off in the other. Justin kissed her hand on parting, telling her to go down to the parlour when she was changed for dinner, which they had been told would be served at five. She glanced over her shoulder longingly as he and Harriet made their way to the family part of the house. She seemed destined for the more recent guest wing.

The familiar sight of Flora unpacking her things gave her some comfort as she looked round the room assigned for her use. It appeared comfortable enough, apart from a couple of mahogany chairs in the angular, Chinese style which lacked cushions to soften the cane seats. But it contained so much lacquered furniture with exotic designs imposed upon every surface that Vinny took it in immediate dislike. To her, the room seemed gloomy.

The four-poster bed was hung with richly embroidered Oriental silk, which smelled dusty, but the mattress felt enticingly soft. She decided there would be time to rest for an hour or so before she need change for dinner. Flora helped her to remove her pelisse and gown and produced her dressing-robe from the depths of a box.

"Shall I order a bath, ma'am?" she enquired.

"Please, Flora, for later; I must be ready well before five. And then take a rest yourself. The unpacking and pressing can wait, provided I have a suitable gown ready to wear. We are both exhausted by the journey, I think. You may leave me now."

Alone, she wandered about the room for a while, pulling out drawers and opening cupboards, all decorated with dragons and swans, peculiar-looking dogs, twisted trees and much more besides. Glancing into an elaborately framed mirror, she saw how disgustingly worn she looked and made for the bed.

Every muscle in her body ached. She hoped the bath water would be more than tepid by the time it was ready for her to use. But the last thing she remembered before she sank into the oblivion of exhaustion was Lord Hazelbourne's dismissive attitude towards her engagement to his son.

Dinner proved an awkward affair, the only real conversation being between Harriet and her mother, the latter requiring a full account of the progress of her grandchildren and demanding that they be brought to Broxwood soon.

Lord Hazelbourne remained taciturn, eating clumsily and spilling food on to his neckcloth and down the front of his velvet jacket. Vinny realised how much this must irk him, for with his crippled hands he could not control his movements precisely. Again, she caught his penetrating gaze fixed upon his son, eyeing somewhat sourly the immaculate white frills visible between Justin's partially unbuttoned waistcoat, his silk neckcloth, a miracle of complexity, his fashionable collar high enough but not so exaggeratedly so as to impede the movement of his head.

"Never expected a son of mine to end up in Bedlam," he announced suddenly into a brief silence which had fallen.

Justin's grip tightened momentarily on his knife, but immediately relaxed again. "Bedlam, sir?" he drawled. He had himself well in hand now, prepared for the worst his sire could do and determined to ride any storm without becoming upset. He had discovered that his father no longer had the power to hurt him deeply, merely to irritate and to anger. Those emotions he could control.

"That's where people who lose their minds go. Place is full of 'em. Drooling, gibbering idiots."

Vinny's gasp brought a sharp, warning glance from Justin. She was forbidden to jump to his defence on this occasion. The other ladies seemed struck dumb by the old man's cruelty.

"They can help their condition no more than can you, my lord," observed Justin mildly, lifting his quizzing-glass to eye with evident distaste his sire's filthy cravat, thrown into stark relief by the light from a branch of candles standing on the table between them. "And do you tell me that you have never heard of the condition doctors call amnesia?"

Lord Hazelbourne drew in a hissing breath. He lowered his spoon with a shaking hand, returning the juicy tart it contained to the safety of his plate, which he thrust to one side.

"Amnesia?" he growled. "What's a fancy name like that got to do with anything?"

"It is a term used by medical science to describe temporary loss of memory, which may be due to many causes. In my case it was put down to a blow on the head, coupled with general injuries and certain other circumstances. No one with any knowledge or sense thought me mad."

"So I don't know anything and I haven't any sense, eh? Sense enough to know when someone's bamming me, sir! Unless," he added craftily, "you are now prepared to remember what happened in Oxford?"

"Oh, yes," said Justin softly. "I can remember. I have just no intention of satisfying your or anyone else's curiosity. Confession would have hurt others more than me at the time, and circumstances have not materially changed. I regret, Father, that my will is just as strong as yours."

"Insolent puppy!" snarled his father. "We shall see!"

Justin smiled. "I shall enjoy the contest, my lord."

Vinny suddenly realised that they were testing each other, behaving like fencers sparring to find an opening. She did not think Justin capable of inflicting a mortal thrust. His father might be. But their rapiers were metaphorically sheathed as Lady Hazelbourne spoke up.

"Can you remember everything now, Henry, dear?" she demanded eagerly.

"Some things have disappeared into the mists of time," shrugged Justin. "I defy anyone to remember every detail of their early life! But more recent events are clear enough to me—except for the period between my falling in battle and awakening in a peasant's hovel."

"How did you fall?" asked Harriet.

"I doubt you really wish to know."

"We do, Henry. Please tell us," urged his mother.

He drew a breath. Vinny saw raw pain enter his eyes, and silently cursed his family's curiosity.

"Very well, Mama, if you insist." He paused a moment as though collecting himself. When he spoke again it was in a level, expressionless tone which hid all the remembered agony of the occasion. "Badajoz had been invested in the middle of March. By the sixth of April the town had been under siege and bombardment for three weeks, and the defenders had had time to fortify the surrounding defensive ditch with mines—and they'd thrown in every piece of dangerous ironwork and machinery they could lay hands upon. We were to storm one of the three breaches our cannons had made in the wall. To do so, we had to cross that ditch."

He paused a moment, gazing down at the table, his face grim in the candle-glow, but his voice remained devoid of emotion. "It was a pitch-black night as we crept forward to the glacis at the edge of the ditch and lowered the ladders," he went on. "Everything was quiet until, suddenly, a flaming carcass flew from the ramparts—the defenders must have heard some sound, the chink of a musket perhaps—and we were discovered."

"Careless," muttered his lordship scornfully.

Justin ignored the interruption. "They immediately discharged fireballs to light the scene and their cannon opened up. The first wave of men going down into the ditch were blown to pieces as shells and powder barrels exploded beneath their feet."

"How dreadful!" quavered Lady Hazelbourne.

"Hush, Mother," whispered Harriet.

"Those that followed were met by such a hail of flying debris, grape shot and cannon fire that very few survived." Justin appeared unaware of their exchange. He stared blankly into space. "Yet still the bugles sounded the advance. I pushed on, leading my men...reached the glacis and the ladders...the ditch had become an open grave...and the last thing I remember is the sound of bugles in my ears, urging us on..."

Towards the end of his recital Vinny had seen the confusion enter his eyes again. His words tailed off and his jaw muscles clenched. She longed to rush round the table and take him into her arms, to offer support and solace, but with the others there such behaviour was utterly impossible. And Justin would not thank her for underlining his vulnerability.

Lady Hazelbourne had her face clasped between her palms, the tears wetting her fingers. Harriet gave a shuddering sigh. Vinny's hands were clenched beneath the table, but she had heard similar stories from Gill, and was better prepared for the horror. Her eyes had sprung tears too, but they stemmed from concern and pride.

Lord Hazlbourne stirred, something in his face at odds with the harsh words he uttered. "You should be ashamed of yourself, sir, upsettin' the ladies with such talk!"

"We desired to know, Papa," said Harriet tightly. "We send men out to fight without having the slightest idea of the horrors they face."

"Should've made peace years ago," grunted her father.

Justin had by now recovered. The attack had lasted no more than seconds.

"I collect, sir, that you are become a Whig, since you would lay the country at Bonaparte's feet." He spoke with icy formality. "Thank God you do not represent the average Englishman, who cannot stomach a coward. Thank God there are still those who would follow in the steps of Pitt!"

"Calling me a coward now, are you?" roared Lord Hazelbourne, attempting to spring angrily to his feet but subsiding, frustrated, and impatiently waving aside the footman who had rushed to his assistance. Doggedly, he started again, leaning his weight on the table and using it for support until he stood upright. "Were I younger, and fitter, you would answer for that slander, sir!"

Justin rose easily to face his angry sire. "I did not call you coward, my lord, merely accused you of following those who behave as though they are. Had the Whigs come to power Napoleon would have crossed the Channel years ago, with none to stop him. We would have been beneath his heel ere now. Is that what you would wish?"

"Certainly not! But a peace treaty—"

"Holding Napoleon's signature would not have been worth the paper it was written on. You must realise that."

Lord Hazelbourne sank down again, rubbing a weary hand across his raddled face. "You may be right."

This was an admission no one at the table expected, least of all Justin.

"I am certain of it, sir," he said quietly. "I am no warmonger; I have seen enough of fighting to be persuaded that there must be better ways for nations to settle their differences—but that would require integrity on both sides. Bonaparte is power-hungry. He seeks to dominate Europe, to impose his revolutionary regime everywhere. When every country is under his heel, he will consider Europe at peace, but not before. And what a peace it would be!"

His lordship made no reply to this. "I will retire," he announced gruffly. "I shall expect to see you in my study tomorrow morning at eleven, Roxborough. I wish you all a good night."

Now he allowed the retainers to assist him to his feet and open the door, exiting to a chorus of parting civilities.

"Henry," said his mother, rising herself, "I believe we will dispense with the dessert course. Do you wish to remain here a while, or will you join us immediately in the parlour?"

"I have no wish to sit alone," smiled her son. "May I offer you my arm?"

Lady Hazelbourne gave him a fond smile. "I shall accept it proudly."

Vinny and Harriet followed them through, their way lit by footmen carrying branches of flaring candles.

"Let us forget the war," cried Lady Hazelbourne, once they were settled. "I vow I find the subject most depressing! Tell us what has happened since your return to England!"

Roxborough obliged by telling them some of the details, drawing Vinny into the conversation whenever possible. "So you see," he ended, "we found ourselves so much in harmony that we decided we must make a match of it!"

"You must perform for us!" exclaimed his mother. "We do not have a pianoforte, but I play the harp. Come! What shall you sing?"

A pleasant hour passed. Justin and Vinny enjoyed harmonising to his mother's accompaniment, and Harriet joined in the chorus of a song when she knew it. By common consent the remainder of the evening was spent in pleasurable enjoyment and gossipy chat. No one wanted to address the more serious problems lurking just beneath the surface.

When she retired for the night Justin escorted Vinny to the door of her room, where he kissed her deeply.

"Do not worry, my love," he whispered. "I believe all will be well. My father is making a great show of antagonism, but I believe I have his measure."

"He is hiding his pleasure," Vinny told him softly. "I have been watching the way he looks at you, my love. Even if he misjudged and despised the youth, he is proud of the man you have become."

"My dearest girl!" Justin tightened his already firm hold on her. "How I wish I could believe you right! And how I wish we were already wed! I shall lie awake tonight aching to have you in my arms."

"I shall long to be there," she admitted shyly. "I would come to you, but—"

"No!" he exclaimed fiercely. "I will not expose you to shame, especially under this roof! The consummation of our love will come after our marriage, not before."

Vinny sighed, partly in gratitude, partly in frustration. "How long must we wait?" she ventured.

"The marriage will take place just as soon as I can arrange it," he promised, so fervently that she had no choice but to believe him.

Chapter Thirteen

Finding herself with nothing better to do, Vinny decided to fill the interval between rising and breakfast exploring the grounds. After the excitements and uncertainties of the previous day she had not slept well and a breath of fresh air should do her muddled head good.

The misty drizzle was already clearing. With Flora's aid she donned her travelling pelisse over a warm morning gown, and chose a crape-covered felt bonnet to protect her hair from the damp. She managed to let herself out of the front door without calling attention, or so she thought, but had scarcely walked a hundred yards before she heard firm steps behind and turned to see who was following her.

"Justin!" The last vestiges of his limp had long since disappeared, or she would have recognised his step. A glad smile lit her face as she held out her hands.

He took them in his own and bent his dark head to kiss the gloved fingers. "I saw you from the parlour," he explained. Releasing one hand, he tucked the other firmly beneath his arm. "You do not mind if I accompany you?"

"I would welcome your company," she assured him and added, unable to prevent a choke of laughter which rose unbidden to her throat, "If you are by my side we can scarcely collide!"

His chuckle confirmed that he too recalled the incident in the grounds of Preston Grange. "But how delightful that collision was! It provided me with my first opportunity to hold you in my arms."

Her pulse leapt at the memories his words evoked, but she managed to maintain a light tone. "And you, sir, made the most of it! Small wonder I thought you forward and encroaching!"

"Did you really?" he enquired with interest. "How perceptive of you!"

Vinny laughed. "You, my lord, are a shocking tease!" She sobered as he began to lead her forward and tugged him to a halt. "But you are without greatcoat or hat! Should you not return for them?"

"I doubt we shall go far, and it is not raining. I am no hothouse plant to require cosseting! Where had you intended walking?"

"Towards those trees—but what lies beyond I have not the least idea!"

"In fine weather, an extensive and delightful panorama! But not today. The woods will be dripping and the view invisible this morning. I suggest we confine our explorations to the walled garden and the orangery. There should be something of interest to see there."

"I need to breathe fresh air," explained Vinny. "I am not particular as to the direction we take!" Suddenly the morning seemed bright, and she felt in spirits.

He brought out his watch, opened and consulted it. "We do not have above half an hour. I could wish for longer in which to enjoy your delightful company."

Vinny's breath caught at sight of the smile which accompanied the return of his timepiece to his waistcoat pocket. "La, sir," she returned lightly, fluttering her eyelashes at him in order to cover her quite shocking awareness. "I do believe you are flirting with me!"

"Of course," he agreed amiably, covering the fingers on his arm with his free hand as he began to lead her forward again. "But then, you have known from the first that I have rakish tendencies."

His eyes danced down at her and she blushed, her agitation deepening at memory of the confusion she had experienced over that first touch of his lips on hers. She had had to protest; propriety demanded it. But she knew now that her indignation had stemmed from disturbed emotions as much as from outraged decency.

"I had hoped you were become a reformed character," she returned severely, the sparkle in her eyes quite at odds with the tone of her voice.

She found his little chuckle vastly comforting. It bespoke an encouraging intimacy of thought and feeling that they could tease each other so.

"I wonder what Lord Hazelbourne wishes to speak to you about?" she ventured, after a few moments of walking in comfortable silence.

"I do not know. But you realise he addressed me as Roxborough, which must have stuck in his gullet, since it was George's title. It means he acknowledges me as his heir."

"He could do nothing else."

"He had no choice but to accept the fact, but need not have addressed me so for all to hear. Broxwood would have done as well."

"Justin," she sighed, "I am becoming so confused with all your names!"

He looked down into her rueful face, a teasing gleam in his eyes. "John Smith became Captain Justin Pelham of the Rifles who is now known to be Lord Henry Justin Pelham Broxwood, Viscount Roxborough, who will one day become the eighth Marquess of Hazelbourne. And you, my dear love, will make a very beautiful marchioness.''

She caught her breath. ''Not if your father can prevent it.''

He stopped, all humour wiped from his expression. They were behind the shelter of a small shrubbery, which screened them from the house. He turned her to him and drew her close. There was nothing teasing in his manner now. ''Do you believe I would allow him to?''

She shivered, despite the comforting warmth of his encircling arms. ''You may not be able to prevent him. He may possess hidden cards...''

''Which I shall not allow him to play.'' His voice held supreme confidence. ''Trust me, Vinny.''

''I do,'' she breathed. Of course she did. It was his sire she did not trust. And even Justin had admitted that he could not win every hand he played...

But his lips were reassuringly warm on hers. Her reticule, hanging from her wrist, bumped his back as she wound her arms about his neck, but he seemed not to mind. Vinny knew that this embrace, too, was a pleasure forbidden by propriety, but remaining within the bounds of good conduct was tedious in the extreme. Besides, no one could see them.

The kiss went on and on, gaining in urgency. Experiencing neither angry, punishing assault nor tender, romantic dalliance, Vinny forgot all her scruples in the exultation of shared passion. She melted in his arms, returning his kisses with uninhibited enthusiasm until at last Justin detached his mouth from hers. He groaned as he pressed her flushed face into his shoulder, quite regardless of both her bonnet, which by now hung behind her head by its strings, and the disorder he was creating in her hair. His heart thundered under her ear, echoing the pumping of her own.

''My darling,'' he muttered unevenly, struggling to con-

trol his breathing. "I believe our union will be a delight
to both of us."

The last of Vinny's doubts on that score had long since
fled. She knew she would find supreme fulfilment as Justin's wife. Provided nothing intervened to prevent their
marriage.

They reached neither the kitchen garden nor the hot-
houses. Vinny hastily rearranged her bonnet and returned
to her room, where Flora, without comment, remade her
coiffure, though the curls she usually wore about her face
were damp past redemption, since there was no time to put
them back in papers. She therefore descended to breakfast
with her hair swept back, though stray tendrils tended to
fall softly about her cheeks. She regretted the loss of her
ringlets, wishing to look her best, but when Justin greeted
her, as though for the first time that morning, his ardent,
admiring glance reassured her.

After breakfast Justin departed to present himself in the
library, which his lordship referred to as his study. Vinny
did not know what to do with herself. She tried to attend
to the conversation between Lady Hazelbourne and Lady
Harriet, but found herself unable to concentrate.

At one point a loud exchange between parent and son
echoed from the library to penetrate even the door of the
parlour, though no words could be distinguished. Amelia
Hazelbourne continued with her needlework, apparently
undisturbed. But her fingers trembled and she exchanged
an anxious glance with Harriet, who shot Vinny a sympathetic smile.

"Papa will not find Henry—" she grimaced "—Justin!
How difficult it is to remember! He will not be so easy to
influence now. He is no longer a raw youth, but an experienced campaigner. Do not worry, Vinny. Justin will come
through."

Vinny nodded, though she felt like shaking her head. He

would not wish to hurt his father deeply. He would never strike a blow fatal to the old man's pride. Nor could he be expected to renounce his heritage. If it came to a choice, he would put family loyalty before everything. Even her.

From the library, Justin strode straight to the stables. Vinny knew because she heard the sound of thudding hoofs from her bedroom, to which she had retired when waiting had stretched her nerves beyond endurance. She had looked from the window to see him disappear into the heart of the estate, galloping as though the hounds of hell were after him.

He must be in a furious mood to ride like that, she thought unhappily; he was not one to vent his frustrations on a hapless animal. Yet perhaps the horse welcomed the exercise. Justin was always most considerate of his mounts and she could not imagine him treating one brutally, even when in the most evil of tempers.

She watched and waited apprehensively. What could have taken place between father and son? That they had quarrelled was obvious. The outcome was less certain.

An hour later he returned from the direction he had gone, the horse lathered and tired, but not evidently exhausted. Vinny hurried down to the parlour, hoping he would seek her there. But he did not appear.

She had to wait until dinner to see him again. Lord Hazelbourne remained in his room.

"He does, you know, when his legs pain him dreadfully," excused Lady Hazelbourne, without much conviction.

Conversation during the meal remained general and subdued. Justin did not mention his interview and the others dared not broach the subject. An uneasy atmosphere pervaded the house. No one wanted to precipitate the storm.

Even Vinny could not draw near to Justin that evening.

So preoccupied was he that even when he saw her to the door of her room she found it impossible to do more than wish him a stilted goodnight. In return, he drew her to him, held her close for a long moment and then kissed her briefly. With that, she had to be content.

Things barely improved the next day. The family, apart from the Marquess, who still languished in his room, attended morning service in the village church. The occasion was remarkable only for the length of time the vicar and Justin conversed afterwards. The two men parted cordially, having, apparently, come to some sort of understanding. Then Justin handed the ladies into their carriage and mounted his horse to return to the house with every appearance of having regained his good humour.

On the homeward journey Vinny discovered that the living, despite the church being that nearest to Broxwood House, was not in the gift of Lord Hazelbourne, but in that of Miss Fanny Allingham of the neighbouring Allingham Court. Uneasily, she wondered what Justin and the vicar could have discussed at such length. And why Justin now appeared so relaxed.

As he handed her from the carriage upon their arrival back he suggested to Vinny that she might like to take another horse and join him in a ride over the estate.

"Oh, yes," she agreed immediately. "I do not have my habit with me, but can manage perfectly well in my travelling gown. I will change immediately!"

He kissed her hand and gave her the first unguarded smile since leaving his father's study the day before. "I will order a horse saddled."

Vinny asked no questions, determined to maintain the renewed atmosphere of ease between them and to enjoy her outing. The estate was extensive, with undulating parkland, pasture and arable fields giving way to untamed hills at its extremes. Cresting such a rise, Justin drew his mount to a halt. Vinny stopped beside him and the animals began to crop the rough grass.

He gazed down broodingly at a large, solidly built manor house, still some distance off, but glowing warmly in the winter sunlight which had replaced earlier mist. With all those windows set in the brickwork it must cost the owner a fortune in taxes, she mused.

"Allingham Court," he informed her quietly.

The shock ran straight through Vinny's nerves. She clutched her reins and swallowed.

"Your former fiancée's house?"

He nodded. "I have arranged to visit her there tomorrow. I have long owed her an apology. If we are to become neighbours, there should be no ill-feeling between us."

"Did...did your father suggest...?" Vinny faltered to a questioning halt.

Justin stirred. "He ordered," he said starkly. "I could scarcely refuse, since I was in the wrong, although at first I told him I would not go."

"What changed your mind?"

"I am not entirely without conduct, my dear. I would account it the height of bad manners were I to evade my duty."

"And I am persuaded that you do not wish to further antagonise your father."

He smiled wryly. "You'll allow that to be no unworthy desire, but I fear I have already done so. He is the one who must come to terms with the situation now."

Vinny was almost afraid to ask her next question. But she forced herself. "And what is the situation, my lord?"

He lifted his brows in disapproval at her form of address. "Why, ma'am, that I make my apologies to Miss Allingham and then marry the Honourable Mrs Davinia Darling at the first available opportunity."

This reply should have satisfied Vinny, but it did not.

The words had been spoken grimly. As though marrying her was another duty he could not escape without being accused of dishonour.

The next morning Justin departed immediately after breakfast. Scarcely had he left the house than Vinny was summoned to the library.

Lord Hazelbourne had emerged from his bedroom and was waiting for her, his body held upright in his chair, rigid with disapproval. His expression did nothing to dispel the illusion that he held her in complete and obdurate disfavour.

Her heart sank. But she stiffened her own spine. Justin loved her. He had told her so a dozen times. Now was not the time to dwell upon her doubts. This old man should not intimidate her!

"You wished to speak with me, my lord?"

"Sit down, girl," he instructed testily. "I have something to tell you."

"I would rather stand."

"Please yourself." He glowered at her from under a furrowed brow. "My son has gone to Allingham Court,"

"I know."

"Did he inform you that he intends to honour his promise to marry Miss Allingham?"

Vinny wished she had accepted his lordship's invitation to sit. Her hartshorn was in her bedroom, for she did not normally require its restorative powers. But even were it on her person she would not give this sour old man the satisfaction of realising her need of it. She clenched her hands into fists and willed herself not to sink.

"He is engaged to marry *me*,' she retorted as steadily as she could.

"Nonsense! He was already contracted to marry Miss Frances Allingham. How could he engage to marry you?"

"He was not aware of the contract, which in any case was dissolved, by mutual consent between the families, many years ago." Vinny forced herself to sound confident, praying that Harriet's information had been sound.

"I am determined to renew the contract. It needs only Miss Allingham's agreement to its resuscitation, which I do not doubt will be forthcoming. The estates will be joined. That is the condition upon which Roxborough's inheriting the means to maintain this one rests. Fernhill is already encumbered. He'll have trouble enough turnin' that one round." He grinned triumphantly, his raddled face taking on the appearance of a grotesquely carved gargoyle. "Roxborough needs the fortune you can't provide, Mrs Darling. When he brought dishonour to this family's name I swore he should never touch a farthing of the Broxwood fortune. It is beyond my power to break the entail, but if he refuses to abide by my wishes now he will never lay his feckless hands upon the means to maintain—or more likely ruin—the estates." He sank back suddenly, relaxing. "He will wed Fanny Allingham," he proclaimed smugly.

"Then sir, he is not the man I take him to be!"

Vinny had long forgotten her wish to faint. She was too full of disgust and anger to notice any other emotion. That a parent could so ignore the wishes and happiness of his son, could virtually blackmail Justin into compliance with his wishes, appeared to her the height of cruelty and injustice. Yet, of course, it had happened before and would happen again.

Hazelbourne's narrowed eyes challenged her. "I believe I may know him better than you do, girl!"

"There I beg to differ!" Vinny did not attempt to hide the bitterness in her voice. "You knew a young man desperate to win your love and approval, which you denied him." Her tone became filled with pride as she went on,

"I know a man who has won the approval and respect of some of the highest officers in the Army!"

"Bungling idiots!" scoffed Lord Hazelbourne.

"I would venture to place their opinion above yours any day!" cried Vinny angrily.

Hazelbourne scowled. "Impertinent chit! If he persists in his scheme to marry you, my girl, he will lose a fortune. Perhaps you should consider saving him from his reckless adherence to a promise made in ignorance by breaking the engagement yourself. It would be best for him in the end."

"No, my lord," said Vinny quietly. "I will never do that."

"Then you will not spend another night under my roof! Go and order your maid to pack your things. You may use my cattle to take you the first stage."

The shock almost undid her, but both Vinny's courage and her pride came to her rescue.

"Had Captain Pelham not learned of his true identity," she said stiffly, attempting in vain to subdue the tremble in her voice, "we should have been wed today. There would have been nothing you could have done, then, to prevent our union. We anticipated living in straitened but felicitous circumstances. How I wish Lady Harriet had not seen that notice in the newspaper!"

"He wouldn't have inherited a farthing!" grunted his lordship. "Would you want him to regret marrying you for the remainder of his life?"

Vinny did not trust herself to reply. Despite her best effort to control them the tears had already begun to spill down her cheeks. She made the merest hint of a dutiful curtsy before turning to withdraw.

Those sharp old eyes missed nothing. "No sense in believin' a shower will change my mind," he snorted. "I ain't that soft. Be off with you, ma'am. Out of my house. Immediately."

Vinny made no reply, but retreated with dignity while she still had it in her power, and sought refuge in her room. Even as she entered it she knew what she must do.

Give Justin back his freedom.

The Marquess was right, although she would never admit it to his face. If Justin married her he would forfeit the means to maintain his estates. They would fall into disrepair. Eventually he would place the blame on her. He protested his love, but would it be strong enough to withstand the bitterness and disappointment which would ensue?

How much of his sincerely professed love was true attachment and how much simple desire she had no way of telling. She loved him so deeply that the thought of cutting him from her life presented the worst kind of torture she could imagine, but male creatures were noted for neither the depth of their emotions nor their constancy. He would be unhappy for a while, but would soon console himself with someone else, probably not his wife, she reasoned cynically. But he would have Fernhill, Broxwood and Allingham and the means to maintain all three. And presumably, despite her years, Fanny Allingham would still be capable of providing him with an heir.

On hearing the door open, Flora looked up from fixing the hem of Vinny's travelling gown, which had come down at the back. She immediately noticed the tears on her mistress's face, and exclaimed, "Dear ma'am! Whatever is amiss?"

Vinny ran a knuckle across her wet cheeks and sniffed back a fresh bout of weeping. "We have to leave, Flora. You may begin packing at once."

Flora's face became a picture of bewilderment. "But the captain—his lordship, begging your pardon, ma'am—is not here—"

"Don't argue, Flora, just do as you are bid while I go and see about the carriages."

She sponged her face to wipe away the last of her tears before descending to the parlour. She did not wish to make an exhibition of herself before Justin's mother and sister.

They looked up expectantly when she entered the room.

"What did he want?" demanded Harriet without preamble.

"To tell me that Justin is to marry Miss Allingham. I am to leave this house."

"Never! Mama, you cannot allow—"

"No." Lady Hazelbourne was on her feet. Her face had lost all colour and the lines of anxiety returned. "I will speak with my husband at once."

"No, ma'am." Vinny's voice was firm. "I believe my departure will be for the best. Justin will not inherit his father's wealth unless he complies with his wishes. I cannot deny him the chance to enjoy his inheritance."

"You love him that much?" asked Lady Harriet quietly.

Vinny drew herself up, her colour high. "Too much too risk his future happiness. To administer both Fernhill and, later, Broxwood without adequate means would be a formidable task. We would have faced it together, had that been the true state of Lord Hazelbourne's finances. But it is not. I fear that Justin would come to resent me because I had cost him a fortune—"

"You do him an injustice, my dear." Amelia Hazelbourne's voice sounded surprisingly strong and firm. "My son is of a just and generous spirit. You must know him well enough to recognise that."

"I do, dear ma'am, but I cannot impose upon his excellence of character. Lord Hazelbourne has ordered me to leave immediately. I am come to ask you to arrange for horses to be put to, to take me the first stage—"

"You cannot travel alone; I will not hear of it!" cried Amelia, scandalised.

"I have my maid. I shall not mind."

"Remain until Justin returns. See what he has to say," advised Harriet quietly.

This was precisely what Vinny wished to avoid. He would be bound to protest his love, perhaps be tempted to defy his father. She could not allow that. She shook her head.

"I shall go immediately to my husband. He must be made to change his mind. This will simply serve to estrange Henry again! That I cannot—will not—countenance! Wait for me here!" So saying, Amelia swept out.

Vinny was stuck. She could not order his lordship's horses herself. She sensed that Harriet would be reluctant to oblige.

"I really must go," she pleaded, her voice quivering woefully despite her determination to control it. "For Justin's sake."

"I believe it would be the worst possible thing for you to do, for both your sakes," said Harriet forthrightly. "While I admit that Papa still wields complete control over his finances and therefore can will his fortune where he pleases, he no longer orders the household. Mama will not allow him to turn you out, Vinny."

"I wish you had been right, Harriet, and that he no longer possessed a fortune to bequeath! George did not run through everything, as you feared."

"No. But until now Father has led us to believe he did! He really is the most curmudgeonly, irascible creature imaginable!"

This raised in Vinny a wan smile. "You should not speak so of your sire! You are sadly lacking in both respect and conduct, Harriet!"

Harriet pulled a wry face. What she would have replied to this gentle raillery Vinny was never to know. At that moment the sound of an approaching carriage crunching to the door caught the attention of them both. They turned to the window with one accord to watch the occupants descend from the post-chaise.

Vinny gave a gasp of glad surprise. "Percy!"

Harriet peered through the glass. "Your brother?"

"Yes! He has arrived at a most opportune moment! But what could have brought him?"

They were not kept long in suspense. Having ascertained that the ladies were at home to the gentleman, Simpson announced their visitor without further delay.

"Percy," cried Vinny when introductions had been made, "what are you doing here?"

"Letter arrived just as I was about to leave for the weddin'. Thought I'd post here instead, see what was happenin'." He raised his quizzing-glass to inspect his sister's woeful face. "You look sadly in the dumps, Vinny. Anythin' wrong?"

"The Marquess has ordered me from his house. You have arrived at quite the right moment, Percy. You may escort me home."

Percy dropped his glass and frowned. "Where is Pelham?"

"Gone to visit the lady he has been ordered to marry."

"Oh, I say, Vinny, doin' it a bit brown, ain't you? He's marryin' you!"

"His father orders otherwise."

"Nothing is settled yet, Vinny," put in Harriet urgently. "Mama will persuade Papa to change his mind, you'll see, and as for Justin, I do not believe he will be so easily diverted from his purpose to marry you!"

"Not Pelham, no," agreed Percy with surprising assurance.

"Roxborough," corrected Vinny absently. "He should be addressed as Roxborough. But it makes no difference what anyone says. I am determined to go. Excuse me while

I see that Flora has packed. You can take me to Blandford in the hired chaise, Percy, and my carriages may follow.''

She left a bewildered Percy discussing the situation with Harriet.

Flora had made a start on the packing, but speeded up the operation at Vinny's urgent bidding. Vinny herself changed into the mended travelling gown. She was just about to tie the ribbons of her bonnet when a sharp rap came as prelude to a loud demand for entry.

Vinny froze. Justin had returned too soon. She did not wish to see him. But he had already thrust open the door.

"Leave us."

Flora gave Vinny an anxious glance. Vinny nodded assent. There was no point in creating difficulties. Justin would have his way, regardless of propriety. The interview, however distasteful, had to be faced. His expression was thunderous.

"What is this I hear?" he demanded curtly the moment the door closed behind Flora. "You are leaving?"

"On your father's orders."

"As I understand it, you have resisted the efforts of both my mother and sister to convince you to remain. Insisted on obeying him because it is best for me, or some such nonsense. Explain yourself, ma'am."

Vinny removed her bonnet and sank wearily into one of the uncomfortable Chinese chairs. Rather than look at Justin's dearly loved face, which might divert her from her purpose, she fixed her gaze on a weird hunting scene pictured on the front of a cabinet. She felt rather like the cornered boar, waiting for the fatal blow to fall.

"If you marry me you will not inherit the fortune needed to maintain your estates. You must marry Miss Allingham. Then your inheritance will be complete."

"I must, must I? My dear girl, I admire your independent spirit and your intellectual capabilities, but I do object to being told what I must do at every turn.''

Her eyes refused to remain fixed on the painting. They moved of their own accord to meet his. Tender mockery had replaced the simmering anger with which he had entered her room.

Relief surged through her. He was able now to treat her tendency to manage him with humour rather than resentment. It had come hard to him to depend so much on others. He had never appeared to lack confidence, but she supposed he had, deep down, until he recovered his memory completely. He no longer needed to climb on to his high ropes over such a paltry thing. And he was mocking her reasoning to scorn. Nevertheless, she thought she should apologise.

''I am sorry,'' she whispered, ''but I cannot help having an opinion of my own. And I have been used to ordering my affairs—''

''Foolish girl,'' he murmured softly. ''Come here.''

She found herself lifted to her feet and securely held in his strong arms.

''Did you truly believe I would, in any circumstances, allow my father to dictate my choice of wife? I will marry you, Davinia, my dearest darling, or no one at all.''

Vinny shook. For her own conscience's sake she had to try once more, however much he might laugh at her. Her voice trembled as she forced out the words.

''But he will not leave you his fortune!''

''If you recall, I was not expecting to receive a fortune. We shall manage, my love.''

''And what of Miss Allingham? You dare not disappoint her again! Your honour will be sullied beneath reproach!''

''More than were I to jilt you, Mrs Darling?'' he enquired interestedly. Then he chuckled. ''Fanny has no more desire to marry me than I to wed with her. We are agreed to forget the past and become friends and neighbours. She gives us her blessing.''

"Truly, Justin?"

"Truly, my love. It is all Father's fancy. He may have persuaded himself that I had gone to offer for her, but I doubt it. Since he could not turn me from my purpose, he intended that you should call off and leave the field clear. And he almost succeeded in his design.''

Vinny gasped. "I—I did tell him that I would never give you up!''

"Good girl! So exactly why were you leaving?"

"I thought about what he said. You would grow to resent me if I caused you to lose a fortune,'' she admitted, shamefaced. "And I wanted you to be happy.''

"Harriet said something of the sort.'' He touched the curls framing her flushed cheeks and stroked her forehead soothingly. "You must believe me the most reprehensible fool in the world to believe that.''

"The realisation of my own foolishness is extremely lowering,'' she admitted on a choked little laugh. "Can you forgive me?''

His voice quivered with answering laughter. "I believe I might be persuaded. Provided you try to forget the whole sorry affair.''

"Oh, Justin! Is this the truth? I can scarcely believe…''

"It is the absolute truth,'' he assured her solemnly. "You were ready to forgo your allowance to marry me. Did you think me so parsimonious and ungrateful that I would consider abandoning you in order to inherit some unspecified future sum of money?''

"N-no. I just thought you might defy your father and regret it later.''

His words, spoken to reassure her, had the opposite effect. Although he still held her in a loving embrace and addressed her in terms of endearment, he had not said he loved her, but implied that he had felt bound...because she had been willing...

"Percy's being here is of the utmost convenience," he was saying. "He can give you away. We will marry tomorrow and travel to Fernhill. I have already sent a messenger ahead. Tonight, unless my father relents, I am certain you will be welcome to sleep at the vicarage. The incumbent and his wife will not object to entertaining my bride and her brother."

"Justin, wait! You go too fast! How can we marry tomorrow? The banns have not been called!" And she needed time to consider the implications of what he had just said.

"Gill arrived with a special licence not half an hour since. He remained behind in London especially to obtain it, and on Sunday I requested the vicar to be prepared to perform the ceremony at short notice." He cupped her face tenderly. "Any further excuses?"

She shook her head. If Justin was as certain as he appeared to be, she would be foolish indeed to continue to entertain qualms about committing her life into his keeping. She wanted above everything to marry him. His father had set the doubts in her mind. She must thrust them aside. Which reminded her...

"But even were Lord Hazelbourne to change his mind I could not remain here, Justin. He has been too cruel." She looked up at him pleadingly. "Can you understand that?"

"I can. I shall find it prodigiously difficult to forgive my father for his treatment of you, my love. But for my mother's sake I will sleep here tonight. She has suffered enough over this business."

She nodded, smiling, as his lips claimed hers in a long breathtaking kiss. He did love her; he must.

His arms tightened around her as it ended.

"Have Flora finish your packing. I will have a team put to your carriage and drive them to the vicarage myself. We will be wed early, before breakfast. Percy will give you away, Harriet will support you, I am certain, and you will have Flora with you. Gill will support me. Nothing and no one shall stop our union, my love."

Chapter Fourteen

Nothing, no one, did. As Justin slipped the ring on her finger Vinny knew a deep, warm contentment. He was hers. His father could not take him from her now.

Even the adverse news from the Peninsula could not mar her happiness, though she knew Justin and Percy to be saddened by another ill-fated, disastrous retreat.

"Wellington has been forced to abandon Madrid, Burgos *and* Salamanca," Percy told Justin gloomily. "Heard yesterday. Word is just comin' through. Shockin' weather, impossible conditions, driven him back on Ciudad Rodrigo again. Spendin' the winter there."

"Where he'll regroup the Army for a spring offensive," predicted Justin thoughtfully. "With Napoleon occupied in Russia—"

"Weather's turnin' bad there, too. He's havin' to retreat from Moscow before his army freezes to death."

"So there is still hope." Justin made an expansive gesture of dismissal. "Let us forget the war, Sinclair. This is my wedding day!"

The nuptial party—which to Vinny's delight included her new mother—returned to Broxwood House for breakfast after the ceremony. Vinny entered its portals reluctantly, but both Justin and Amelia Hazelbourne assured her that the Marquess would not refuse his heir's wife hospitality.

"I rang a peal over his head yesterday," said Amelia with a grim little laugh quite at variance with her size and comfortable appearance. "You could have slept here overnight, my dear daughter, but I do understand your reluctance to remain under a hostile roof."

"Thank you, ma'am."

Amelia smiled, though her expression remained somewhat grim. "My husband will accept the inevitable in the end. He is feeling his age. Administering the estates is become too much for him." She glanced fondly at her son. "He needs Justin."

"I pray you are right, ma'am, for I would not like to feel Lord Roxborough cut off from his family estate, as well as disinherited from a fortune, because he married me."

"We shall see. Meanwhile, do have some meat with your rolls, to sustain you on your journey."

Lord Hazelbourne had been given no hint of the ceremony which had taken place. Amelia had thought it best to confront him with a *fait acompli*. He seldom appeared for breakfast and that morning did not deviate from his habit of taking early refreshment in his room.

Before departing for Fernhill Justin took his bride's hand and together they went to face the old gentleman, who had by then been helped downstairs and settled in his usual chair in the library. Justin put his arm across his wife's shoulders as they entered the room. Amelia followed them in and closed the door.

Justin released Vinny in order to make his duties. Vinny, acutely reminded of the unpleasant interview of the previous day, curtsied without looking at Lord Hazelbourne.

"Good morning, my lord." Justin spoke with exaggerated formality. "I have brought Lady Roxborough to bid you farewell. The Viscountess and I are leaving for Fernhill within the hour."

The Marquess gripped the arms of his chair. Blotches of angry colour stained his cheeks, which shook with emotion. "What is this, sir? You have ignored my expressed wishes and married this woman? How dared you, sir? You will regret this defiance!"

"I beg leave to doubt that, my lord. I love Davinia more than life itself. I want no other woman for my wife."

Vinny felt her heart glow and melt. She turned a radiant face to her husband. He had answered her last doubt as to his feelings. "And I love your son, my lord," she declared huskily, gazing deeply into Justin's brilliant eyes.

Justin took her chin in his hand and kissed her lips. The exchange held, if possible, more commitment than the vows they had so recently made before God.

Amelia had been unable to stem her tears in church, and now they flowed freely again.

"How can you be so blind, Hazelbourne?" she demanded on a choked sob. "I informed you last evening that I would not tolerate your forbidding my son this house again, and now I include his wife! You will accept Vinny as your dear daughter and stop behaving in such a non-sensical manner!"

"Sentimental nonsense! Love!" grunted his lordship disgustedly. "Don't matter who you marry, so long as she's of good stock, able to breed and brings a decent dower. Find your amusement elsewhere."

Justin's face had turned to stone. His jaw clenched. "Is that what you did, my lord?" he enquired acidly.

Hazelbourne darted his stricken wife a furtive, uncomfortable look. "Maybe. But I can't stand spineless non-entities, even though they be female. Your mother changed after you walked out, Roxborough. Stood up to me. I can respect that. Haven't strayed for years.''

''My dear!'' Amelia moved to put her hand over her husband's, where it still gripped his chair.

Justin replaced his arm about Vinny's shoulders. ''I, sir, am persuaded that I shall have no call to look elsewhere. I have every intention of remaining a faithful husband.''

Vinny's sudden exclamation, and the way she pressed herself against him, brought a responsive, tender smile to his lips. He kissed her again, lightly, ignoring his father's snort of impatience. He looked up from the caress to eye the Marquess coldly.

''And I would remind you, my lord, that I did not walk out. I was cast out.'' He drew Vinny closer still. ''We will take our leave now. But I must make it clear that in due course we shall be returning to visit my mother.''

Hazelbourne's colour had returned to normal. To Vinny's absolute astonishment his face suddenly cracked into an approving grin.

''Found some spunk from somewhere while you've been away, my boy. Got yourself a plucky wife, too.'' He waved an irritable hand. ''Took a chance, didn't you? But you win. Take over Broxwood. I'm past it, and that fool of an agent needs a goad behind him. See what you can make of it. I'll vouchsafe you'll not be short of funds.''

Vinny felt Justin's arm stiffen, then relax as he let out a pent-up breath. But he made a guarded reply. ''I collect I may have a free hand. There are new ideas abroad which I may wish to employ. I shall certainly put them into practice at Fernhill and Ashlea, my wife's estate in Kent.''

''You'll be too occupied to become a rakehell, like your brother.'' He shot a look upwards to Amelia's startled face. ''You thought I wouldn't let myself see what George was, but I did. My children have all proved a great disappointment to me. So far. I look to you, Roxborough. Save the family name and fortune. I don't care how you do it.''

Justin released Vinny to go to his father. He dropped to one knee and took a gnarled fist between his own slender, capable hands.

''I will do my utmost not to disappoint you in future, Father. And do not despise Harriet. She is a good, strong, loving woman. She was not responsible for Shatton's misdeeds, she merely suffered for them. She deserves your affection, and needs your help to raise your grandchildren.''

''We'll see,'' was all the promise his father would make.

Vinny suspected that the Marquess merely wished to maintain his curmudgeonly attitude a little longer. He could scarcely cave in completely at one sitting!

Percy was staying on for a few days, until Harriet was ready to return to Hertfordshire, for he had gallantly offered to escort her on the journey. The fact that Jane had returned to the vicarage, which lay scarcely twenty miles from Lady Harriet's home, had done nothing to discourage his gesture. The Reverend Mr Rosedale had travelled to Devon to meet Lord and Lady Marldon, and taken his daughter back with him to prepare for a spring wedding.

Vinny bade her brother a fond farewell, promising him to take her new husband to Preston Grange to meet their parents as soon as conditions allowed. They would visit Harriet, too, and an exchange of visits was agreed all round.

At last they were on their way, alone in the landau with Flora and Gill travelling in the chaise behind. Vinny sank back against the cushions, her head cradled on Justin's shoulder.

''Only one day late,'' he murmured into her ear.

''Oh, Justin! Are you certain you have no regrets?''

''My dear one, why should I have?''

"Because...although your father does seem to have come round considerably. I told you I thought he was proud of you, however reluctant to admit it! Perhaps, in the end, you will not suffer for marrying me."

"I shall suffer nothing but happiness, my love. And I engage to cause you no greater suffering than I experience myself!"

He kissed her to reinforce his point. Then he grunted. "My father still fears I am a rakehell, I believe."

Vinny snorted in a most unladylike manner. "How can he?" She reached up to touch his cheek with loving fingers. "There is no trace of dissolute behaviour in either your face or person!"

Justin caught her kid-covered fingers and kissed them. "He is not beyond disregarding the evidence of his eyes. And he does not know the lesson the business with Shatton served to teach me."

She peered up at him in surprise. "You knew of Shatton's gambling? I inferred that you did not. You were out of touch..."

She felt his chest heave in a sigh. "Not when it began. I should have warned Harriet, but I thought to save her pain... Shatton was in Oxford while I was there. He was a few years older than I, more worldly. In debt over his head and carrying on an affair with an engaged woman."

Vinny sat up. "This is the explanation of what occurred in Oxford?" she asked.

"I have never told another soul, but you should know, my love. I was reckless enough, in debt myself through—er—carrying on affairs with a series of high flyers—hum—"

"I am familiar with the term," Vinny informed him primly.

He grinned at her flushed face. "They cost me a fortune," he admitted. "As Harriet said, there was a superficial resemblance between Shatton and myself. At a distance we could be mistaken for one another. When gossip linked my name with his lady love I wanted to deny the charge, but he begged me not to. Harriet, you see.''

''Poor Justin! What a coil!''

He gave a mirthléss bark of laughter. ''A coil indeed. Her fiancée challenged me, but neither of us was any use with weapons. I suggested a game of cards. We played for money, and when his ran out the lady became the stake. He lost, as I had known he would. I told him he was welcome to the whore, I did not want her. Inexcusable.''

He paused, while Vinny tried to control her whirling thoughts.

''I imagined, you see, that I could defend my honour and still give him what he wanted, though she was not worth his regard,'' he continued at length, self-condemnation lacing his voice with bitterness. ''I was shattered when I learned that he had thrown himself into the river. I should not have cleaned him out, nor thrown her infidelity in his face. Shatton had left, having settled most of his debts with the chief portion of my winnings. In any case I could not have placed the blame where it belonged, for Harriet loved the fellow.''

Vinny took hold of his hand. ''It might have been better if you had, my love.''

''It did not seem so at the time. When I had settled my own debts I had nothing left. Are you not disgusted with me, Vinny?''

She lifted his hand and pressed it to her lips. ''No. You were foolish, but you acted from love of your sister. And I can see that you do not wish to cause Harriet unnecessary grief now. You are right to remain silent.''

He gave a vast sigh and drew her against his chest. ''You cannot know what a relief it is to admit the truth after all these years.''

"Even to just one person?"

"Provided that person is my wife."

They arrived after dusk had fallen. Thus much of the moderately sized building which was Fernhill House still remained a mystery when the time came for them to retire.

Candles flickered and glowed warmly in the small drawing-room where they had just partaken of a light supper.

"Are you tired?" asked Justin, regarding her pensive face with concern.

"Not particularly," said Vinny, blushing. Her husband's rueful grimace brought sudden palpitations to her heart. The moment she longed for yet dreaded was approaching too fast. She had believed all her doubts and fears quite laid to rest, but found them rising again to plague her.

"I had hoped we might retire early." His voice was softly neutral. "Did you find your room adequate?"

"Oh, yes! Perfectly adequate, thank you. Was yours?"

"It lacked only one thing."

She waited, but he did not enlarge. "What was that?" she asked at last.

"The presence of my wife."

Her colour flared, but she could not control the choke of laughter which released her tension as she protested, "My lord! Really!"

He grinned, and all the mischievousness, the mockery, the tenderness and love he had ever shown shone from his eyes.

"Is that desire so terrible? You once offered—"

"Sir, you are no gentleman to throw such an indiscretion back in my face!"

"I am a rake," he reminded her. He sprang to his feet. "It is high time I began to live up to my reputation!"

He swept her up into his arms. She did not struggle, but threw hers about his neck. Laughter overcame confusion as he carried her from the room and along the corridor to the master suite, which was on the same floor. During the journey she became acutely aware of the masculine scent of him, of the strong muscles holding her so easily, of his hand splayed beneath her breast as he carried her to his room and laid her on the huge four-poster bed. Leaping flames from the fire added warmth to the light from several candles scattered about the room.

"Stay there!" he ordered.

Vinny had no intention of moving. Her breath was coming fast, her heart pounding. She felt deliciously abandoned. He had precipitated the moment and now it was upon her she found herself revelling in his mastery. He was so very different. And yet...

A door communicated with her room. Justin opened it and spoke to Flora. "You may retire. Lady Roxborough will not be requiring your services again tonight."

Gill was in his lord's dressing-room. He too was dismissed.

"Now," announced Justin, advancing on the bed purposefully, "you are at my mercy, my lady."

"Oh, sir!" cried Vinny in anguished tones. "Spare me!" Her dark eyes, the pupils enormous in the dimness, laughed up at him, but strain and shyness lurked in their depths. Or did the flickering light deceive him?

Justin picked up a candle and held it over his wife's reclining form. "Beautiful," he murmured, and saw the colour rise to stain her cheeks.

She had done her best to respond to his light-hearted banter, but his purpose of funning her out of her nervousness had failed. He had not been mistaken. She was shy. And apprehensive. He could see her trembling. He supposed that must be natural, though to him it seemed absurd. But he would need to woo her gently if he wanted to enjoy the fruits of the passion he knew to be inherent in her nature. He had roused it before, when she had been unprepared and her response unguarded. Now she was waiting, expectant—and uneasy. He frowned slightly. He really could not understand why. Was she afraid to let her feelings run free? Afraid of disgracing herself as a gentlewoman? She must realise that he would not condemn... And she knew what to expect. She had, after all, been married before.

Perhaps the answer lay there.

"Relax, my love," he murmured, replacing the candle. All teasing had left his manner. "I shall not hurt you. First, I must remove your gown..."

He proceeded with infinite patience, and not a little skill, Vinny noted in amusement tinged with jealousy. She was by no means the first woman he had disrobed. Charles had been clumsy, for he had not previously dallied...

She shut the thought of her first husband away in the back of her mind, where it could not intrude. She should rejoice in Justin's experience.

When she was naked, Justin lifted the candle again. Vinny, suddenly all too aware of her deficiencies but most of all of her vulnerability, drew her knees up and swung them sideways, crossing her arms over her breasts.

"Don't hide from me, wife! Beauty such as yours deserves to be admired. You are extraordinarily beautiful, you know."

His voice caressed. Vinny's confidence grew and she smiled.

He put the candle down and began to throw off his own garments. So tightly fitting were they that he had more trouble discarding them without help than he had experienced in dealing with her buttons and ribbons. He cursed softly as he peeled off his jacket, easing his shoulders and arms from its snug confines. He searched for and found the forked implement for removing his boots, and things became easier after that.

Vinny watched, fascinated, as her husband's clothes disappeared into the shadows. A gleam of candlelight caught his rippling muscles, showed her again the scarring down his shoulder and arm. He removed his breeches and linen with his back turned. By the time he approached the bed again Vinny's eyes were closed. Her hands clutched the covers on either side of her straight, tense body.

The bed dipped as Justin laid his length beside her. His hands and lips gentled and roused at the same time. Before long the wild passion Vinny had already experienced in his arms rose again to blot out every other thought. Her own hands roved, exploring the ridges where he had been hurt and other, more intimate parts of his body, her courage growing as the moments passed.

Justin sucked in his breath and groaned. "Oh, my love! You cannot imagine what you do to me!"

Vinny's hand stilled. "I am sorry."

"No!" he gasped. "Don't stop! You make me feel I want to die of love!"

"That is how you make me feel," she acknowledged shyly.

He groaned again and renewed his attentions to her quivering body. She urged him on, willing him to complete their union. When he did not, but continued with his seductive wooing, rousing—rousing, but not fulfilling—she began to panic.

"Justin," she whimpered. "Justin, you must...please!"

"I must what, my love?" he murmured, still able to tease although almost demented with the effort to control his body. He raised himself above her. "This?"

She gave a small cry, partly of pain but mostly of sheer exultation. For a moment Justin lay still within her. Then he began to move again and she forgot everything but the

wonder of his possession, responding with all the passion
pent up in her for so long.

Afterwards, holding her close, his breath warm upon her
forehead, he asked the questions she had been dreading.

"Did I hurt you, Vinny?"

"No," she whispered. "Hardly at all. You have made
me so happy, my dearest husband! How could I possibly
object to a little pain?"

"Why didn't you tell me you were still virgin?" His
voice cracked. "How could I guess, when you had been
wed for months to a young man—?" He broke off and
began again. "What happened, my love?"

"Charles...couldn't," she choked. "Justin, it was so...
so lowering. He was most ardent before our marriage, and
he...he tried—but he could never... I thought it must be
my fault."

"How could it be?" growled Justin.

"Well, it could have been that I did not excite him, but
I discovered that he had never had a mistress or any-
thing..." She sighed. "He would not discuss the problem.
He had so little conversation of any kind."

"My poor little love! You should have sought an an-
nulment—"

"Oh, no!" exclaimed Vinny quickly. "I could never
have faced the scandal! And I hoped that perhaps, one day,
he would be able to produce the heir his family demanded.
I would not have minded how seldom...then..."

Justin gathered her even closer. "And you feared I might
fail, too?"

Vinny hid her flushed face. "I realise I was idiotish in
the extreme, especially after...but..."

He chuckled, tilting her chin so that he could kiss her
tenderly.

"Having demonstrated my ability once," he murmured,

"I shall now prove that I am quite able to repeat my performance as often as you like, my wife—within reason…"

Vinny gave a gasp of sheer delight as he proceeded to put his boast into rapturous practice.

* * * * *

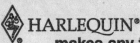